Rain began to leak ~~on the path glowe~~ **revealed a smatter** **the bridge of her nose.**

"I find that I would not mind flying away with you," he admitted.

Nor would he mind kissing her. He ought to have summoned a chaperone. This was dangerous ground he was treading.

Hell, not treading so much as dashing headlong over. Helpless to do otherwise, he lifted his hand, smoothed away the raindrops from that fine, sharp nose with his fingertips.

"I say we do." She smiled, winked. "Let's ruffle our feathers and take to the sky, just the two of us."

"Yes...well..." He shook his head, trying to clear it of the delightful fog swirling in his brain. "It would be a great scandal if I kissed you."

Had he murmured that aloud?

"Immense... But only if someone knew about it."

She was bold and sassy.

She completely captivated him.

Author Note

Thank you for picking up a copy of *The Earl's American Heiress*. I know life can sometimes feel like a race with all the places we need to go and all the things we need to get done. I'm very grateful that you have chosen to give a bit of your valuable spare time to Clementine and Heath. I hope their story takes you along a road you would not otherwise have traveled.

It's certainly not a road Clementine planned to travel. Not at all! One day she was in a classroom in Los Angeles happily fulfilling her dream of teaching, then the next she was crossing the ocean to marry the Earl of Fencroft.

It was not the road Heath Cavill, suddenly the sixth Earl of Fencroft would have traveled, either. He found contentment in tending the family's country estate. But with his brother's death, here he was in London, awaiting the bride who will save them all from financial ruin.

As roads tend to be, our couple's is twisted and they often feel as if they have no idea where it will end up. I'll bet you do, though. Since you are reading a romance, you have the assurance that in the end all will be well.

It is my sincere hope that you enjoy their journey and also that all your own twisted roads will lead to contentment.

Very best wishes from Clementine, Heath...and mostly me.

CAROL ARENS

---

*The Earl's American
Heiress*

Recycling programs
for this product may
not exist in your area.

ISBN-13: 978-1-335-63526-6

The Earl's American Heiress

Printed in U.S.A.

Carol Arens delights in tossing fictional characters into hot water, watching them steam and then giving them a happily-ever-after. When she is not writing, she enjoys spending time with her family, beach camping or lounging about a mountain cabin. At home, she enjoys playing with her grandchildren and gardening. During rare spare moments, you will find her snuggled up with a good book. Carol enjoys hearing from readers at carolarens@yahoo.com or on Facebook.

Books by Carol Arens

Harlequin Historical

Dreaming of a Western Christmas
"Snowbound with the Cowboy"
Western Christmas Proposals
"The Sheriff's Christmas Proposal"
The Cowboy's Cinderella
Western Christmas Brides
"A Kiss from the Cowboy"
The Rancher's Inconvenient Bride
A Ranch to Call Home
A Texas Christmas Reunion
The Earl's American Heiress

Visit the Author Profile page
at Harlequin.com for more titles.

Dedicated to Brielle Mary Iaccino,
our sparkling, happy earth angel.

Chapter One

Santa Monica Beach, an afternoon in May 1889

One did not need to open one's eyes to appreciate the majesty of the Pacific Ocean.

It was better, in fact, to keep them closed. Doing so made it easier to ignore the hustle and bustle of high society as it went through its prancing and posing at the Arcadia Hotel, grandly squatted three hundred yards down the shore from where Clementine Macooish stood.

With closed eyes one could better feel the rush of a cold wave across one's bare feet and the tickle of shifting sand between one's toes as the salt water retreated into the sea.

"Once the ocean laps at your toes, it will summon you home forever," she muttered softly, even though no one was within shouting distance. "Or with one's dying breath—no, not that—with one's first gasp of eternity!"

That last was a vastly more positive thought. Beautiful thoughts often came to her when her eyes were closed. She would write this one down and share it with her students at Mayflower Academy.

Moist air, the cry of gulls circling overhead... Sensation became sharpened without the distraction of the outrageously incredible vista glittering all the way to the western horizon.

Without sight, what a simple thing it was to draw in a lungful of salty, fish-scented air and imagine being as free and weightless as a pelican gliding over the surface of the water. Free to dip—free to swirl in feathered—

"Clementine Jane Macooish! What in blazing glory do you have on?"

She opened her eyes and turned when she heard the voice she loved above all others approaching from behind.

"Good afternoon to you, too, Grandfather." She fluffed the gaily dotted ruffle of her bodice. "This is a perfectly respectable bathing gown, and you know it."

"Respectable for underwear. Cover those bloomers with a proper skirt, girl."

"Don't look so shocked. If you walked the shoreline from the hotel you've seen this costume a dozen times on other ladies."

"I came down the cliff steps, every blasted ninety-nine of them." Her grandfather was trim, fit and in excellent health, so she doubted the stairs had been a burden on him. "Besides, those women are wearing stockings and booties. Your feet are bare as hatchling birds. And your hair! Surely you've not come without a hat."

"It's around here someplace." She glanced about and didn't see it. Perhaps it had tumbled away with the on-shore breeze or been carried away by a gull. "Stand beside me and close your eyes."

She snatched his sleeve to draw him closer.

"Folderol," he grumbled, but did as she suggested.

She plucked the bowler hat from his head and tucked it under her arm. "Now there, doesn't the ocean breeze feel lovely gliding over your scalp? The sunshine so nice and warm?"

With a sidelong glance, she noticed a smile tugging one corner of his mouth. Truly, he was far more handsome than most seventy-year-old men. With his gray beard and mustache, neatly trimmed, and dark brows arching dapperly over intelligent brown eyes, it was no wonder he drew the attention of ladies of all ages when he passed by.

"Fine for me," he said, opening his eyes and pinning her with one arched brow. "I'm bald on top while you've the hotel ball to prepare for. I can't think how Maria is going to do a thing with that thicket of hair, not with salt and sand stuck in it."

"In that case I might have to stay in my hotel room tonight."

Of course Grandfather would never permit it, but it was what she wanted to do, and she was duty bound to say so.

"Do not test me, child. You are a well-bred Macooish woman and will represent the family as such. And besides, you are quite lovely, even given the dishabille you are now in."

Grandfather would think so, of course, since he had been the one to raise her. The truth was, her hair was far too red to be considered fashionable, her eyes green rather than the desired blue. But it was her nose that was her biggest beauty fault, being a bit too sharp. Unless she was smiling, her countenance had a slightly severe appearance, bordering even on arrogance, or so Grandfather had warned.

Her younger and prettier cousin, Madeline, had a nose that looked sweet no matter her mood.

And Clementine's temperament? She was far too direct and opinionated to be considered socially graceful. Truly, she smiled only when she felt like it, not when it was required. Her smiles were quite genuine, to be sure, but never given away simply to put someone at ease during an awkward conversation. Sadly, on those occasions she tried, the gesture came out more as a grimace.

Madeline was far better at playing the hostess. Indeed, she excelled at charming people. Her cousin was petite, with fairy-blond hair. Her blue eyes were lit from within by a gracious spirit. Madeline had a gift for making a stranger into a friend.

It was why Grandfather had elected Madeline to be the one to cross the ocean and marry a peer of the realm—a lofty earl, no less.

Every morning and night Clementine thanked the good lord that she was not the charming granddaughter.

Which allowed her to be the one who was free to stand on the beach in her bathing costume, wiggle her bare toes in the sand and dream of being a pelican.

Since she was not doomed to become a countess, Grandfather had given his blessing on her desire to become the schoolteacher she had always yearned to be. Truly, she wanted nothing more in life than to direct young minds toward a sound future.

And of equal importance to her, marriage could wait until she was good and ready for it.

"If I do stay in my room, no one will miss me." She returned her grandfather's arched brow with one of her own. It must be a family trait, that—putting someone in their place with a lifted brow. Her cousin didn't share it, though. Only she and Grandfather used the expression. Perhaps her parents and Madeline's had it, but they had all died so long ago that she knew them mostly as portraits in the formal parlor. "Madeline will make up for my absence."

"Madeline has run off."

All of a sudden she could not hear the surf crashing on the sand, and the gulls went silent.

Run off?

"To the dressmaker, no doubt."

"She's run away with some charlatan. Left a note admitting it."

Clementine ought to have suspected that might happen.

While she and Madeline both tended to be freethinking, as Grandfather had raised them to be, her cousin's temperament sent her flying headlong into adventure.

Clementine was of a settled nature, happy to be at home, cozy and content in the smallest room of the sprawling mansion she had grown up in. Her best nights were the ones when she managed to hide away from Grandfather's many social gatherings. The back garden had private nooks and lush alcoves where she'd spent many a warm summer evening undetected.

Now Madeline—the intended countess—the one to fulfill Grandfather's plan for the safekeeping of the family, beyond that which could be found by mere fortune alone, had freely taken wing and fluttered happily away from her duty.

And Grandfather was looking at Clementine in a most peculiar way. She feared the battle of the arched brows was going to end up with her becoming the Countess of Fencroft.

No! No! And no!

But the merciless, twisting knot in her stomach made her suspect that Grandfather would win the battle, because she was, above all things, distressingly loyal.

Drat it.

Near Folkestone, England, at the same moment,
May 1889

The sixth Earl of Fencroft stood on a rock, staring out at the sea. The light of a full moon suddenly emerging from behind a cloud illuminated the crests of unsettled, ink-like water for as far as he could see. It was a violent yet beautiful thing to behold.

And to hear. The forceful crash of waves hitting the rock ten feet below where he stood suited his mood, which, like the approaching storm, was darkly brooding.

Cold wind snapped his cloak about like a pair of wild, flapping wings. Mist from the crashing waves dampened his clothing, soaked his hair and dripped down his face. He felt the sting of salt water in his eyes but didn't dare to close them.

If he did he would see the fifth Earl of Fencroft's face, still and pale in death.

In life, his brother's face had never been still. In spite of a lifetime of ill health that face had always been smiling.

Laughter—not always appropriate laughter, to be sure, but laughter just the same—was what he was known for.

Even though no one had expected Oliver to make old bones, his death had seemed sudden.

The lung condition that had plagued him all his life had grown worse so slowly that it hadn't been noticeable day to day, not until Oliver slumped over his cards while playing whist with the estate accountant, Mr. Robinson, and died.

No, Heath could not say that he had not known the mantle his brother carried so jovially would fall upon him one day. He had understood it since he was old enough to recognize that his brother lived in a damaged body. Nonetheless, it was shocking and bitterly sad.

Even if sorrow were not perched upon his shoulder, he would not be happy. Believing in a vague way that one day he would replace his brother as earl was a far different thing from actually doing it.

The last thing he wanted was his new title, especially given how grievously he had come by it.

Death certainly had a way of altering life.

His life had been rather ideal when the main requirement on his time was to oversee the estate in Derbyshire. Those rolling green acres of pastureland were paradise.

While his presence in London was often necessary, he had been excused from much of the city's social rigor.

Now he would be required to attend Parliament in Oliver's stead.

He'd be required to sit among the nobility, arguing unsolvable issues.

Glancing back over his shoulder and up the stark cliffside, he watched smoke curl out of the chimney of his coastal retreat.

The seaside cottage was as much home to him as the estate in Derbyshire was. Certainly more than the town house in London was.

All the upstairs lamps had been put out. Only the kitchen window remained aglow.

He looked back at the sea, watching the blackish surface peak and foam.

Somehow, knowing that the children slept sweet and safe inside made him feel more peaceful.

He'd get through this, learn to be all he needed to be for everyone who depended upon the Earl of Fencroft for their survival. How many were employed by the estate and the town house?

He didn't know. Oliver and Mr. Robinson had taken care of everything having to do with the business of running the earldom.

A hail of small pebbles hitting rock rattled from behind.

"Yer Lordship, sir!"

Turning, he saw a boy scrabbling down the steep hillside.

"What is it, Georgie?" The eight-year-old was thin but not as thin as he'd been the first time Heath had encountered him. "You should not be out in the dark. It isn't safe."

"Not so dangerous as before in London, sir. And here—"

The boy extended a sheet of paper, already damp and limp with sea spray.

"It's from the telegraph office, and coming so late as it is, Mrs. Pierce reckoned it must be important."

Indeed. A message sent at this hour could indicate an emergency. He opened it slowly, half fearing to know what it said.

Brother, come back to London at once. The accountant has fled and left chaos in his wake.

What kind of chaos? It would have been helpful had his sister explained further.

He hoped she was just being overdramatic. Olivia was Oliver's twin. She had been understandably distraught since his death. Still, getting news that Robinson had fled could not be a good thing.

Heath hadn't let the fellow go after Oliver's passing three weeks ago. With the knowledge he had of the estate, he was invaluable and Heath had had every intention of keeping him on.

"Hold on to my hand, Georgie. The rocks are slippery."

At the cliff top, with the child's footing secure, he let go of the small fist. "Go tell my coachman we're off for London at first light."

There was no point in dragging anyone out into the dark of night. Whatever problems the fellow had left behind would wait until a decent hour.

As it turned out, a full eighteen hours passed before

Heath finally entered the study of the London townhome. The servants were abed but a small fire glowed in the hearth, apparently kept in expectation of his arrival.

The weak flames gave off scant warmth and even less light. Shadows hovered in the corners of the room; they swirled about his heart like mist.

It was too easy to imagine Oliver still sitting at the desk, a blanket draped across his shoulders and a cloth close at hand for him to cough into. The scent of cigar smoke lingering in the room made Heath feel that if he but blinked, his brother would be there.

"At last! I feared you would not come."

His sister's voice crackled with worry. It hadn't always sounded so vulnerable, but Oliver's death so close on the heels of her husband's had changed her.

Death changed everything. To this day grief for Wilhelmina came upon him at unexpected times. Of course, it was not only his fiancée's death that haunted him, but the secrets she kept in life.

"We made decent time given the storm." In fact he would give the coachman extra pay for having to bear the cold and the wet in order for him to get here and deal with Olivia's perceived "chaos."

"No doubt you were loath to leave your mistress."

"I don't have a mistress."

"No?" Her bow-like mouth pressed tight. It was hard for his sister to accept that not all men were like her late husband. "So you say, but I think you spend too much time at Rock Rose Cottage not to have one stashed away."

Everyone faced betrayal at some point in life. His sister had trusted and adored her husband, until the day he passed away in the bed of his mistress. Given all Olivia had been through, Heath tried to smile past her suspicions.

He strode over to where she stood in the doorway,

dipped his head and kissed her cheek. "I'd have been here sooner but the roads were complete muck. I'm just lucky my driver was skilled enough to keep us from getting stuck like so many others were."

"Just remember, brother, a mistress and the devil are one and the same."

"Let's sit while you tell me what chaos Mr. Robinson has left behind."

Since he could not tell her the truth about his business at the seashore, he did not argue further about there being no mistress, even though he was quite weary of her continued accusations.

He sat down on the divan. Olivia eased down beside him with a deflated sigh.

What he must remind himself was that she was a widow, that she and four-year-old Victor were dependent upon him for everything. Truly, a woman without a man to protect her was helpless in society.

Willa's face flashed in his mind. The helplessness in her sad brown eyes had always made him feel protective of her, even when they were children. In the end that expression had been his undoing.

"Solicitors have been pounding on the door and demanding payment for debts that they claimed Oliver incurred. Three of them two days ago, and one this morning. I sent them away as best I could."

"With their ears red and ringing, I imagine."

She shrugged. "It's no more than they deserved, but I fear the obligations are valid. I loved Oliver—you know I did—but he could be irresponsible."

"I think he wanted to squeeze as much living as he could out of his failing body."

"Perhaps, and who could blame him? But really, our brother ought to have hired someone more capable as our accountant. What did Mr. Robinson really have to recommend himself other than being Oliver's chum from Cambridge? I didn't think so much of it at the time but looking at it now I ought to have. The pair of them laughed and indulged in spirits when they worked on the ledgers."

He did not know that, but it hardly surprised him. Oliver sought gaiety above most everything else. No doubt that pursuit had hastened his death. Doctor after doctor had warned him to leave the caustic air of London for the sake of his lungs. He would not consider it because he found country life dull. He used to claim all the charming, lively ladies lived in town and that was where he would reside.

"Our brother did enjoy a good time."

"I thought," Olivia murmured with a sigh, "that was the reason he wanted to marry that rich, flighty American, for the thrill of doing something risqué. But I see better now. We'll need an auditor to know for sure, but I fear we might be bankrupt."

"I'll wire James Macooish, let him know that our brother is gone and he need not bring his granddaughter. I suppose I ought to have done it straightaway, but with—"

"You will not. The girl is coming to marry the Earl of Fencroft. Fifth or sixth, it hardly matters."

"It matters a great deal when you are the sixth."

"Don't be selfish, Heath. You have a duty to the Fencroft estate. Without Miss Macooish's fortune we will be utterly lost. How many people will be left in ruin if you do not marry her?"

"The woman would have suited our brother. He always did like brightly feathered birds. From what Oliver had to say about her I believe she is quite freehearted and pretty, and no doubt frivolous. You know me better than to think we would make a good match."

"That hardly matters. I made a love match and look where that got me. Believe me, little brother, better to set your sights low and not be disappointed. If you won't think of all the souls Fencroft Manor supports, consider the well-being of your nephew. He might be the one to take over the title one day."

"If I marry the heiress, her son will inherit."

"Don't be silly. American women are notoriously infertile. They will be the ruin of the aristocracy. It's what everyone says."

Life had certainly spun Heath about and dropped him on his noble head. Unless he wedded Madeline—wasn't that her name? Truthfully, until this moment he'd given his future sister-in-law little thought, but unless he wedded her, there would be nothing for Victor to inherit. His hardworking tenants and all of Fencroft Manor's trusted servants would be cast out onto the street.

For all that he longed to leap off the couch and dash off a telegram to Macooish, he sat there long after his sister kissed his cheek and went to bed. He watched the dying flames until the room finally went dark.

Chapter Two

London, nine weeks and a dozen and a half ball gowns later...

"Loyal to a fault," Clementine muttered while sitting on the balcony of the apartment Grandfather had rented and gazing down at the midnight stillness of the garden below. "Exceedingly and preposterously loyal."

Excessive was what it was. She had never considered herself to be a weakling, but surely any woman with a backbone would have refused to even consider Grandfather's scheme.

And yet here she was, sleepless in London, with a notebook on her lap and a lantern glowing on the table beside her. Grandfather's handwriting on the pages blurred before her eyes. The more she stared at the instructions on how to address the titled, the wavier the letters became.

From down below, she heard the soothing tap of water in a fountain. Squinting through the dark, she could see how large it was. It might rightly be called a pond.

This building was vastly elegant, as was the garden that separated it from Fencroft House on the other side. In fact, Grandfather had rented this apartment because of its proximity to the Fencroft place. Perhaps he thought she would fall in love with the environs and look favorably upon the man.

That remained to be seen, but the garden did look appealing by moonlight. The landlord had told Grandfather that the garden was shared space between the apartment and the town house.

If she looked hard she could see the outline of the three-story brick building across the way.

As late as it was, even the servants were abed. No one would be the wiser if she slipped outside.

Within fifteen minutes she was sitting on an ornate iron bench three stories below her balcony.

Fresh, cool air washed over her face, a welcome change from the stifling yellow fog that had clung to everything earlier in the day.

Truly, there had been moments when it hurt to breathe. She'd felt great pity for those forced to go about their daily business muddling through it.

Thankfully, at about sundown a fresh wind had blown it away, allowing the moon to shine down, to cleanse and bless everything with its pure, cold light.

The thought was quite poetic and it made her smile. She hoped she would remember it when she went back upstairs and took her pen and paper out of the secretary.

She might not, though, since she was in no hurry to leave this tranquil spot. It would be nice to sit here until the first rays of morning light peeked over the rooftops, but she was fairly certain it would be forbidden.

Given that Grandfather had cautioned her to observe every social rule, appear beyond reproach in everything she said or did, she doubted she ought to be down here by herself for even a moment.

Still, who was to know that she sat here blissfully listening to the rustle of tall shrubbery in the breeze, and the tinkle of the fountain?

Not a single soul. She was free to sit here and wonder what she was doing in London in the first place, why she had even considered Grandfather's outrageous request— not demand. She was free to sit here and wonder what she was doing in London in the first place, why she had even considered Grandfather's outrageous request—not demand.

And yet here she sat, somewhat contentedly listening to the sound of pattering droplets hitting the surface of the large pond when she ought to be seething in indignation.

But it was soothing, and while not as dramatic as the crashing waves of the ocean, it was lovely in its own way. Perhaps if she viewed events as an adventure, at least until she made up her mind about them, she could find a bit of peace within herself.

To that end she must make a point of sneaking out every night.

Solitude was something that even Grandfather's fortune could not purchase. Closing her eyes, Clementine listened to a symphony of frogs accompanied by the twitter of a nightingale. London might be a pleasant place after all. In time she might—

"Curse it!"

A man's exclamation cut the peace of the moment. He sounded startled more than angry. The sudden rustling of brush gave way to a husky gasp.

She leaped off the bench, ready to flee. Who would be creeping about in the hedge at this hour unless he was an intruder up to no good? Perhaps a thief or a pillager?

A cat dashed across the walkway at the same moment the dark-clad figure tumbled into the fountain. She could not be certain, but she thought he hit his head on a stone going in.

Oh, dear!

The pond was only knee-deep, but the man was floating facedown in it.

It was possible that he was a villain, or equally possible that he had a very good reason to be out here, the same as she did. In any case, she could hardly let him drown.

Running, she came to the edge of the water, stepped into it, slippers and gown forgotten—but not forgotten enough not to feel horrible for the servant who would have to make them presentable again.

Reaching for the man's shoulders, she had to kick aside the long black coat he wore because it floated about him, getting tangled in her skirt and restricting her movement.

Giving a solid yank, she managed to get him on his back. Mercy, but he was heavy and, oh, my—

If he was a villain, he was a dashing one, with dark hair and a sweep of black, seductive eyelashes. Until this moment Clementine hadn't known a man's lashes could be seductive.

No doubt his villainy consisted of sneaking home from a tryst.

She patted his cheek. "Wake up, sir!"

All at once he lunged, caught her about the hips and dragged her down.

She beat on his forearms. "Why! You great lurching oaf! Let me go before I scream!" Which she could not do without everyone knowing she had come outside in the dark. It would not be well received to be found in the fountain in the slippery embrace of a man.

The most amazing eyes she had ever seen focused on her face. Slowly, as if shuffling through dense fog, the fellow came back from wherever the blow had taken him.

"Wh-what?" he stuttered, wiping his face and then reaching for his hat, which bobbed about on the surface of the water.

"As best I can tell, you were startled by a cat." She snagged the soggy headwear and handed it to him. "You hit your head after you fell through the bush and into the pond. There is a bit of swelling above your right eye, but so far it doesn't appear too horrid."

What was horrid, and funny at the same time, was that she was sitting side by side with a stranger in a fountain, the pair of them blinking away water dripping down their foreheads.

"And who do I have to thank for my rescue?" he asked, swiping the hair back from his face.

Certainly not Clementine Jane Macooish! The scandal would be enormous were anyone to find out about this.

"Jane—Fitz."

"Thank you, Lady Fitz." Heath did not recall anyone by the last name of Fitz among the titled but he had no wish to offend his beautiful rescuer by assuming she was not. Clearly she was an American but she might still be titled if she was married to a peer.

It was difficult to determine the color of her eyes in the darkness. The shade of her curly, tumbled hair was disguised as well, given that it was dripping wet and dappled with moonlight. Fortunately the midnight dousing appeared not to have dampened the lively spirit shining from the lady's eyes—no, not that so much as lively and serious all in one suspicious glance while she studied him.

"Miss Fitz will do nicely, I think."

The right thing to do would be to rise from the water and offer her a hand up, but she was gazing at him with her head tipped ever so slightly to one side. He found her fascinating, so all he wanted was to sit here and look at her.

"I believe—" her brows lifted in a slender, delicate arch "—it would be polite to introduce yourself so that I do not decide you are a criminal bent on mayhem."

"I assure you that I am not."

That admission did not mean he would reveal himself as Fencroft. How would he explain his reason for dashing through the garden at this hour like a fleeing criminal? Better she thought he was bent on mayhem.

If his business of the evening came to light, lives would be threatened, the Fencroft estate ruined.

"My name is Heath Ramsfield." The first surname to pop into his mind was his butler's, so he used it. "You are shivering, Miss Fitz. We should get out of the water."

He stood, reached for her hand and saw that it was bare, but he clamped his fingers around it anyway. The last thing he wanted was for her to slip and be injured, which would force him to seek help. Anyone he called upon would recognize him.

"I can only wonder, Mr. Ramsfield, are you always so skittish of cats?"

"It did appear rather suddenly."

He stood a respectable distance from her, although barely, being captivated as he was by moonlight reflecting in the beads of water dotting her face. She had a beautiful nose, not pert as so many desired, but straight and elegant. It might have given her a stern demeanor were it not for the good humor warming her eyes.

"Oh, yes." She squeezed her fingers around the hank of hair dripping over her shoulder and wrung out the water. "They do tend to do that."

Water dribbling from their clothing onto the stones chimed with the droplets sprinkling in the fountain. A breeze scuttled through the shrubbery, making him shiver. It would be wise and proper to part company now, but he found he did not want to.

Who was this woman and why was she here in his garden? It was not as though he could come right out and ask, not without admitting he had a right to know.

"I suppose I have ruined your evening, and your gown."

"Oh, I think not. I've never rescued anyone from a fountain in the middle of the night before. It was a riveting distraction."

He laughed quietly. When was the last time he had done that? "And I thank you. But what did you need distracting from? Perhaps I can help?"

She was silent for a moment, holding him with her gaze, judging to determine if he was worthy of her confidence, he imagined.

The woman seemed as wise as she was attractive. Probably as different from the one he was contracted to marry in every way there could be. It was harsh of him to judge his future bride before he ever met her, but if she appealed to Oliver, he doubted Madeline Macooish would suit him.

"That is unlikely unless you know how a common-born woman would address, well, let's say an earl or a viscount, in case she passes him in a hallway or on the street."

Or in a water fountain with the night so close and intimate about them.

"I suspect he might just appreciate 'Good day.'"

If only he were free to pursue a woman of his choosing! It couldn't be this woman, a commoner and a poor American—society would never recover from it—but one like her. If there was one like her to be had.

"That sounds delightfully simple. But now that you know why I was in the garden, I'd like to know what *you* are doing here."

She spoke to him with boldness and he found it quite appealing. Would she do so if she knew him to be the lordly master of the house next door? He was glad she didn't know it, since the very thought was as pompous as a strutting rooster.

"There are some things a gentleman cannot reveal. Let's just say I thought it an inviting path to take on my way home."

"Yes, until you encountered a cat. I can't be sure but it appeared to have been a black cat. I hope you do not also encounter a string of bad luck."

"To tell you the truth, Miss Fitz, tripping over the cat and coming awake in the pond with you was the nicest thing to happen to me all evening."

The nicest thing to happen to him in a very long time, in fact.

"Being plucked from certain death is nice of an evening."

"Quite," he murmured. Then, since he could hardly keep her here shivering all night, he said, "Please, let me pay for your ruined gown."

"It's far from ruined, only wet. It will dry out right as rain."

"I'll see you home then." He crooked his arm thinking how silly it must look, two dripping people in the wee hours of the night observing the formal gesture.

"There is no need." She arched a brow, shaking her head. "I'll be fine on my own."

"I assure you, I'm not a blackguard, but they are out there." He waggled his elbow at her. "You saved my life. I will escort you home."

"As I said, there is no need." She glanced over her shoulder at the apartments on the far side of the garden. "I am completely capable of walking from here to there."

But she didn't walk. She lifted the hem of her drenched skirt, spun about and ran. Her slippers made squishy noises across the stones.

She opened a door mostly used by servants, nodded to him and then vanished inside.

And like a dream in the night, she was gone. Who was this woman? A servant? Not likely, given she was an American. A lady's companion hired by someone renting one of the apartments across the shared garden? More likely that, or something of the such.

While he stared at the door, a fairy-tale character came to mind. The mysterious Cinderella. Although Cinderella was not seductively dripping but merely missing a shoe.

Leaves rustled. The cat leaped from a bush. It crossed in front of him, tail waving smartly in the air.

Was it good luck or bad luck that he had met the beautiful and self-minded American?

Heath supposed he would never know for certain. In his sphere, the titled and the common people lived side by side but in vastly different worlds.

Since breakfast was a private affair, Clementine ignored proper etiquette and propped her elbows on the table. She folded her fingers under her chin and stared across at Grandfather.

He seemed distracted, glum. It bothered her to see him so downcast. It was uncommon for him to be anything but cheerfully confident.

She lifted a biscuit from a dainty plate and spread clotted cream on it while she thought how she might best cheer him up.

But given that she was one of the reasons for his frown, it might be difficult.

Surely he must understand that he could not simply decree that she would take Madeline's place and marry a stranger in a foreign land and expect her to smile blissfully and fall into line with his wishes.

She had wishes of her own—dreams that his ambition had ripped from her—of teaching children, to put a fine point on it. Every day she wondered how her students in Los Angeles were faring with the new instructor. She hoped he would be patient with Billy's slow speech and Anna's progressive mind.

Would it even be possible to teach again once she bowed to Grandfather's demand? She honestly had no idea what a countess was and was not allowed to do. She did know it was a rather lofty position in society, so maybe she could do as she pleased and no one would speak against it. Then again, perhaps everyone would speak against it.

She wished she could ease her grandfather's mind by agreeing to the marriage before her next bite of biscuit and cream, but she was not quite ready to make that commitment even though she had crossed the Atlantic Ocean to that supposed end.

Indeed, she was less ready this morning than she had been last night.

For some reason the man she'd pulled from the fountain was capturing a good deal of her attention. No matter how she tried, she could not put away the image of water dripping off the corners of his mouth, of the handsome turn of his lips when he smiled or of the easy conversation that sprang so naturally between them.

It was not an easy thing to make a decision to marry a man when another fellow's face was all one could see.

What a shame Mr. Ramsfield was not the earl. Her outlook on the marriage might be slightly different if that were the case.

At the heart of it, Grandfather's heavy spirit was not her fault. It was Madeline's. Had her cousin lived up to what she had been groomed for rather than running off, Grandfather would be celebrating an engagement rather than fearing there might not be one. Also, he would not now be fearful that Madeline would come to a desperate end.

Yes, it was all completely Madeline's fault. Clementine was only here in London facing a decision that might break Grandfather's heart because of her cousin's reckless decision.

"Life for a bastard child is—" Grandfather's voice faltered. "I only hope that Madeline will remember and behave—"

He would know this since he had been one.

The circumstance of his birth was not something he spoke much of—not in words—but the struggles of his young life had formed the man he was.

To his mind, amassing a fortune was vital. At the same time he believed that no amount of money would keep his granddaughters secure.

After all, wealth hadn't helped his mother. At eighteen she had made a brilliant match, at twenty she had become a widow, a year and a half later her solicitor had squandered her fortune and left her pregnant.

"Madeline will do the right thing, Grandfather. You raised her to be strong and resourceful. She will not make that mistake. I know she will not."

For all that she said so, she knew her cousin had acted rashly and followed her heart as she tended to do. Clementine wondered if she had given more than a passing

thought to what might happen to her by going off with—
well, a stranger. No matter what Madeline might feel for
the fellow in the moment, he was surely a philanderer.

"Maybe so, but she's used to having money to rely
upon and now she does not. She might cling to the wrong
sort of man."

Was he picturing the faces of the many wrong sorts of
men his mother had clung to? If the faraway look in his
eyes was anything to go by, he was remembering them.

"Madeline," she pointed out, "is not your mother."

"No, but she is a woman and thereby helpless."

"Well, she does take after you in being resourceful.
I'm sure she will be fine." As long as the Pinkerton agent
found her before she was not fine.

"A woman is only as fine as the man in charge of her
funds is honest. You'll know that a part of the reason we
are here is because I'm going to earn a fortune in Scotland. You being titled will ensure the venture is a success. But Clemmie, my girl, it won't be enough. Wealth
on its own will not keep you secure."

"So far it has."

"Because I'm a man. All I ever earn will be mine. All
I give you will belong to your husband. But a title will
protect you."

"But why is this business in Scotland so important
to you? Surely there is money to be made back home."

"Diversification. You'll recall that I've lost a fortune
and then gained it back again. By having ventures in
more than one country I am not depending upon only one
country to be prosperous. I'll be more likely to stay afloat
financially with ventures in other parts of the world."

"If your business succeeds, I'll be financially secure
on both sides of the ocean and have no need to marry."

"Did you not hear me when I said money can vanish

in an instant? Look at your cousin. She was a wealthy young woman a short time ago, and now? You must marry well, Clementine."

She must not have looked suitably convinced, for a worried expression flitted across his face, which made her more than uncomfortable.

Grandfather was the most confident man she'd ever met. She had never seen the anchor of the family defeated in anything. His strength had always been her refuge.

Many years ago—she'd been only three then—he had snatched both her and Madeline from certain death while a flash flood washed the rest of the family away. He had held them secure in his strong arms while hell surged all around. He would not give them over to the killer current. She vaguely remembered how his muscles trembled, how he groaned with the effort to keep them locked to his chest. Even though he was being pelted and cut by debris, he'd shielded them and refused to let death have them.

Afterward, those wounded arms had held them through the grief of losing their parents, even while he dealt with his own. Over the years he had kept them fed and clothed, despite being busy rebuilding the fortune he'd lost.

He'd raised them and loved them. Truly she and Madeline owed him complete devotion.

And now he was asking her to give up everything.

While she did owe him everything, could she really pay the price he wanted?

"We'll have word of a good outcome soon enough," she said, focusing the conversation on Madeline.

Someone came into the dining room and set a plate of bacon on the table between them.

Grandfather did not speak again until the servant had left the room.

"Do you understand the reason you will marry the earl?"

She understood why he wanted her to. Things from her perspective looked a bit different.

"You cannot assume that I will. I do have a say in it. For all we know the earl might be as greedy as most of the suitors I've already crossed paths with. You are aware that they wanted your fortune and not me?"

"I am, indeed. Still, you'll need to marry someone. And have you forgotten that I've met Fencroft? I'd hardly arrange a marriage that was not in your best interest. I will not see you bound to a common fortune hunter."

"But you would a titled one?"

"Yes, indeed, I would. Please understand that a title is more enduring than money. No matter what, your children will never face one day of humiliation. They will never go to bed wondering about their next meal or what might go bump in the night. The respectability that comes with being a peer will be a hedge about them."

"My children! Surely you are ahead of yourself. The earl is a complete and utter stranger."

And surely not half as compelling as the stranger in the garden last night. Given that she was here in London to consider wedding an earl, she was giving far too much thought to the intriguing fellow.

"He's not a stranger to me. I spent considerable time with him during the negotiations. He's a decent sort, and while not in the best of health, he enjoys his entertainment. In fact, he would have suited your cousin quite well had she given the union a chance."

"And you truly believe I would be happy doing so?"

"I do, Clemmie. We would not be here if I thought otherwise."

"While that assurance might be fine for you, I can't

simply hand my life over to some man! Why, I don't even know what he looks like."

"Oh, he has a pleasant face. Fair hair and friendly brown eyes. He's slight of build."

Quite unlike the tall, muscular man in the pond whose eyes were—well she didn't know the color, but they were quite mesmerizing.

"He seems a merry fellow who laughs easily and does not look at life in an overserious manner. He attends all the grand balls."

"You know I dislike grand balls."

"Yes, I do know that, Clemmie. The earl would have suited your cousin grandly. It's why I picked the man for her. But here we find ourselves. Try to look at the good side of this. You will have a fine London town house— there it is. You can see it just out the window across the garden. If you don't like that there is a lovely country estate, even a seaside cottage, I've been told. I'm certain that would be to your liking. A lovely spot by the seashore?"

Truly, there was not much she would not do for the man she loved above anyone else—but this?

How could she possibly?

As he walked in the garden late at night, Heath's steps felt heavy. His fate was nearly sealed.

He was to become betrothed, again.

As much as he tried not to think of Willa it was impossible not to, given the turn his life had taken. He'd always been smitten by her, he supposed. As a boy his heart had swelled whenever she deigned to look his way. He'd grown and given his heart to a few others for a time, but he'd never really forgotten her.

Nor would he now. She continued to influence his life in a way he would never have imagined.

Heath walked slowly about the perimeter of the garden, reliving what had happened.

He shook his head. For once the tinkling of the fountain did not bring to mind his former fiancée's desperate weeping.

Apparently Cinderella in all her dripping glory had replaced the grim reminder with something delightful. She had become a happy vision in his mental angst.

He didn't often dwell on Willa's betrayal, but with another marriage looming, it all came back.

It had seemed a miracle at the time: his Willa seeking him out after so many years. They had become engaged within a week—she was in a hurry to marry him. Not for any tender feelings she had toward him, he'd discovered later on, but because she was pregnant. She confessed it before they wed, so he thought she must have come to care for him a bit. Even so, it was not the fact that she was expecting a child that made him break the engagement. He might have accepted it had Willa loved him. But she did not. He'd been broken for a bit by the way she'd used his affection.

Heath sat down on a bench and watched as wispy clouds drifted across the moon.

While he hadn't gone through with the marriage, he could not find it in him to cast her out. He'd put her up in an apartment away from everyone she knew, so that her shame would not be exposed. He visited her, brought her what she needed to live in comfort. Oddly enough, a friendship had grown between them during that time, a true one. He wanted to confront the cad who had left her in this state, but she would not say who it was.

One day, when he paid his weekly call, Willa was huddled in her bed, weak and feverish. She admitted to giving birth the day before and walking two miles to Slademore

House to give her baby over to the charity there, run by
Baron Slademore. As soon as she'd done it, she regretted
it. She looked in desperate condition, cursing Slademore
in her near delirium. Perhaps he was the culprit and that
was why she had taken her child to him and not because
it was a well-reputed orphanage? Willa claimed it was not
true, but still, Heath had wondered. In the end there was
nothing to be done but send for the doctor.

Even now, sitting here on the bench, he felt the cold
lump that sickened his belly when the doctor reported that
Willa would not likely see the dawn. She'd wept, clutching
Heath's shirt, and begged him to bring back her daughter.

That trip to Slademore House had changed his life in
a way that nothing ever had before.

It had surprised him when Baron Slademore—a man
respected by the highest members of society—denied re-
ceiving a newborn. Perhaps Willa, in her fevered state,
had imagined she'd come here. If not, the baron was lying.
But why? Was Heath correct and the baby his? Was he
lying to keep from being caught out?

In any event, he had to try to bring Willa's baby home.
When it seemed the orphanage had gone dim for the night,
he'd gone in search of the child. Luckily someone had left
the back door open. Indeed, he'd sensed a presence just
out of sight, seeming to lead him down this ill-lit hallway
and down another until he came to the half-open door that
led to a dark, dank room. He found the baby there, wail-
ing in a strident newborn voice. While there was no nurse
present, there were other children sleeping on cots with
thin blankets offering scant warmth. It was so different a
picture from how he'd seen them treated earlier that day.

He'd snatched up Willa's child, tucked her under his
coat and raced back to the apartment. Willa had held her
daughter to her heart for an hour before she passed away.

Baby Willa was the first orphan to be kidnapped by the villain whom the papers named "the Abductor," and the first he sheltered at the seaside in Rock Rose Cottage.

That had all happened two years ago, and now, suddenly, marriage was in his future again.

"Hello, cat," he said to the feline twining about his trouser leg. It looked a bit like the one that had spooked him in the dark and led to his meeting with his mystery woman.

"What do you think?" he asked the fluffy creature looking up at him with great, dark eyes. "Perhaps a marriage of convenience is for the best. No secrets, no expectations. No heartache, either."

No passion, no love. Eyes wide open. The cold, formal circumstances of this union were for the best.

The cat, in apparent agreement, gave a hollow meow and then went on his way toward the fountain.

Earlier today he'd gotten word from James Macooish that he was in London and prepared to present his granddaughter at Lady Guthrie's intimate gathering a few days hence.

From past experience, he knew that the intimate gathering would be grand rather than cozy. He wondered if his future bride was any more prepared for this meeting than he was.

As vibrant and socially accomplished as he understood Madeline Macooish to be, he could not help guessing that the duchess's soiree would be different than what the American would be accustomed to. For all that the lady was admired in America, England was a vastly different place. He feared she might be shunned by the other women because she was an outsider. And not just any outsider, but one who threatened to dash their ambition of gaining a titled marriage.

Heath pitied his bride-to-be as much as he did himself. He could not imagine why she had agreed to marry Oliver. It was not as though her family would fail without the money like his would. And not only the family of his blood but those he was now responsible for: parlormaids, footmen, butlers, cooks and farmers. Even the merchants Fencroft frequented could suffer if he failed to keep the estate solvent.

If he could choose the direction of his life, it would not be this.

Heath was far better suited to the bucolic life of the estate. Helping farmers tend the land and the livestock—it was all he'd ever needed of life. He'd been grateful to be born the second son.

None of that mattered now. There was a crown pressing on his head and the legacy Willa had unknowingly bequeathed him burdening his heart.

It hurt his brain to think about everything all at once. He'd rather let his mind wander to Cinderella. He'd come out tonight, half hoping to see her again. Thoughts of her had interfered with his daily duties; they'd even invaded his nighttime dreams.

If he could only see her one more time, discover who she was.

He glanced the length and width of the garden. While he'd been woolgathering, fog had rolled in. The vapor swirled brown and ugly in the light given off by a gas lantern beside the gate.

A movement caught his eye. A woman stood beside the fountain dabbing her eyes with a white apron. He heard her softly weeping.

She was not the lady he sought, but a chambermaid who worked on the third floor. He recalled seeing her hustling about her duties.

Since he could not turn away from a weeping woman, he approached her.

"Miss?" He spoke softly but still his voice must have startled her, because she jumped.

"Oh, Lord Fencroft, sir," she sniffled. "I beg your pardon for being out here but, but I—"

"May I be of help, Miss—?"

"Oh, I'm Betty, sir. And no one can help, I fear."

"Is there a problem with your employment?"

She shook her capped head, and her breath shuddered when she inhaled. "No, not that—I shouldn't trouble you about it."

"As Fencroft, I'm the one you ought to trouble about it." Maybe he could not help in any way but to listen, but perhaps he could.

"It's to do with my cousin, sir. She's a sweet and trusting soul but gullible to go with it. Well, the poor wee girl trusted the wrong man. She gave birth to a child and now has no way to support it. No one will hire a fallen woman. She's gone to leave the baby at Slademore House. Not to speak ill of the sainted charity—they'll care for the wee one fine enough—but I fear the grief of the parting will send my cousin headlong into the Thames."

Betty did not know how wrong she was about the charity being "sainted."

And why would she? Heath would think the same had he not stumbled upon the truth while searching for Willa's baby.

He would have been as blind as the rest of society, believing that Slademore House was exactly what it appeared to be.

Living luxuriously was easier, he supposed, when one thought one's donations went to ease the lives of those who did not. It was the only reason he could think of that no one ever looked beyond what their eyes saw when it came to the place—or the man.

Slademore House might appear to be a haven for the hopeless, but in truth it existed for the purpose of feeding the baron's lust for wealth and prestige.

In Heath's opinion, the baron put on a display of opulence to disguise the fact that his social position was a few steps below that of a duke or a viscount.

The fellow drew attention wherever he went. Even the small dog he toted about wore jewels on its collar.

Where everyone else seemed to see an angel in Slademore, Heath saw the devil. Who else would house children in poverty while keeping the gifts of the wealthy to benefit himself? What kind of man would allow a sick child to die before he would spend money on a doctor's visit?

Or might it not be giving up a few pounds so much as having a doctor suspect the conditions in which the children really lived?

Well, he would not get away with it forever.

"I will keep your cousin in my prayers, Betty. And if there is anything I can do to help, you may call upon me."

"Thank you, my lord. I only fear things have gone too far by now."

After a quiet moment, Betty nodded and hurried across the garden, her image weaving in and out of the fog. He heard the door to the back stairs of the town house open.

The door hadn't closed before he dashed for the stables.

Chapter Three

"It's the devil's own night, my lord," stated Charles Creed, the only coachman Heath trusted to accompany him on the night's errand.

"Not so different from any other night so close to Whitechapel," he answered, tugging the brim of a black hat low over his brow. He withdrew the dark mask he was about to tie over his face and gripped it tight in his fingers.

"It's just that the fog is so yellow and foul. An evil presence is what it is. Who can tell what wickedness it's hiding."

"It's hiding us."

"And a lucky thing. Looks like the baron is getting worried. There's two guards by the back door tonight."

Heath would ask if Creed wanted to wait a few streets away but he already knew the answer would be no.

They sat side by side, pretending to be laughing at some ribald joke as they passed the door. The guards glanced up and then away.

"Wish we knew when the girl was bringing the baby," Creed whispered when they rounded the corner of the building. "It's not safe business circling the block."

"Nothing about this is safe."

"Which is why you should quit and leave it to me," the coachman said.

No doubt Creed was correct. Heath was a man under great obligation.

"It takes two of us to get the children safely away."

"I'll be right relieved when we can expose the black-guard for good and all."

Exposing a supposed saint would be a difficult thing to do, especially in this case.

The baron had several benefactors of high rank. He was highly respected by all of society. His good deeds were touted in the newspaper on a regular basis. Even his cousin was a judge of much influence in London.

No, anyone who went to inspect Slademore House would see what Heath had when he'd first gone to ask for Willa's baby: well-cared-for children doted upon by a loving staff, and fed tarts and treats on a regular basis. They would be gratified to see their generous donations being put to good use.

But they would not have seen what Heath had when, his mind full of questions, he'd gone looking further.

Clearly no one suspected a man who sat in the first pew at church every Sunday to be a greedy soul.

"Don't you wonder, Creed, why no one ever questions how Slademore manages to dress in such riches? Why that little dog he carries about wears real jewels in his collar?"

"Oh, aye, many times. I think folks are just blinded by him being so angelic-looking."

Yes, and hadn't Satan been reputed to be the same?

Leaping off the bench to the ground, Heath nodded up at Creed.

"We have help, though," Creed said. "There's our informer. It's not only us to help the children."

Without this mysterious ally, they could do nothing.

Heath could only assume it was the person who had left the door unlocked for him when he'd rescued Willa's daughter.

Without the notes Creed received, they could not do this.

While Heath climbed into the interior of the carriage, Creed changed his coat and his hat. The same pair of men in the same coach would draw the attention of the back-door guards who would be on alert since they had been here only nights ago—the very night he had met Cinderella in the garden.

Drawing back the curtain, Heath spotted the bent figure of a woman clearly weeping while she made her way to the back door of Slademore House. She appeared to be carrying a bundle close to her chest.

Creed must have noticed her, too, for the carriage slowed down.

Heath snatched up a pewter-tipped cane. The thing was a weapon as much as a prop. While the carriage creaked along, he jumped out on the side facing away from the guards.

With his shoulders hunched, he limped along the cobblestones, his head dipping toward the ground to hide his mask. He hoped he appeared to be no more threatening than a drunk having trouble maneuvering his way.

He intercepted the woman when she was but thirty feet from the guards.

One of them glanced up; the other yawned.

Heath made a tripping motion and pretended to catch his balance on the lady. He slipped an arm under the baby.

"Come with me," he whispered.

"You're him—the Abductor!" She opened her mouth to scream but Heath covered it with his palm.

"It's him!" called the guard just finishing his yawn. He jerked his coat aside and withdrew a pistol.

Heath yanked the baby away from the woman, believing she would follow.

She did, screeching and yanking on the end of the blanket. He snagged her elbow with his free arm and dragged her toward the moving coach.

"Your cousin, Betty, sent me." The familiar name silenced her scream.

A shot rang out. He heard the bullet hit a stone on the street. Because of the fog it was hard to tell how close the pursuing footsteps were. Close enough to raise the hairs on his arms, though.

"Get inside!"

Thankfully she made the leap. He handed the infant to her on the run and then dragged himself in after her.

He heard the whip crack over the horse's ears, felt the lurch of the carriage when the animals jolted into a gallop. Wood splintered when a bullet connected with the back corner of the carriage.

It took three blocks for his heartbeat and his breathing to slow enough to reassure the trembling woman that he was not kidnapping her but taking her and her infant to safety.

Half a mile away from the town house, Creed slowed down to let him out. The coachman continued at a slow, leisurely-looking pace, bearing his charges toward the seashore and the haven of Rock Rose Cottage.

How could she possibly?

And yet here she sat on the balcony overlooking the very lovely gardens of Fencroft House with the dratted notebook in her lap.

Her brain nearly ached with the studying she had been

doing. If it had not been for pleasant memories of a darkly handsome man flitting through her brain at odd times, she would be completely addle-brained by now.

Where had he come from—where had he gone to?

Sheaves of paper fluttered on her lap. The afternoon breeze lifted the scent of roses from below. She shook her head. It didn't matter about the man.

She was not intended for him, knew nothing about him. For all that she stared down at the fountain she was not likely to see him again.

Glancing back at the notebook, she frowned, wanting to rip the pages to shreds and rain them down on the garden.

She felt part saint for going along with Grandfather's machinations, also part pawn, and completely a fool.

If she felt a fool to herself she would appear thrice so to others. She was a foreigner to the ways of the British aristocracy in every way she could be.

"Correct forms of address," her grandfather had written in the bold script he always used.

She had read it so many times that the paper was limp. How did Londoners keep everyone straight? Perhaps one had to be born to it.

If she closed her eyes and thought hard she recalled that she would address the earl as Lord Fencroft, but only for the first meeting. After that she would call him "my lord" or, perhaps in time, Fencroft.

But under the stress of a face-to-face meeting she might forget. The American in her might blurt out something like: *How pleasant to meet you, Mr. Cavill.* Or what if she accidentally called him Mr. Fencroft—or Oliver! That might result in a great scandal.

But if she became his wife? What did she call him then? Something a bit more personal than his title, she hoped. And if that familiarity was allowed, was she permitted to use it in public or only in private?

And what would he call her? Madeline? She had urged Grandfather to send a telegram to the earl informing him that it would be Clementine who was coming and not Madeline. He'd only laughed and said it was not necessary because Lord Fencroft was a lucky man to get either of his girls.

Pressure built in her head, pounding behind her eyes. She could see it all too clearly—after she made a fool of herself and disgraced Grandfather by incorrectly addressing the earl, she would need to address his siblings.

"Lady Olivia" would be right and easy, or perhaps it was "the Lady Olivia"? She squinted at the note Grandfather had written in the margin. Olivia had married Victor Shaw—the younger son of an earl—which meant she retained her own precedence.

What did that even mean?

Does that change what I call her? Would not "Mrs. Shaw," or Heaven help them all, "Olivia" suffice for most occasions?

The one thing she did know for certain was that Grandfather was going to regret bringing her here. No doubt he was going to have to take her home a shamed woman without the title he considered so vital to the survival of the Macooish line—which at this moment in time did not exist beyond her and Madeline.

Lost in puzzling out exactly why she had agreed to cross the ocean in the first place, other than perhaps being a martyr to Grandfather's cause, Clementine found her mind drifting back to the stranger in the garden—again.

She was prone to do that far too easily. Truly, she had no business considering marriage to anyone until she could put that dashing fellow out of her head.

With a sigh she returned her attention to the notebook on her lap and reminded herself that one day she would have to live her life without her grandfather. And how could she possibly do that knowing she had let him down?

She could not and so here she was.

But even now all she had committed to do was to seriously consider the marriage. She would need to meet the earl before she would make such a monumental decision.

While Grandfather had agreed to offer his granddaughter to Oliver Cavill and the earl had agreed to accept her—well, not her so much as Madeline—she, the granddaughter sitting on a balcony in Mayfair needed to know that the man she would spend her life with was someone she could respect.

Love might or might not follow wedding vows and the marriage might still be adequate. But without respect? No, without that a union could only end in misery.

Grandfather seemed convinced that she would be content with his choice for her groom.

Indeed! He'd been confident enough to have invested a fortune in the venture, surely half of it in ball gowns. He would need to succeed in his Scotland venture in order to recoup the cost.

Since Clementine was not convinced that fluff and satin ruffles would ensure happiness, or even basic contentment, she was withholding her final decision. Or so she told herself.

Deep down she knew the Earl of Fencroft would have to be quite unworthy in order for her to break Grandfather's heart.

So, for now, she had to practice. "It is lovely to meet you, Lady Olivia, or whoever you are in whichever social situation is at hand." Being alone on the balcony, she allowed a frustrated and unladylike snort to escape her lips. "I'll need to marry quickly so I can call you good sister and be done with it."

"And in the meantime Lady Olivia should suffice nicely."

Clementine turned her cheek up for her grandfather's kiss.

"Is not your new home grand?" He grinned at the impressively stately building across the way.

Oh, it was grand, but not so formal-looking as to be unwelcoming. A pretty vine twined up the west side of the house while flowering trees bordered a private patio on the east side.

Still, to call the town house home was premature.

"And tomorrow, your season will begin."

"What was that?" Absorbed in looking at the town house as she had been, she must have misheard.

"Your social season. Your coming out, so to speak."

"You will recall that I am twenty-three years old and a good five years past time for that."

"Folderol. I do realize it is late in the season but I still hope to have you presented at court."

"No, Grandfather. Perhaps I will wed to your liking, but I will not be paraded about like a blushing innocent. It would be humiliating."

"You are an innocent, are you not? And in the moment you are blushing. I've got to warn you, my dear, that as an American you will be suspect. As a foreigner sweeping in to claim a plum of a prize you must observe all the customs." He reached down and swiped a curl behind her ear. "Do not be surprised if you are resented by the families who have raised their daughters to fill the slippers you are standing in."

"Well, they most certainly have my blessing because

I will not be presented at court. Asking me to quietly marry an earl is one thing, but no one will be better off because I look like—"

"A good and loyal child who deserves every advantage a title can bring. Just think, Clemmie, your children will never suffer from having been conceived of an accident of birth."

"That is one of the most outrageous things I've ever heard you say. I don't know that one can consider being conceived in an adulterous liaison an accident of birth. And do you truly believe I would allow that to happen?"

"I'm certain my mother did not intend it to happen, and yet it did."

And he had lived with the unfair label of bastard because of it.

She wished she had not rebuked him so flippantly. The lack of a respectable birth had been his burden and what formed his values. Grandfather craved respectability in a way that most people did not.

And yet she had to point out, "I could marry the corner constable and my children would be respectable." Was the man in the fountain a constable, perhaps?

"But not protected against life's unpredictability. I thought you understood, Clemmie. A title gives you power, protection. And I am convinced you will be happy with the earl."

"There is one of us, then. I've yet to even meet the man."

Judging by the wide smile on his face, Grandfather was confident that all would go as he willed it.

"I told you the truth about him. He's a fine fellow— an outstanding chap. You will get along well together."

Oh, she didn't hope for that much. Only that they would share a mutual respect.

* * *

If Lord and Lady Guthrie's casual gathering was this grand, what would one of their famous balls be like? It would glitter to the heavens, Clementine figured.

The Macooish mansion in Los Angeles was lovely, a well-known gathering place, but it did not glow with half the formal elegance of this home.

She clenched her fingers on Grandfather's coat sleeve. As long as she remained attached to him she might get through this—this presentation, this being shown off like a new variety of flower, or bug.

But really, she was far from the first American lady to invade the aristocracy in order to save a peerage from financial ruin.

"How is it that you got us invited to this 'little gathering'—isn't that what you called it?" Clementine glanced about the ballroom that Grandfather escorted her into. There had to be a hundred people or more milling about in lively conversation.

And one of them was very likely the fellow expecting to marry Madeline.

She feared the poor earl was in for a disappointment. Grandfather had touted a bride who was as pretty as a butterfly and as lyrical as a sweet melody.

Clementine was neither of those things. The earl was bound to be dissatisfied with her if a woman like her cousin was who he wanted.

"The duke is interested in the Scotland business." He shot her a wink. "Nothing like a good financial bond to open doors that would have remained closed."

Money had always been Grandfather's greatest tool. At least Fencroft would not be disappointed in that part of the bargain. The Macooish fortune in ironworks was beyond respectable.

And yet, Grandfather did not trust that alone to ensure the family's security.

"Do not be surprised to find other men competing for your attention tonight since no one knows of the arrangement I made with Fencroft. But keep in mind that I have made a bargain with him."

"As long as you keep in mind that I have yet to agree to anything." Of course, she would not be here if she did not seriously consider his wish, would she? "Is the earl here?"

Grandfather shook his head. "I don't see him, but perhaps he is in the parlor, where the gents are gaming."

If only Oliver Cavill's absence was not as much relief as it was disappointment.

Also, it did weigh on her that if he was in the parlor it meant he was a gambler. She would feel better about the man had he not been gaming. She hoped there would be other things about her potential intended that she would come to respect.

But it could not be denied that one thing she would have respected was to see him waiting to greet her instead of going into further debt.

"Do you not think a more formal meeting would have been appropriate, Grandfather? It is all rather haphazard, having us meet so casually."

"To my mind, it's more comfortable this way."

As if there could possibly be anything "comfortable" in any of this.

Walking under a huge, exceptionally glittering chandelier, she was aware of people staring at her, the women from under veiled lashes and the men with ill-disguised interest.

"They'll have heard that you are an American."

"They aren't staring at you."

"I'm not an heiress come to snatch up a peer. I'm sure

the debutantes and their mothers are quaking in their dancing slippers wondering who you have set your sights upon."

"Sneering behind their smiles, more to the point."

He turned her chin with his fingertips, pulling her gaze away from the frown of a middle-aged woman peering at her through a huge arrangement of orange-and-yellow chrysanthemums. "Clemmie Macooish, keep your chin up just so, and don't forget that you are the most beautiful woman in this room. It's no wonder some of them are jealous of you. Why I'll wager your gown cost more than three of theirs put together."

Heaven help her, it was probably true. Being a man, Grandfather would not realize that the extravagance gave them even more reason to be resentful of her.

"Put on your best smile. Our hostess approaches." He patted her fingers where they clamped onto his arm. She suspected that under her gloves, they were as bone white as the lace was.

"Your Grace?" she asked under her breath. This was where it would be revealed whether her studying had been for naught.

Grandfather nodded, his smile bright for the approaching duchess.

If other women's smiles at Clementine seemed forced, the duchess's did not. Lady Guthrie was clearly gifted at making a guest feel welcome.

Clementine prayed that her return smile would indicate that she was pleased to be here, especially given that she was not.

While Grandfather led the way with formal pleasantries, Clementine gazed over Her Grace's shoulder at the garden beyond the open doors. If she became overwhelmed, she would escape to that torchlit paradise and find a private place to catch her breath.

Perhaps once she met her earl the flutters in her belly would settle. What she needed to bear in mind was that the opinions of daughters and mammas did not matter so much in the end. If Fencroft approved of her all would be well.

If she approved of him, all would be very well. For all that she struggled against Grandfather's insistence that she become a countess, she did want to give him what he wanted most, if it was within her power to do so.

This man she owed everything to had been horribly betrayed by one granddaughter. If she could ease his grief over it, she would. Of course, she had yet to meet Fencroft, so she could not say for certain.

But she would try. She did know that much.

"Come, let me introduce you," Her Grace declared.

Grandfather's arm fell away from under her hand.

She prayed that her lips formed a bright and twittering smile.

Grandfather walked toward a group of gentlemen engrossed in lively conversation across the room. She was utterly on her own.

Even though the duchess was leading her to a gathering of women near the garden doors, sanctuary felt miles away.

Heath strode into the grand entry hall and handed off his black coat, hat and gloves to the servant standing in waiting.

"Thank you, my good man," he said with a nod.

The fellow returned the nod but did not speak. Now that Heath was Fencroft, life was more formal. He'd been set on some blamed pedestal that kept some people at arm's length. At the same time other people who had barely spared him a glance in the past attached themselves to him.

His mind returned to the woman in the pond. She didn't know who he was and so she showed him no deference. It was almost as though he was simply Heath Cavill, second son again. What would he not give to be strolling on a moonlit path at the estate in Derbyshire instead of traversing these marble floors?

What would he not give to hear his brother's congenial laugh one more time? But death changed everything and so he would not.

By custom, he ought not to be here. He was still in mourning. But in mourning for Oliver. His brother would encourage him to laugh and enjoy his first meeting with Madeline Macooish.

It wasn't likely that any of the women here would object to his break with tradition. They would think he was looking for a wife, which, in fact, he was.

Going into the ballroom, he felt the gazes of a dozen blushing girls settle upon him. Then again, not him so much as the Earl of Fencroft.

Somewhere among this assembly was a vivacious, blue-eyed heiress who assumed she was about to meet a fellow who was as fun-seeking as she was.

One of the ladies milling about this room was willing to give up life as she had known it for the honor of being called countess.

He rather thought she might regret that choice. Chances were the lady did not understand the restrictions that would be put upon her. Not by him so much as by the rules of polite society.

Other American ladies had made the same choice and

later regretted it. The gossip sheet was full of their marital misery.

He would do his best to see that his wife did not suffer by giving herself and her fortune to him, but there was only so much he could do in the face of social opinion.

There was also the matter of surrendering his heart to a wife. He'd done it once, given it quite freely to a fiancée who only pretended to cherish it. He did not wish to go through that despair again.

Which, it suddenly occurred to him, made a marriage by arrangement appealing. While he would be committed to his wife in being faithful to her and providing her with a comfortable life, she would not expect him to invest his heart in the agreement. There was every possibility that she would not want to invest hers, either.

A marriage of convenience suddenly seemed a fine thing.

"Lord Fencroft!" For a split second, Heath expected to hear his brother's voice answering the greeting of the matron chugging toward him, her freshly presented daughter in tow.

"Lady Meyers," he answered, cringing at the gravity in his tone while recalling the genuine pleasure Oliver took in making the acquaintance of a debutante. It was the job of an earl to make people feel welcome in his presence. If the half-panicked expression on the girl's face was anything to go by, he was failing miserably. "What a pleasure it is to see you tonight. I hope you are well."

"Quite well." For some reason her smile sagged. "As well as a mother can be when her son goes into trade, I suppose. But here, please meet my daughter, Emily. I'm sure she will find a match to make us all proud."

"It's a pleasure to meet you, Lady Emily." He bowed

over her hand, certain he felt the heat of her blush through her glove.

"As it turns out, Emily has one dance free on her card—the next one in fact. It would be a lovely chance for you two young people to get to know one another."

The right and decent thing to do would be to refuse the dance given that he was here to meet the woman he would marry.

But he'd been neatly boxed in by the matron. Unless he wanted to insult them both, there was nothing to do but graciously agree, or appear to at any rate.

He danced with Lady Emily, half embarrassed by the furious blush reddening her cheeks through every step of the waltz. The last note had barely sounded before she nodded, turned and fled from the dance floor.

Emily's mother might think her daughter ready for marriage, but the person Heath saw was still a child.

While the girl hurried over to half a dozen young ladies whose heads were bent in apparent gossip, Heath scanned the room for a blond, elegantly coiffed head. He'd learned from Oliver that Miss Macooish was a confident sort, a lady whom he imagined would dance until her feet blistered.

Still in mourning for his brother, Heath would have been excused from dancing, certainly. But mothers continued to come forward asking to put his name on their daughter's dance card.

While he had no intention of waltzing until his toes blistered, he would dance to honor his brother. Sitting in a dark corner would not serve that purpose. If Oliver were looking down upon the gathering, he did not want him to be frowning.

Debutante after debutante came into his arms, every one of them sweet and pink-cheeked. He could barely tell one from another. A proper earl, like Oliver, in fact, would know every name, what rank and family they came from.

Once or twice, through the whirl of dancers he caught a brief glimpse of a red-haired lady on the arm of an older gentleman.

She was not the one he was looking for. Somewhere there was supposed to be an older man, James Macooish, with his lively blonde granddaughter on his arm.

He would ask his hostess who she was, but how would he explain his interest in her? The arrangement with Macooish was private and he would prefer to keep it so.

He did not see anyone matching Miss Macooish's description.

Ah, but he spotted the red-haired lady standing with the duchess and being introduced around.

She was new to society, he thought. He would recall that shade of hair had he ever met her. She stood out as a red rose in a bouquet of pink.

He nearly chuckled out loud at the poetic thought because it was something his brother might think. And then, just like that, in a blink, he wanted to weep.

After two hours he no longer felt poetic and the weeping had to do with the blisters he had vowed to avoid.

From the corner of his eye, he spotted Lady Meyers snatch up Emily's hand and begin an advance upon him.

With the garden doors standing open and only a few feet to his left, he rushed—no, hobbled—through them into the cool sanctuary of the night.

Music faded as he walked along the torchlit path, making his way deep into the garden.

Clementine sighed and leaned back against the garden bench. Everything smelled green and as soothing as it did in the Los Angeles garden. A good bit cooler, though.

Gazing up, she was reassured to see that the night sky looked the same wherever one traveled.

Misty-looking clouds raced across the face of the moon, making it appear ethereal, fairy-like.

She hadn't told Grandfather she was escaping to the garden. She should have: it was quite improper to be out here without a chaperone.

The wonderful solitude would not last for long. Knowing her as well as he did, Grandfather would quickly figure out where she'd be.

Even when he did, it would take him a long time to locate her given how very deeply she had wandered along the path and how many secret places the garden hid.

Judging by the rustle of shrubbery and a hushed sigh she had heard while walking along, she assumed she was not as alone out here as it seemed.

She had to admit it was a lovely, late-summer night, just right for romance.

At least it would be for a little while longer. A cool breeze rippled along the stones and made the leaves in her private spot whisper. The hem of her skirt fluttered. She glanced up to see a dense bank of clouds move slowly across the face of the moon.

How quickly did storms advance here in Mayfair? At home one had hours of warning before rain began to fall, which it rarely did this time of year.

But yes, just now, the scent of the air changed. She felt its moist hand brush her skin. And there in the distance? She was fairly certain she saw a flash and, seconds later, she heard the faint rumble of thunder.

This was exciting, since she could not recall the last time she had heard thunder. Two years ago, or three?

In considering whether or not she could be happy in

England, she had not anticipated the wetter climate. Rainy days were her favorite.

So, to the positive side of her mental list of reasons she should wed the earl, she added rain. She saw the word in her mind right there beneath afternoon tea and cakes, and strangers in fountains. Since this was merely a mental list, she allowed the handsome stranger to remain on it.

But his inclusion in the list created a problem on the "reasons to sail for home" side of the list. She had liked the fellow, for all the little she knew of him. He reminded her that liking one's spouse was paramount. At this point she did not know that she could even tolerate the earl—a man who did not show the common courtesy of leaving the gaming room to meet the woman who had the funds to save him from financial ruin.

Even though she held no illusions that the earl was going into the marriage for any reason but monetary gain, she was disturbed by the contrast between the behaviors of the pair of men who were lately on her mind. One of them had gallantly offered to walk her home in the wee hours of the night, while the other had ignored her presence.

Marriage implied a particular kind of intimacy. She did not think she could allow free access of her body to a man she did not at least think highly of.

Recalling how appealing she had found Heath Ramsfield for those few moments she spent with him, she wondered if perhaps she ought to stand firm for a love match.

Wondered until she recalled how Grandfather's arms had held her through that flood. Held on with a love so fierce she had not been swept away.

That memory, and everything else he had done for her, weighed heavily in her decision.

If only there was someone she could speak with—a trustworthy confidant. Once again, she sorely missed her cousin, even though if she saw her this moment she would chastise her.

Footsteps crunched on the path.

"Excuse me, my lady," said a deep voice from the shadows. "I did not realize this space was occupied."

Chapter Four

It was her, the woman with the red hair Heath had caught mysterious glimpses of throughout the evening. He was not sure why it was that she had caught his interest more than any other beautiful lady in the room tonight.

His voice must have startled her because she gasped, touching her throat with lacy white gloves.

"I apologize for intruding on your solitude."

"It's quite all right. I was just about to go inside." She stood up, and then all at once her green eyes—even in the dark he could tell that they fell somewhere between emerald and peridot—blinked wide.

"Mr. Ramsfield? Heath Ramsfield?"

If she was startled to see him, he was doubly surprised to come upon her in the duchess's garden. How was it that this lovely commoner came to be dressed in satin, lace and exceptionally exquisite jewels?

"Miss Fitz—is that you?" Yes, he was nearly certain it was and yet… "What are you doing out here?"

"Seeking answers to a dilemma. And you—have you run afoul of a cat again and come here to escape it?"

He could hardly be offended, not when she looked up at him with good humor winking in her eyes.

"Also seeking answers to a dilemma."

She sat back down, turning a fraction to the side to make way for her small, fashionable bustle. She patted the bench.

"I recognize that it isn't proper to be alone together in the garden, but I do not happen to have a chaperone at the moment."

"At the first sign of footsteps I promise to dive beneath that bush." He indicated a large, dense rosebush behind the bench. Thorns be damned, he wanted to spend time with this lady who, he expected, was far different than the one he would be wedding in a very short time. "Will you not be missed?"

"No doubt I'm being sought as we speak—but I am in no hurry to be found."

Did she not value her employment? Although she hardly appeared to be in service.

Still, sitting down beside Miss Fitz seemed the most natural thing in the world to do. Had he been in the same situation with anyone but this forthright American, he would have immediately fled. Being alone in the dark of night with one of the debutantes would have found him at the altar within a fortnight.

At the altar with expectations of love and romance. Much better he wed the heiress and be free of such entanglements.

"Nor am I." He smiled at her. It might be the most genuine pleasure he'd taken in that gesture since he'd last seen her. "You look quite fetching, by the way."

Fetching in a very expensive way. Odd, that.

"My grandfather has been very lavish in making me look like an exquisite doll."

"I tip my hat to him. He has succeeded beyond measure."

"Grandfather always succeeds when it comes to me. I do his will quite obediently on most occasions. It is my downfall, I'm afraid."

"I find it hard to believe you are submissive."

"Loyal, I think, rather than that."

"And what loyal act are you hiding from out here?"

"Marriage." The thought flashed through his mind that some fellow was a very lucky man. "He has arranged one for me and I am not at all sure the fellow and I will suit."

He had more in common with Jane Fitz than she knew.

"Have you spoken to him about how you feel?"

"I've told him I would only go through with the marriage if I found the man was someone whom I could respect. My fear is that I will not even find him tolerable."

"You should not marry a man you cannot tolerate. I support you in that."

"Do you? I appreciate your saying so. I've been quite alone in my concern over it. I can scarce believe I've told you, a stranger, about it."

"It's because I am a stranger. I think it's easier to speak one's mind openly to someone one does not know. Although I do feel we are no longer quite strangers. But tell me, why do you believe this fellow will not suit?"

"We were supposed to meet for the first time tonight and yet he has not had the courtesy of emerging from the gaming room." Wasn't that one of life's odd coincidences? He had yet to meet his bride as had been arranged, either. "I believe he might not be the most stable of men. I have no wish to act the fellow's keeper."

Heath had taken a brief walk through the game room tonight. Slademore had been in attendance, but surely he was not the man she meant. Which of them could she have been speaking of? None of them appeared to have anything in mind but cards, or, if he was a footman, serving the gentlemen.

Gentleman or servant, none of them seemed to be anticipating meeting a bride for the first time.

"Perhaps circumstances prevented him from meeting you."

"I sincerely hope not." Her brows arched. Her chin lifted while she looked steadily into his eyes.

"I'm sure it's only that he had a duty—"

"A duty to his cards? Never mind. Time will tell if I consent to wed him or not." She lifted her shoulders with a sigh, gave her head a slight shake. "And what drives you out into the night, Mr. Ramsfield?"

"Much the same thing as you. Apparently we are kindred spirits." Somehow, speaking to Miss Fitz seemed comfortable. Even knowing he should not be out here alone with her, he wanted to talk all night long. "Shall I call for a chaperone?"

"I'm hardly a blushing child. Besides, we've been alone long enough already to be thoroughly compromised. Calling for a chaperone will only draw attention to the fact. No doubt we would be forced to marry and I surmise that you are promised to another?"

"Bound and fettered." He should not have revealed that. It was a thought best kept to himself.

Overhead, he heard the soft pattering of raindrops. Dense leaves of the rosebush growing over the arbor kept the moisture from penetrating, at least for the moment.

"I must say—" she arched one pretty brow "—that attitude does not bode well for a blessed union."

He nodded. "You understand that, I believe?"

"Sadly, I do. Still, I do not have to go through with it. Although it will be at the cost of crushing my grandfather's heart. He's had one granddaughter do that already. But you, are you so bound that you cannot walk away from it?"

A drop of water must have hit her nose because she lifted her hand and brushed it off. If only he had been the one to whisk it away. For some reason he desperately wanted to feel the warmth of her skin under his thumb.

"Yes, I am. There are many people who would be destitute if I walked away from my duty."

"Birds of a feather are what we appear to be, Mr. Ramsfield. If only we were free to take wing and fly away."

Rain began to leak down the leaves. A torch on the path glowed dimly on Miss Fitz's face and revealed a smattering of raindrops across the bridge of her nose.

"I find that I would not mind flying away with you," he admitted.

Nor would he mind kissing her. He ought to have summoned a chaperone. This was dangerous ground he was treading.

Hell, not treading so much as dashing headlong over. Helpless to do otherwise, he lifted his hand, smoothed away the raindrops from that fine sharp nose with his fingertips.

"I say we do." She smiled and winked. "Let's ruffle our feathers and take to the sky, just the two of us."

"Yes, well." He shook his head, trying to clear it of the delightful fog swirling in his brain. "It would be a great scandal if I kissed you."

Had he murmured that aloud?

"Immense—but only if someone knew about it."

She was bold and sassy.

She completely captivated him.

"Or if we were legally bound to others," he foolishly pointed out. Had he lost his mind?

"I have yet to give my word on anything."

"And I have yet to meet my ball and chain." He cupped the back of her head, felt the slickness of the rain on the strands of her hair. Lifting her chin with his fingertips he bent toward her rain-dotted lips. "Fly away with me, Jane Fitz."

"Clementine Jane Macooish!" At the sound of the deep voice, Heath's head jerked up. "Have you lost your mind?"

He stared into the furious expression of an older man.

"Take your hands off my granddaughter, sir."

What? Oh…he was still cupping the back of Jane's head. As if under water, good sense stroked toward the surface of his brain. And what had the man called her— Macooish?

"On the contrary, Grandfather." Jane, or Clementine, slowly stood up, her brows arched in a most becoming, if rebellious, way. "I'm quite certain I've just found it."

"Have you found her?" asked a voice Heath recognized.

Now might be the time to leap for the rose bush.

"I tell you, I only stopped for a conversation with Lady Claremont and she disappeared from my—"

The duchess's face popped into view. Her mouth sagged open.

"Lord Fencroft!" Feeling rather like a worm in the grass with everyone staring down at him, he stood.

Her Grace's eyes blinked furiously while she sought words appropriate for this compromising situation—this horrid breach of hospitality.

"Fencroft?" Miss Macooish spun toward him.

"Macooish?" He swiveled his gaze toward her.

Miss Macooish's mouth worked silently. Not for lack of words, he thought, but because of an abundance of them. He imagined she did not know which ones to fire at him first.

* * *

Clementine hardly knew what to say. Words fumbled on her tongue vying for utterance.

Grandfather, however, suffered no such confusion.

"Charlatan! Scoundrel! Seducer!" He stood nose to nose with the man, poking his chest with a stab of his finger upon each heated word. A roll of thunder might have been taken as agreement. "Reprobate!"

Appearing somewhat blanched, the duchess tugged on Grandfather's sleeve.

"Mr. Macooish! You are speaking to the Earl of Fencroft!"

"What foolishness is this?" Grandfather swiveled his gaze and settled it on Lady Guthrie. "I've met the earl and this is not him."

"You met my late brother." The deceiver's handsome mouth turned tight and pale at the corners. "Did you not read about his passing in the papers?"

In spite of what was happening, in spite of the hot fist squeezing her belly, it could not be denied that he had a handsome mouth and that she had nearly kissed it.

All of a sudden she saw the bluster rush out of Grandfather, and the words that the man had spoken settled in her brain.

Oliver Cavill had passed away? It could not be! His poor family must be devastated.

Considering how the new earl must be wretched with grief, she decided it would not be right to hold his deception too harshly against him.

"Ah, well, we have been traveling and not caught all the news." Grandfather withdrew his finger, curled it into his fist and took a backward step. "My condolences on your bitter loss, my lord."

The earl nodded curtly.

"Macooish?" he asked in a gruff voice.

Footsteps crunched on the pathway. The lovers she had heard cooing at each other earlier were no doubt retreating from the rain. Lady Guthrie turned to look at them when they slowed down to gape at the unfolding scandal.

Clementine could not see the expression the duchess shot at the pair but they hurried away.

"James Macooish." Grandfather nodded. "The young lady you were accosting is my granddaughter, Clementine."

In all honesty, *accosting* was a harsh word to describe what had happened. She had been a willing participant, at least until the point when the man's true identity had been revealed.

She was certain Grandfather had not brought up the word idly. No, she knew well enough that he was trying to point out that the current earl had overstepped his bounds and must now live up to his brother's agreement.

He had to, of course—or face ruin.

For a time the only sound was rain pelting leaves and stones.

Then the earl pinned her with a glower.

"Jane—Fitz, was it not?"

Oh, no, titled or not, this man had no right to judge her.

She arched a brow at him as imperiously as she knew how. The fact that Heath Cavill was in mourning did not excuse his behavior and given the hardness in his expression…well, sympathy did have its limits. "Mr. Ramsfield?"

"You do not look at all the way my brother described you—Madeline."

"No, I would not since I am not. Madeline has run off rather than marry for a title. An event that leaves me as your ever-so-wealthy ball and chain."

"Clementine." Grandfather spoke in a soothing tone. "I'm sure no lasting harm was done. There is no need to be—"

The duchess huffed. Being the closest to the woman, Clementine was certain the sound disguised a curse.

The Earl of Fencroft spun about and walked away with his shoulders hunched against the rain. He stopped a short distance away, staring at a bush.

Thunder pounded closer than before. Clementine felt the echo of it shiver through the stones under her soaked slippers.

"Fencroft," Her Grace stated, her tone blade-sharp. If he spoke one word in his defense—of which there could be none—he would be cut.

He whirled around, his black coat swinging wide. After staring hard at the three of them, he strode back.

"I'm willing to carry on with our agreement." This he stated, locking gazes, not with Grandfather, but with her.

"Why, that is very magnanimous of you, my lord." Surely everyone heard the distain—all right, the sneer—in her voice. "But as you recall I told you that I would only wed a man I could respect. Therefore, I do not agree to this marriage."

"Clementine!" Grandfather's gasp sounded as shocked as she'd ever heard. But what was she to do? Marry someone who concealed his identity and then tried to steal, or coax, a kiss? How would she ever trust him?

"That, my dear," the duchess announced, "is no longer a matter of choice for you. The damage to both of your reputations is done."

"I believe I will survive it."

"And so you might," she said with a very noble-looking tilt of her head, "were you back in America. But here you are in my garden."

And that was all she had to say to Clementine.

Shifting her attention to Heath Cavill, the duchess said, "You may announce the engagement tomorrow. People will assume the two of you were overcome with romance and give this lapse in judgment a wink. The wedding will be three weeks hence and not a day later."

The duchess placed her hand on Grandfather's arm, looking composed even in the midst of the transgression tainting her garden and a deluge of rain coming down upon her head.

Watching Grandfather hitch one shoulder and then the other while he walked away, she knew he was grinning like a loon in mating season.

For one dreadful moment she and the earl simply stared at one another.

"Her Grace is right, you know," he said at last. "There is no help for it. We'll have to wed."

This changed nothing for him since it was his intention all along. But she had anticipated having a choice—or at the very least the appearance of a choice.

She spun away from His Earlness.

"Bound and fettered, indeed," she muttered and then walked the path back to the mansion, keeping ten paces ahead of him.

Midmorning sun cast leafy shadows across the garden stones. It seemed to Heath that there had to be at least a dozen birds in each bush, every one of them in full song.

It might have been a perfect morning, for all that it mattered. Miss Macooish's parting words were still ringing in his ears.

Bound and fettered, indeed.

Oh, he'd expected to marry—was obligated to do so. The problem was, he hadn't anticipated this scandal to go with it. What was more, he had not expected to take such a great deal of pleasure in the heiress's company.

Not at all. This marriage of necessity was supposed to be as devoid of emotion as—as an egg—as the stone under his boot.

He strolled along the path leading from the patio to the fountain, kicking at a pebble and cursing his luck.

Had the intended Madeline been his bride, he could have simply filled her days with shopping and her nights with entertainment and then neatly set her to the back of his mind. She would live her life and he would live his, together and yet apart.

Not so with Clementine. He'd foolishly wished for someone like her to marry. He doubted that he would ever be able to confine that lady to the back of his mind.

Had he not, even at this moment, been scanning the balconies of the apartments on the other side of the garden hoping to get a glimpse of her?

Not that he expected her to look down with smiles and blow kisses in pleasure at seeing him. Nor did he want that if it happened. Life with his beautiful and intriguing bride was going to be a difficult thing as it was.

Given nurture, he had no doubt that a bond could grow between the two of them.

He did not want a bond—could not form one if he did.

He and Creed could hardly respond to their informers' notes while he had to explain his absence to a wife who shared his bed.

Somehow he was going to have to find a way to keep his bride out of his heart and out of his bed.

It was not going to be easy. Clementine Jane Macooish had already taken a long step inside his heart before he knew to post the No Trespassing sign.

A movement from one of the balconies three floors up snapped his gaze toward it.

It was not Miss Macooish but her grandfather.

Coming to the edge of the balcony, the sturdy old man placed his hands upon the rail, took a deep breath of morning air and smiled down.

"Good day to you, my lord," Macooish said. "I trust you slept well."

With the exception of the night his brother died, he could not imagine one worse.

"Yes, and you?"

"As well as one can when one's granddaughter is stomping the halls at all hours. She is a sweet thing, loyal to a fault, but strong-willed to go with it. I expect you ought to get that special license before she sets sail back to America."

Macooish was grinning when he said it, so Heath tried not to stress overmuch that she actually would.

"My solicitor is paying a visit to the Archbishop of Canterbury as we speak, sir. We'll have the wedding within the duchess's time allowance."

There was more he needed to say, but how?

In the end it was Macooish who spoke first.

"Clementine is finally asleep, so I'm free to speak." The old man lowered his voice but it carried well enough for Heath to hear if he strained. "I know this marriage isn't what the two of you planned for your futures. It was supposed to be Oliver and Madeline. I was sure they would suit or I'd not have made the arrangement. Now here is my Clemmie bound to someone I don't even know. I do expect you to treat her well."

"I had no wish to marry, but my brother's death forced it. You are quite correct in that. Even though this is not what I would have chosen—not what she would have chosen, either—be assured that I will honor my wife. In fact, I like your granddaughter quite well."

"Yes, indeed. So I witnessed last night." The old fellow's smile tipped up. He winked one eye and arched the opposite gray brow. "I'm an astute judge of character, Fencroft. It's my opinion that all has worked for the good. My sweet girl will be a good match for you. Better even, I think, than Madeline would have been for your brother, may he rest in God's loving arms."

Unless he missed his guess, Oliver was not resting but rather gleefully laughing at what was going on down here.

He could hear the sound as though his brother stood beside him. In his mind he saw Oliver holding his side in mirth because he could see the very thing that Heath feared.

That being so, he and Clementine would be an excellent match and he would not be able to resist her.

"I know this is an unusual situation and if—" Heath had to clear his throat because words seemed to be strangling him "—if I had behaved like a gentleman things would be happening much more to custom. And so I find myself asking the most important question of my life in an unconventional way. Sir, I most humbly request the honor of your granddaughter's hand in marriage."

"Granted," Macooish stated quickly. "In a sense, I'm not unhappy with the turn of events last night. I know now that you are not cold when it comes to my Clemmie. If I thought you were, I'd not go through with this. At the least, now people will not think that my granddaughter is an object of barter."

Others might not but Clementine certainly did.

"No, but they will think she's been compromised."

"Not that so much as desired—as she should be."

It was the truth. He might as well face it. He had desired her—had cast away good sense because he had.

"I give my blessing to your union. Good day, son." James Macooish grinned, turned with a sharp half salute and went back inside.

Good, then, Heath thought as he walked the path back toward the townhome. That was one issue resolved.

Still, he worried about Miss Macooish's acceptance of the inevitable marriage. Would she refuse even though Lady Guthrie decreed that she would wed?

Clementine was an American and not as likely to be as influenced by the duchess's command as one of the daughters of the aristocracy would be.

Perhaps he ought to make some grand romantic gesture to ensure she did not refuse. Then again, that might be the very last thing he ought to do.

A merely friendly gesture, then? An olive branch.

A quick movement on the low stone wall of the patio caught his attention.

Victor, a sunbeam catching and reflecting in his blond hair, clambered over. Hopping down, he then ran headlong at Heath and caught him about the thighs.

He swung his nephew up and around, enjoying the joyful squeal Victor made.

"Did you eat a horse? You feel heavier than you did yesterday."

"Noooo! I like horsies. Well, not to eat, though." Victor latched his arms about Heath's neck. "Mother says I can be witness for you at the wedding since Uncle Oliver is in Heaven and I'm next to be earl."

"I can't think of anyone I would want more." For his witness and his heir.

Heath stepped over the wall, coming face-to-face with his sister. She wagged a newspaper at him.

"That horrid Abductor!" Her cheeks pulsed pink but her mouth was pinched and pale. "He has kidnapped another child. Stolen the baby right out of his screaming mother's arms."

Yes, he had done that and was proud to have done so, even though the act would be reported as an evil deed. No doubt good folks were bemoaning the mother's fate, not realizing that she and her child were safe.

"I'm sure justice will be served," he said, setting Victor down. The boy promptly scampered after a squirrel chattering in a tree on the far side of the patio.

Heath only hoped it would be done to Garrett Slademore.

"They are searching the river for the poor woman's body," his sister whispered. Victor was beyond hearing range, but only barely. "The reason the two guards did not rescue the infant is because they feared the woman meant to do herself harm. So they followed her instead."

"It seems to me that they ought to have split up. One of them could've rescued the child and the other, the mother."

"And face the cutthroat alone?"

"The guard was armed. I think he was safe enough."

"What makes you say so? I'm certain Lord Slademore has stated his guards are not armed, for the sake of a shot going awry when the children are so close by."

"I don't know what I can do about it in any case, sister." He sounded pathetic in saying so, but he'd revealed too much in mentioning the weapon and needed to cover for it.

"You can make sure your American goes through with the marriage so we have the funds to keep our people from the fate of that unfortunate woman."

Olivia snapped the newspaper down on the patio table.

Apparently by slapping the table she was demonstrating what she would like to do to the Abductor. She stomped toward the open parlor door.

"I'll do what I can, and Olivia?" His sister spun about. "My American has a name. She's called Clementine, and she has given up a great deal to come here. Please keep that in mind."

As he would. The trouble was, keeping it in mind opened the door to his heart more than a crack. If he was not careful she would walk right in, set up housekeeping and capture his affections more completely than Willa ever had.

An open heart might lead to secrets learned.

Chapter Five

Clementine sat on a stool, watching in the mirror while her maid thrust a pin in the coil of hair she had just placed in a stylish whirl on top of her head.

For mercy's sake, she was only going for a stroll to try to settle her nerves from the knot she had done herself up in.

Back in Los Angeles a walk in the sunshine never failed to relax her. Surely a stroll in Mayfair would accomplish the same thing.

"While I do thank you for your effort, Trudy, you needn't go to the trouble. I'm only taking the air." She gave her servant a smile to reassure the woman she meant no criticism of her handiwork. "Besides, I am simply going to cover it with a hat."

"Yes, my lady." Trudy studied her handiwork, clearly wanting to add more curls. With a subtle shake of her head she pinned the hat to the coif. "I'll just get my coat."

"Don't bother yourself. I'll be fine on my own."

"But, Miss Macooish—"

Perhaps a woman in her position was not allowed to take a simple stroll unaccompanied.

No matter, life would not fall to pieces if she did.

"Take an hour to yourself, Trudy," she said and hurried out of the bedroom, down the stairs and out into the open air.

The first thing she noticed upon going down the steps was that the sun was not warm upon her shoulders. The next was the noise.

The grind of dozens of wagon wheels on stone, the shout of drivers and the call of vendors selling their wares did not bode well for a bit of quiet contemplation.

But the park was only across the street. Surely it would prove to be more tranquil.

Moments later she padded along a wide pathway. Tall, ancient-looking trees growing along each side of the path formed a canopy, the leaves only beginning to hint at the fall beauty to come.

In itself the setting might have been one of the most tranquil she had ever walked. Creative words to express the natural beauty ought to be overflowing her mind.

But the path was also crowded with people walking in both directions.

They laughed merrily, chatted gaily—and stared at her!

It was impossible to know if people looked at her because she was a gauche American heiress come to ruin polite society, or if it was because gossip had spread of her disgrace in the duchess's garden.

Either way, it was disconcerting.

Her maid had tried to dissuade her from venturing out alone, and now, feeling eyes on her back, imagining what whispers behind hands were saying, she felt she ought to have perhaps stayed in her bedroom.

But honestly, how could she have guessed that a simple walk in the sunshine would cause a scene.

If a potential countess went out walking back home,

it would only raise mild interest. At the moment she felt quite on display.

There was only one thing to do, other than flee back to the apartment—which she was not going to do—and that was to draw upon her cousin's sense of adventure.

Madeline would not feel a thorn in society's side. No, her cousin would breeze through the park and not return until she had won the affection of everyone who crossed her path.

"I'm going no farther than the garden from now on," she muttered, because in the end she was nothing like Madeline and could not pretend she was.

"If I may say so, Miss Macooish, you are doing admirably. A born and bred peer could not keep her emotions disguised half as well."

She started at the voice. How long had the man been walking beside her without her noticing?

"Good morning, Lord Fencroft." For the sake of politeness she ought to add how lovely it was to see him. But it was stressful more than lovely.

How did one deal with a man who went from mysterious friend, to betrayer, to presumed fiancé, in the space of a moment? Certainly not with a fluttering heart!

What was wrong with her?

And now people were openly frowning.

"I assume I am not to take an honest walk in the park unescorted," she muttered.

"It is frowned upon." His mouth tugged up, but only on one side.

"I think you are enjoying my embarrassment."

Why did his smile have to be so appealing—make her want to return it?

It was only with the greatest effort that she did not. And truthfully, it was a relief to have him walking beside her even if the heat of censure from passersby was increasing.

"I'm enjoying their outrage."

That was not the answer she expected to hear. The man was part and parcel of them, after all.

"You do not feel it is a slap in the face of decency for a woman to walk in the park alone?"

"Not decency, but perhaps safety."

"It's a lucky thing you came upon me, then. One can never tell when a ruffian will pop out from behind a tree."

"Not as lucky as you might hope, Miss Macooish."

Did she detect a slight tone of resentment when he pronounced her name? As if he resented the fact that she had not used it upon their first encounter—the one in which she saved his life?

"Perhaps you are right, Lord Fencroft."

"You see all these raised brows?"

How could she not—in fact she could not help sending a superior gesture back at the pinch-faced matron passing by on a gentleman's arm.

"Those scowls aren't because you are walking alone." He smiled at her, winked as if they were on some grand lark. "It's because you are walking with me."

"Because you seduce strangers in duchesses' gardens?"

"Because for an unmarried woman, walking in public with a man is worse than walking alone."

"I ought to go home."

"I'll escort you."

"Across the Atlantic?"

All of a sudden his expression sobered. It must have occurred to him that if she did his family would be left destitute.

"If that is what it would take to win you, then yes."

What a romantic statement that would have been had it come from his heart and not his bank account.

"I've asked your grandfather for your hand." He stopped dead in the path. People flowed around them as if they were a boulder in a stream.

His blue-green-eyed gaze all but swallowed her up. She had to curl her fingers into her fists to keep from losing herself in it.

"That's grand, my lord," she answered. "But you have yet to ask mine."

He blinked, opened his mouth and closed it again before remaining silent for a full thirty seconds.

Honestly, he ought to have something to say to that. She was certainly not going to help him by speaking first.

Suddenly, for no good reason one side of his mouth twitched as if he were trying to repress a grin.

Well, then. She spun about and walked back toward the apartment alone.

Which, apparently, was less of a sin than walking with him.

By afternoon, heavy clouds were sweeping over Mayfair.

Grandfather had gone to some gentlemen's club to discuss business with Lord Guthrie, which left her on her own with nothing to do but listen to the clock tick.

She could summon a carriage and go shopping. Bond Street might have a pretty hat or dress to distract her—if she was one to enjoy such a pursuit, which she was not.

Even Madeline had not been able to convince her that shopping was a fulfilling pastime and her cousin was nothing if not persuasive.

Besides, it was starting to rain. The thought of curling up in a chair beside the window with a book was far more appealing.

She picked up a blanket, swirled it about her shoulders and then sat down in the chair.

Rain tapping on the window sounded soothing, and the blanket felt like a warm hug. She picked up her new copy of *A Tale of Two Cities* and let it lie open on her lap.

In the moment, with everything so soft and lovely, her mind wandered, drifting of its own accord to something that occupied too much of her attention.

The kiss that never quite happened. It seemed like it had for all that Mr. Cavill's lips never actually touched hers. But intimacy had been there in his eyes—the desire to share something forbidden with her, the gentle pressure of his fingers on the back of her neck...

"Lord Fencroft is in the parlor, Miss Macooish," the butler announced, standing at attention in the doorway. When had he rapped on the door? Probably in the instant she indulged in the unfulfilled and imaginary kiss.

"Shall I tell him you are at home?"

"Here I am, so I suppose you must." Odd, how she wanted to see him and not see him in equal measure.

All she could hope for in the moment was that the flush would fade from her cheeks before she entered the parlor.

"If I might point out, miss, one can be present without being at home to receive callers."

"Thank you, Bowmeyer. You may inform the earl I will be down in a moment. And please inform the kitchen there will be two of us for tea."

Bowmeyer presented a polite half bow in acknowledgment and then went to do her bidding.

Clementine stood and squared her shoulders. Clearly the earl was here to propose and there was nothing she could do but accept. No one would be better off if she refused. And in the pit of her heart, there was a quiver that suggested she might do worse than marry Heath Cavill.

Which was not happy news since good judgment suggested that he might turn out to be a man she could not respect.

Did he often accost women he didn't know? Although, to say that he accosted her would not quite be the truth.

Crossing the house and entering the parlor, she recognized that she had behaved with abandon in Lady Guthrie's garden. She could not put the blame completely on Fencroft's shoulders.

No, and now coming upon him standing on the exact center of the rug, hands behind his back and a nervous smile on his handsome face—well, it did occur to her that it was a shame about that kiss being cut short.

"Good day, Miss Macooish," he said. "It's lovely to see you again."

She nodded. "Good day."

"I've come to…" His voice trailed off as he seemed to be searching his mind for what it was.

Propose, she wanted to prompt but instead said, "Would you like to sit down, Lord Fencroft? Tea is on the way."

"Thank you."

She settled on the divan, spreading her skirt to show off the sweep of a satin ribbon.

He sat down on the chair straight across, drumming his fingers on his knees. She hadn't noticed how masculine his fingers looked, quite unlike the smooth, pale skin many gentlemen had.

No doubt Grandfather ought to be in attendance for this meeting. A chaperone was certainly called for.

In the end, what did proper form matter really, since in a few more minutes she and the earl would be engaged?

A beam of sunlight broke through the clouds and streamed through the window, igniting rich brown highlights in his dark hair. At least her future husband was handsome—uncommonly so. There was something about his eyes—they gazed out from under his brows in an intriguing mixture of sobriety and humor.

And then there was his smile… Well, she did not dare look at that overlong.

"It's a bit late, but I do owe you an apology." He glanced away and then back again.

The tea cart, with its one warped wheel, thumped down the hallway, clattering the china.

"As I recall, Your Lordship, I share half of the blame for what happened in Lady Guthrie's garden."

A footman placed the cart between Clementine and the earl and then went to stand beside the door in case he was needed.

He would be a chaperone as well as anyone.

"No— I took—" He shot a sidelong glance at the footman, who gave every indication of being deaf and dumb. Still, when Fencroft spoke it was in a whisper. "I took unfair advantage of you. Please forgive me."

"I imagine I must since we are to—" No—she was not going to be the one to bring up the proposal. It was up to him to do it. "—to take tea together."

If only Heath Cavill was not the most handsome man she had ever seen, she might have come up with something a bit more witty to say. Sadly, looking into those somber blue-green eyes made her somewhat blankminded. Except for the part of her mind that continued to wonder what that kiss would have been like.

Perhaps when he went down on one knee she would find out. She imagined sealing an engagement with a kiss would be appropriate.

"Well." He cleared his throat as if the words he meant to say had somehow gotten tangled up. "I've come for a particular reason."

Best to get it over and done with, she supposed. Things were what they were and it was time to move forward.

He reached into his pocket and withdrew a delicate little box with a bow on it.

Clementine felt as nervous as the earl looked. It was not every day that a lady became engaged. She smiled and, to her surprise, the gesture felt natural. She'd always known Grandfather's fortune would have a big part in whom she married. And just now, she thought—just maybe—she was not sorry about it.

If the butterflies in her middle and the quick thump of her heart were anything to go by, she was half-pleased.

Given that she had been all but trapped into this marriage, she might be feeling a good deal worse about it.

Heath Cavill tugged the satin bow between his thumb and his finger for a moment before he handed the package to her.

He made no move to kneel. No, he simply leaned forward a bit, his elbows braced on his knees and his gaze intent upon her face.

Did the aristocracy not go down on bended knee to propose? Or was it because she was an American and a commoner that he did not?

She felt her smile sag a bit at the thought.

"Please, will you accept this gift as a token of my regret?"

Regret?

At asking for her hand?

If she didn't need something for her hands to do while she thought of how to respond, she might not have opened the gift.

Had he changed his mind about the marriage since he'd spoken to Grandfather? From all she knew he could not. Not without leaving himself bankrupt.

"Thank you," she said of the comb she cupped in the palm of her hand. It was a pretty thing, etched with gold flowers and embedded with a swirl of tiny pearls. "It's very lovely."

Lovely, but far from the engagement ring he ought to have presented.

She stood up, signaling that the visit was at an end.

The earl stood after she did. Stepping around the cart, he leaned close. Inappropriately close, in her opinion, since they were not engaged.

He took the comb from her fingers, stared at it for a moment while caressing the pearls with his thumb.

Evidently he was regretting parting with the bauble.

She frowned because, really, any other expression would have been false.

He needn't worry about the loss since she had no intention of keeping it—not without the courtesy of a proper proposal first.

Turning, she intended to regally walk from the parlor, then run upstairs to her bedroom and quite possibly weep, but he caught her hand, flesh to flesh.

"One moment, Clementine." He placed the comb in her hair and secured it behind her ear.

She watched the muscles in his throat constrict, go slack and then constrict again.

"It looks as lovely on you as it did on my mother."

Heath stood on the balcony of his bedroom, enjoying the sunset—or so he told himself. Had that been the truth he'd have been gazing west at the fire-red ball dipping below the tree line, not at Miss Macooish's flame-hued hair as she sat on a bench beside the fountain.

With the wind rising, strands blew loose from her mound of curls in a glorious crimson fury. With her posture straight and her hands folded demurely in her lap, was she a tigress or a kitten? He could not decide. She might be either or both. What she was, was unexpected.

Only a short time ago his only worry was behaving like a proper earl. Standing here now, he was trying to sort out how he would be a husband.

The special license was in the hands of his solicitor and, curse it, he had yet to propose!

Any man worthy of Miss Macooish would have asked for her hand right away after speaking to her grandfather.

Ordinarily, having been granted Macooish's permission to wed would have been all the formality needed. The deal would have been made no matter the lady's opinion on it.

But Miss Macooish was far from ordinary. Clearly she expected a proper proposal, where she would have a yes or no say in the matter.

That was what she had expected when he'd given her the gift of his mother's comb yesterday. In his mind it had been a peace offering of the most precious kind.

His sister had warned him that it would not be well received, not when the heiress was expecting an engagement ring. Olivia insisted that the gift must be presented after the engagement was agreed to.

Olivia had also pointed out that he needed to put the scandal behind them and soon, else Miss Macooish would take her fortune and return to America.

He was an oaf.

Grunting, he squashed the urge to flee to Derbyshire, to forget everything and walk the peaceful pastures along with the sheep.

Obviously, the duty set before him in the moment was to make things right with the beautiful woman below.

With a decisive turn, he left the balcony and walked across his chamber, snatching up the ring that had been displayed on his bureau for two days.

Going down the stairs he felt he walked a razor's edge between the conflicting duties of being Lord Fencroft, protecting helpless children and becoming a husband. He'd turned into a puzzle in which the pieces did not match up.

He crossed the patio and stepped over the low stone wall, determined to seal his fate. Officially, anyway, since he'd actually done it when he'd indulged in temptation in the Guthries' garden.

Miss Macooish sat with her back to him, her face angled toward the side, and that strong, lovely nose lifted to catch the light of the fading sun.

With her eyes closed, she mumbled something. The wind, growing more boisterous by the second, ruffled the pages of what appeared to be a journal resting on her knees. She clenched a pencil in her fingers and, looking down, tried to write something on the snapping pages.

"Good evening, Miss Macooish."

She snapped the notebook closed while pivoting on the bench to look up at him.

"Good evening, my lord." She smiled, but somehow the gesture did not reflect pleasure in seeing him. "I trust you had a pleasant day."

"Most pleasant. I trust yours was, as well."

"Indeed."

This might be the stiffest conversation he had ever been a part of.

"May I sit?"

"You may."

This was not quite a gracious invitation to share the sunset, but he took it anyway and sat down on the bench beside her. Maybe a bit of friendly conversation would help.

He had come to propose but he couldn't simply blurt it out, not with the brittleness between them at the moment.

"What is that you are writing?" he asked.

"Oh, just some observation on the sunset. I'm one for preserving my more poetic thoughts. I used to share them with my students back in Los Angeles."

"You were a teacher?"

"Happily so, until Madeline ran away." And she ended up bound to his title. He heard the words even though she did not speak them.

"And what did you do, my lord?" The false smile fell away. Her expression softened. "Before the sad loss of your brother?"

"I suppose you would call me a farmer, at the heart of it. I saw to the running of the estate in Derbyshire. Tended the crops and the livestock, helped the tenants."

"I'm sorry for both of your losses. You must grieve terribly for your brother and for the life you knew."

"Yes, London and Derbyshire are vastly different from each other. Life is different. And my brother? Everyone liked him. You would have, I'm certain."

"I like you."

She did?

Probably. The smile she gave him seemed sincere.

"I appreciate the gift of your mother's comb. It's very beautiful and I'm afraid I was not as appreciative as I ought to have been."

"I might have bungled my intentions."

A gust of wind rippled the surface of the pond, rushed between them with a chill that hinted of autumn.

"Would you read it to me—what you just wrote?"

In the dimming light, he thought he saw her blush, but she opened the notebook, sighing. "If you are sure you want to hear it?"

"Please."

She shrugged. "'Leaves, dried from the first bite of autumn, tumble over stones. The orange-red glow of the sun sinks behind lush garden trees. A sight of great beauty, stifled and choked by stinging, yellow fog.'"

"In Derbyshire, the air is always fresh—" He looked north, imagining the emerald pastures, the soft shadows of sunset. "The air in Los Angeles isn't tainted?"

She shook her head. "Sometimes the breeze comes in off the ocean so fresh that it seems you are standing on the seashore."

"Would that we could fly away like we spoke of, Miss Macooish."

"Like a pair of free-sailing birds?"

"Just so." If only it were truly possible.

The wind seemed to be coming from east and west at the same time, swirling about the garden like a dervish. They ought to go inside, but he'd come out here for a purpose and would not retreat until it was accomplished.

Reaching inside his pocket he went down on one knee.

"Miss Macooish, will you do me—"

All at once a great gust caught the journal, spun it up and away.

Miss Macooish jumped up from the bench, reaching for it even though the flapping pages were well beyond her reach.

He made a lunge for it but the notebook twirled higher as if carried by an invisible fist. It snagged in the crook of a tree branch ten feet above the bench.

He bent his knees, leaped and caught the lowest branch.

He hauled himself up, limb by limb. It seemed suddenly urgent to rescue what was clearly very important to her.

The V the book was wedged into lay at least nine feet out of his reach. Lying flat, he scooted along the limb, pretty certain he looked like an inchworm making slow but determined progress.

He glanced down once. Clearly, the similarity hadn't escaped Miss Macooish. Why else would she be quietly laughing while trying to hide her mouth behind her hands?

She could not hide her eyes. Nor could he guard his heart against the green merriment flashing in them. The woman had him entranced.

How had that happened?

Reaching out, he snatched the flapping pages and held the book with his teeth while he scooted backward over the limb. It was risky business with the wind whipping the tree every which way.

At last he bumped against the trunk. He made his way to the bottom branch.

The endeavor was more taxing than one would expect. His energy was spent. He rested a moment with his cheek on the buffeted branch, a position that brought him face-to-face with his intended.

He plucked the notebook from his mouth and handed it to her. Surely it was his imagination that she tapped her fingers over the spot where his lips had been?

Surely so.

"Thank you, brave sir." She pressed the journal to her heart.

If he had ever seen a woman more appealing he could not recall the event. With half of her hair in tidy curls and the remainder lashing about her face; her cheeks nipped pink by the slapping wind; and laughter sparking in her eyes—he could not be blamed for being more than a little overcome.

A strand of her hair blew against his mouth. He caught it and twirled it around his finger.

"Miss Macooish—Clementine—will you do me the great honor of becoming my wife?"

She tipped her head, gazing at him intently while the fate of the Fencroft estate teetered upon her answer. "Do you mean to kiss me?"

"Yes, I do."

"Oh, then by all means, I will marry you, my lord."

He thought he felt the branch give, maybe even heard a crack, but in the moment all he could think about was her mouth. He wanted to feel her lips, to nibble them and see if they were as warm, as moist as he thought they were.

Leaning forward, he tasted her, indulging in the dizzy sensation.

And there it was, proof that she was every bit as sweet as he'd feared she would be. No matter, he would enjoy the intimacy this once and then never again.

The pleasure of the marriage bed would be denied him—and her. It wasn't right, but what could he do? There would be times when he would need to leave her bed—how would he explain it?

What he did in the night was considered a heinous crime. If he was caught and she knew about it, she would be condemned along with him.

No. It was essential for him to stay out of her bed altogether. For her sake she was, and would remain, forbidden—even as a legally wed bride.

At least until he found a way to shut Slademore House down.

When he drew back and looked into her eyes, Heath's

heart nearly stopped. He feared abstinence would prove to be impossible.

All at once the branch snapped at the trunk and dumped him on the ground.

"Oh!" Miss Macooish knelt beside him, lightly brushing her fingertips over a fresh swelling on his forehead. "Are you hurt again, my lord?"

"Heath," he clarified. "Call me Heath."

He would have that familiarity of her if nothing else.

Chapter Six

Eleven a.m., September 1, 1889. The grand entry at Fencroft House

Clementine stood beside Heath at the head of the reception line, a married woman of one hour.

Grandfather was aglow, his grin as wide as the Cheshire cat's.

The only one grinning wider would be the seamstress who had accepted a huge sum to put off her other customers in order to create a gown to rival the one the Queen's granddaughter, Princess Louise, had worn in July. One could only guess that Grandfather had spent a fortune on just the pearls decorating it.

Of course, Clementine could not confront Grandfather about the cost, given that she was the one to have asked for a few pearls to be sewn on the collar and cuffs—as a simple complement to Heath's mother's comb. She hadn't expected a few pearls to become a sweeping expanse across the skirt and around the hem.

While walking up the aisle of the church, she had the distinct sensation of gliding within a shimmering white cloud.

In that moment Grandfather had moisture standing in his eyes. Apparently he was overcome by giving her away in marriage, like he had always dreamed of.

Oddly, for an instant she thought she saw moisture spark in her groom's eyes as well, which had to be a trick of candlelight, since she was not likely the bride he had dreamed of.

And was there someone he had dreamed of? A lady he had wanted to marry but now, because of circumstance, could not?

Who among the guests might she be? She scanned the crowd looking for a young lady gazing at her groom in forlorn misery.

She did not see one young lady, but several.

With a start she realized that she was—although she did not know how it could be, but yes, certainly she was—resentful of their longing gazes.

"You're frowning, Clementine," Heath murmured in her ear. "Are you so unhappy?"

Was she? Perhaps she had been forced into this marriage, but seeing genuine care in his expression, watching the lines of his forehead crease over eyes the color of deep turquoise, she could not say for sure that she was. Only time would tell for certain.

"We can speak of it later."

In the bridal chamber. She felt heat rise from her chest, curl up her neck and flood her cheeks. Now that she was a married woman she no longer had to dash away the thoughts that flitted through the mind of a maiden.

"Are you sure you are well?" He swiped the backs of his fingers across her cheek. "You feel warm."

Indeed.

"Later," she whispered and had the distinct impression that he saw her thoughts, every tantalizing one of them.

Oddly, her new husband was frowning. From all she had ever heard, a man looked forward to his wedding night—intensely.

"Heath, this is talk for another time. And look, here comes Lady Guthrie. Let's put on our brightest smiles so that she does not think she made a terrible mistake."

He glanced down the line of well-wishers, saying something when he spotted the duchess. But he said it without sound, moving only his lips.

From her time spent as a teacher, Clementine had learned to read the lips of her students quite well.

So she had no doubt that what he had silently uttered was "I do not believe that she did."

And why would that make her suddenly feel that she was, once again, not touching the floor but floating within her cloud of pearls and satin?

Truly, at times life made no sense whatsoever.

Looking into his bride's eyes, sensing the thoughts in her mind and feeling his body react to those thoughts made Heath wonder how he was to approach this marriage.

He wanted this woman, and might even have chosen her of his own free will had their paths crossed in a different way.

Had Lady Guthrie made a terrible mistake?

"I do not believe that she did," he mouthed silently, while turning his face down the line of well-wishers toward the duchess, who at all times seemed in control of her world.

There was nothing to be gained by denying the truth. It would only make the future harder to face. Besides, not even Clementine, who stood at his elbow, would know what he said. Over the laughter and conversation of dozens of people and the strains of the orchestra playing in the next room, no one else would, either.

"I simply adore weddings," Lady Guthrie declared, stepping forward and patting his cheek with her gloved fingertips.

Given the way her garden was designed, with winding paths and secret alcoves, one could only wonder how many hurried vows it had been responsible for.

"My dear Lady Fencroft, I welcome you to London society." With great show Lady Guthrie kissed Clementine's cheek. She then murmured something in his bride's ear, but standing so close, Heath heard it, too. "May God help you, my sweet girl."

Perhaps this show of the duchess's favor would aid Clementine's launch into society. If it did not, he only hoped that whispers born of jealousy and gossip in dark corners would not become known to his wife.

She was doing a great good for so many people and he did not want her to suffer for it.

But she *was* going to suffer—and by his own hand. Or more precisely, the lack of his hand. The thought of the way he would neglect her made him want to leap into the Thames.

Lost in self-loathing, Heath failed to notice the next guest in line.

"My best wishes to you, Lord Fencroft."

No matter how deeply Heath reached, he could not find an answering smile for Slademore.

Willa…

The man's mouth might be exhibiting friendliness, but his eyes were as cold and gray as a snake's. But no, snake eyes were a reptile's and nothing more. If one looked deeply into Garrett Slademore's eyes, one saw evil. But the fellow was beautiful in a way that he seemed to disarm people.

Willa… Heath suspected she had never looked deeply enough to see the cruelty. Never looked deeply into the heart of another man, as well. She'd gone to her death without revealing who the father of her baby was.

Because he could do nothing else, Heath gritted his teeth and uttered, "May I introduce Baron Garrett Slademore."

"May he never darken our door again," he added by further introduction, but only in his mind.

"It's a great pleasure, Baron." Clementine extended her hand. "I've heard of the generous work you do for poor children at Slademore House."

She looked so happy to be speaking to the baron, praising his good work. It bothered Heath that she did not see the heart of the man, no more than anyone else did.

Heath put his hands behind his back and clenched his fists because what he wanted to do was squeeze them around the baron's neck.

"The pleasure is completely mine, Countess. I do hope you will remember us in your charitable giving. The children are always so very grateful when they are remembered." The baron bent over her hand for too long, lowering his mouth too close to her fingers.

If he kissed them, Heath was certain he would have to knock him to the floor, causing a new scandal to replace the old one, but fortunately that didn't come to pass.

"He seemed a pleasant fellow," his bride declared, smiling after Slademore.

Heath had the strongest urge to rip off her glove and send it to the laundress. With the greatest effort, he nodded and focused his attention on the next guest.

Or tried to. From the corner of his eye he watched Slademore take the arm of an elderly lady and with deliberate care escort her toward the breakfast room. He smiled at her and bent his head as if what she had to say was of utmost importance to him.

Heath could stand on a chair right here in the reception line and tell the world what he knew.

He could—but in doing so he would reveal Willa's fallen state. After protecting her secret he would not now shame her. Besides, he had no proof.

When he came forward to condemn Slademore, it would be with proof that could not be argued.

What kind of life had he got himself into? Heath was compelled to express neither his budding affection for his bride nor his animosity toward his enemy.

There were times when life made no sense whatsoever.

Olivia drew open the door of Clementine's new bedchamber.

"I've had the countess's chamber prepared for you. I hope it suits. It has been slept in by the mistress of Fencroft for generations," she pointed out while Clementine walked past her. "The master's chamber is two doors up the hallway, far enough for him to have his privacy but close enough in the event he feels inclined to visit."

In the event? Olivia had been married, was a mother. Surely she understood that a husband might feel inclined to—well, to linger.

Even Clementine, pure as a newly dawned day, understood that much.

Oh, but the room was lovely, decorated in yellow with accents of red. A vase of tall flowers on the entry table sported the same hues. Even with full dark fallen outside, with only the lamps and the amber glow of the fire in the hearth for illumination, the place appeared cheerful.

The bed looked like a pillow. She guessed it would be like sleeping on a cloud.

"That is the most beautiful window. I'm sure I could sit beside it all day." Clementine nearly sighed over the inviting spot.

And the chairs tucked into the bay? She feared if she sat down on one of them she might spend all her time gazing at the garden below.

It was especially appealing at the moment since wedding guests had lingered even after the food ran out.

"Mother used to. Oliver and I would sit on her lap and we'd watch the—" Olivia pursed her lips, frowning. "Well, it was a very long time ago."

"This is the most inviting room I have ever been in, Olivia. Thank you for all you've done." Truly, she could not have wished for a nicer suite.

"It's the very least I could do." Olivia's crystal blue eyes swept the room. "It's we who should be grateful to you. My brother—Oliver, I mean—he was a good person at heart but he could never resist a good time and in the end…"

Her gaze shifted, settled again on Clementine. "In the end he was a man."

It was evident that Olivia's comment was born of personal experience. Since Clementine barely knew her sister-in-law, she did not feel it right to ask further about it.

"I'm sure Heath and I will be comfortable here," she said instead.

"Yes, I'm sure but…" Olivia sighed, shaking her head. "It's not my place to give you advice. But you don't have your mother to do it. Given that I've been married, I hope you don't mind getting some from me?"

"I would thank you for it—I'm rather green at being a wife."

"Most of us are. We foolishly go into the arrangement

with our hearts wide open. But take heed, sister, it's a risky thing, giving yourself over to a man."

"Is there something in particular you think I ought to know?" Olivia must certainly know her brother far better than Clementine did.

"I shouldn't say."

But she wanted to. Clementine knew a secret on the verge of being exposed when she saw one.

A soft knock rapped on the door. Heath entered the chamber before Olivia could blurt out the thing she should not say.

"Good evening, ladies." He glanced about the room, seeming to see his sister's handiwork for the first time. "You've done a beautiful job in here, Olivia. I thank you."

Olivia looked back and forth between her and Heath, a delicate wrinkle creasing her smooth, fair brow.

"Well," she declared. "I'll leave you to your evening."

She left the door open when she went out.

"I've the feeling my sister shared her thoughts on marriage."

"On men."

"She has good reason to be bitter. Her husband was often unfaithful—and Oliver? In a sense, he betrayed her, as well, by mismanaging the estate and leaving her and her son vulnerable." Heath glanced over his shoulder down the darkened hallway and then back at her. "I don't think she trusts me, either, not completely. Did she say anything?"

"No." But she nearly had.

Heath closed the door, turned the lock.

The click sent a shiver over Clementine's skin because somehow that act was more intimate than any she had ever experienced.

She was a married woman, alone with her new husband for the first time. What did he expect of her? What was she willing to give him?

Pivoting on his heel, he smiled while he loosened his collar.

"I don't know about you, Clementine, but I could use a few hours to sit and just breathe." He indicated the chairs beside the window with a nod. "May I?"

"I'm sure you are free to sit anywhere you like." Such as on the bed.

He settled onto the plush cushions, rolling his shoulders while he beckoned for her to sit down across from him.

As soon as she did, her muscles melted against the back of the chair and she realized how weary she truly was.

"Marriage is exhausting business," she admitted with a sigh.

"And we've only begun."

Something stirred inside her belly, because did he mean—?

She stole a glance at the bed.

Her groom's gaze wandered in the other direction, to the darkness beyond the window, so she suspected he was not thinking of the pursuit of carnal knowledge.

"Clementine, I need you to know something. I might not be a perfect husband, but I promise you, I will always be faithful. You will not end up hurt the way my sister has been. For all that our marriage was not of our choosing, I will not betray my vows to you, or to God."

It was good to hear him say so, because Olivia's attitude had made her a bit ill at ease.

"Nor will I." She nodded. "I'm exceedingly loyal by nature."

"I'm sorry for getting you into this, Clementine. I know this marriage was not what you wanted and that you expected to have a choice in the matter."

He could not possibly know what she wanted, since she, herself, did not.

"It remains to be seen whether this is what I want or do not want," she said but his gaze slid away from the window, his blue-green eyes seeming troubled. "It might prove to be that I do not, but it might also prove to be that you and I will find happiness in our situation. Our marriage is less than a day old, after all. Far too soon to know anything for certain."

Rain tapped lightly on the window, carried by a gust of wind. Water drops rolled down the glass. It was interesting to see how they hit the glass singly, rolled for a bit and then melded with another drop. Mingled, the drops became one and moved together.

She didn't point it out to Heath, but she thought it a perfect analogy to marriage. Tomorrow she would write it in her journal.

"And yet I would expect you to resent me for compromising you. It was unconscionable for me to take away your choice."

"I wonder, Heath, if I only had the illusion of a choice. Eventually a man would have married me, and very likely it would have been for my grandfather's fortune. I'd rather it be this way than to believe I'd made a love match and then later find I'd been duped."

The fancy concoction of curls on top of her head felt suddenly heavy, and itchy. Carefully, she removed Heath's mother's comb and set it on the small table beside the chair. Then she made quick work of plucking out the hairpins. The mass plopped upon her shoulders and she shook her head to loosen it.

If the locking of the door had felt intimate, this felt more so. Without a vow, this was something she would never— even under dire circumstances—do in front of a man.

Perhaps, rather than being trapped, she was liberated. Apparently one could be quite free with a husband.

No doubt it would even be acceptable to loosen the top buttons of her wedding gown. What a shame they were located on the back of her gown.

If she reached around, struggled with them, he might help her—the backs of his fingers would brush the skin on her neck. He might take the gesture as an invitation.

Did she want it to be? Her thoughts lately had certainly led that way—but did she truly want to do something she could not go back from?

She did not know.

Clementine set the hairpins on the table next to the comb. Unbound hair was enough familiarity for the moment.

For some reason he was staring at her, mute as a bug, so she picked up the conversation.

"It seems to me you have had less choice in the matter than I had. From the moment you lost your brother, you have been bound by duty."

"And so here we find ourselves." Reaching across the distance between their knees, Heath cupped her hands in his and squeezed. "Once again, I thank you. Olivia and I are so very grateful."

"You are hardly alone when it comes to gratitude. In case you failed to notice, Grandfather is beside himself with joy. He's convinced that his grandchildren for generations to come will be secure."

And there, so swiftly that she nearly missed it, he glanced at the bed. Perhaps it had been bold to bring up children. She hadn't done it by accident. Of the many issues needing to be settled in their marriage, this was a rather big one.

He let go of her fingers, settled back in the chair and folded his arms over his chest.

"Given our circumstances, I will not press you on the physical aspect of our marriage. If there is to be no heir, I can accept it. You didn't choose me and I would not force myself…" Another glance at the bed. "It's not as though— at any rate, there is my nephew, Victor."

Damn the bed! He ought to have had this conversation somewhere else.

He ought to go to his own room. It was not as if he could not come up with a reason to— Such as, as— Dammit! He couldn't come up with a single thing that made sense.

No doubt it was because the last thing he wanted to do was go to there. It was a big lonely room.

This one was cozy, and his wife was here.

Heath yanked his gaze away from the inviting piece of furniture only to have it settle upon the cascade of red curls falling across Clementine's chest.

The sight of it was no less tempting than the bed had been, so he focused his attention on the slippers peeping out from under her pearl-embedded gown.

But the pearls reminded him of his mother's comb and how lovingly his bride had touched it when she took it out of her hair.

Intimate emotions for her were dangerous. He needed to guard against them—but when she smiled at him the way she was doing now? Was there any kind of defense for that?

"I caught a glimpse of the boy crawling under the food table at our wedding breakfast." She said this with her gaze focused on the fingers of flame leaping in the fireplace. "No doubt he'll make a fine earl one day."

"He's a sweet child and I suppose he will."

Would not his wife desire the same thing? To bear a son and see him inherit the title? Of course she would want daughters to arrange fine matches for and grand-babies to cuddle in her arms.

He was her husband and honor-bound to give her those things. But at what cost?

Risk having her go to jail with him if he were caught? Having forced her to be his wife would he now damn her to a life in prison?

Or retire from giving rejected children a chance at life?

Maybe give up on finding a way to expose Slademore?

No, doing so would make him the worst of men. He could not possibly indulge in the joys of being married and all the while know that children were suffering. In some way that would make him as bad as Slademore was. To know and do nothing—his conscience would never allow it.

He had no options that were acceptable.

"I wonder, Heath, what will my duties be?" she asked. "Your sister seems to run the household efficiently." Clementine looked away from the hearth and pinned him with a green-eyed blink. "I cannot think she will welcome my interference."

"If you wish, I will relieve her of her duties. Hand them over to you."

"That would be highly unfair, don't you think? A woman needs a purpose and I would not take hers from her."

"It is your right to run your household if you please to. You are Lady Fencroft now."

"Yes, I am. A peer of the realm—a countess, no less." She sighed and he thought it was in resignation.

The position in society that a thousand women coveted was one that he knew she would rather not have.

They shared that bond. Earl and Countess of Fencroft, reluctant heirs to the title.

"And if not to run the household, exactly what are my duties to be?" Her fine brows arched in accent to her question.

Duties? That was something he hadn't given a great deal of thought to, beyond delivering the fortune to save them all.

"There are social calls to be paid, balls and parties to be planned, and shopping. Yes, a hundred shops depend upon your patronage."

"It sounds perfectly frivolous." Clementine stood up, paced to the bed and back, the pearls on her gown reflecting the glow of firelight.

Looking down upon him, she clamped her hands at her waist and tapped her fingers on the white satin.

"You might as well send me to Bedlam tomorrow, for that is where I am headed. Social calls! Shopping! Is that all I am fit for? And I detest balls."

In that moment, his heart caved. Clementine Cavill, to his way of thinking, might be a perfect woman.

What a gift she was, and yet she was as untouchable as the moon.

"What is it that you want?" He didn't know. He thought he'd mentioned everything a lady could desire, except the obvious thing.

Dammit, he had to stop glancing toward the bed.

"I would like to do what I was doing before—teach."

"Teach?" he repeated dumbly, because it was the last thing he'd expected to hear her say. Although, giving it a second of thought, it was exactly what he should have expected.

"School. I'd like to teach school." She arched her brows, a clear reaction to his frown. "Instruct children."

"I'm afraid that is not possible."

"Are there not children in need of instruction?"

"The young peers have tutors."

"What about the children of the servants? Surely in these progressive times, they will require an education."

"I'll need to ask Olivia, but I don't believe our servants have young children." On the country estate where life was less formal they did, but not here.

"I see." Judging by the way she narrowed her eyes and looked down that elegant nose at him, he suspected that it meant she did not see his point at all.

"I don't think that would be—"

"I'm not asking for this, Heath, I'm demanding it. I will have my way in something."

Heaven help him if he wasn't beginning to fall in love. A thing he could not possibly allow to happen.

Heath stood up. He cupped her cheek. As soon as he felt the velvet texture, the warmth and the way she turned ever so slightly into his palm, he knew he should not have.

But she was his wife and he, too, would have his way in something.

"It is simply not within my power to give you what you ask. If it was I'd give you a whole school full of children."

"How perfectly chivalrous." The sweetness of the moment vanished.

He turned on his heel, took two steps toward the window and stared out at the garden. It was too dark to see the fountain where they first met, but raindrops reflected the golden light in the room and slid down the pane, a wash of sparkling amber.

"That sounded pompous and I'm sorry." He sensed that she had come to stand beside him, because the air felt warmer, smelled like roses. "You have given me everything, Clementine—your hand, your fortune, your future. And I have given you shackles."

"Perhaps you ought to have consulted more thoroughly with my grandfather before you married me. He'd have warned you that I don't do well with shackles."

"The truth is, it's one of the things I appreciate—" more than that, hold dear "—about you. I find that I like your forthright spirit."

"And a lucky thing, if we are to make a go of this marriage." It touched him deeply to see her smile grow warm again. "And as far as the shackles are concerned? My grandfather might also have told you that I take after him in that most of the time, I get what I want."

"I doubt that you wanted to be forced to marry me."

"And yet," she murmured softly. "Here I am."

And all of a sudden it wasn't Clementine in shackles, it was him.

Chapter Seven

The next morning, Clementine stood in front of her grand wardrobe mirror, hoping the simple day gown reflected in the glass was elegant enough for a countess to wear. Her maid would have offered guidance, but Trudy had taken the day off on a family matter.

No doubt Madeline would know how she ought to dress but—

"God, protect my cousin," she whispered and then returned her attention to the problem in front of her.

As it was, she expected she would only discover the appropriateness of the gown by observing the sidelong glances the servants cast her way.

Being the granddaughter of a wealthy man was far simpler than bearing a title. As the American Countess of Fencroft, there would be consequences to what she did: gossip over her every word, deed and fashion.

Picking up her late mother-in-law's comb from the table, she slid it into her hair. Over her shoulder, the mirror reflected the rumpled blanket lying across the back of the chair where her newly avowed husband had spent the night.

And what a restless night it had been. She did not believe he'd slept much. She knew this because she also had not. She'd lost count of how many times she peeked up from the pillow to peer at him.

Every now and again he would twitch like a worm on a hook and she would have to suppress a giggle. In girlish wedding night fantasies, she had never imagined doing that.

With a pat to her modest hairstyle, Clementine turned from the mirror and walked across the room to the pair of chairs beside the window.

Picking up the blanket, she brushed it across her nose. While listening to the tap-tapping of rain on the glass, she breathed in the scent of Heath Cavill.

Rather than being tortured by the chair all night long, he might have gone to his own suite of rooms.

Might have, had it not been essential for the marriage to be consummated—or appear to have been.

She was under no delusion that her groom dallied in her room because he could not bear to be apart from her. Oddly, she found she did not mind him being here, no matter the reason.

Placing the blanket back on the chair, she turned to leave the room, but not before she lingered a second, trailing her fingers over the soft wool.

It was a lovesick gesture, even though lovesick was the last thing she was.

Only a fool would allow feelings to grow for a man so quickly. Clementine was wise enough to know that one did not toss one's heart at the feet of a fellow until she knew he could be trusted to not tread upon it.

She hadn't needed Olivia's wedding night advice to know it. Madeline had demonstrated it in a way that had changed not only her own life but Clementine's, as well.

Whatever her cousin's life was in the moment, she

doubted it involved the rascal she had run off with. If it did, Clementine was sure it was not in a good way.

Out in the grand hallway, she glanced this way and that. It seemed that countess-hood ought to come with a guidebook for those who were not born and raised for the job.

How was she to occupy her time?

At the top of the stairs she met a kitchen maid coming up carrying a breakfast tray. The girl curtsied without sloshing warm chocolate over the rim of the cup.

"Good morning, Lady Fencroft," she said. "Forgive me for being late. I did not know you were an early riser."

Why, it was nearly nine o'clock. As it was, Clementine felt a slugabed for lounging under the covers until eight.

"No need to apologize, I'm sure."

"But did you not wish to take breakfast in bed now that you are a married lady?" The poor girl glanced between her and the breakfast tray in confusion.

"Oh, why…" Maybe when she understood how things worked, she would write her own rule book for the American heiresses coming after her. "I do appreciate your trouble, but if you wouldn't mind I would prefer to take breakfast in the conservatory."

Back home she preferred the garden, but given that here there were so many rainy days, the indoor garden would suit nicely.

"Yes, my lady." The maid curtsied again and turned to go back down the stairs.

"Thank you, Miss—?"

"Oh, Mary, ma'am."

"I'm sorry to cause you extra work, Mary."

"'Tis no trouble at all. Not a bit of it."

To Clementine's way of thinking it was a bit of trouble to carry a tray of food three flights up the stairs.

"Are you happy working in the kitchen?" When it came to desirable employment, menial kitchen work was not top rung.

"Oh, I'm more than grateful for the job, my lady."

She followed Mary into the conservatory, noting that being grateful was not the same thing as being happy. Perhaps her job would be to see to the well-being of the staff, making sure that Fencroft House was a pleasant place to work in.

But perhaps Olivia was already seeing to that. It would not do to take over her sister-in-law's duties.

Stepping into the conservatory was a bit like entering an enchanted garden, Clementine decided while sitting at the table where Mary placed her tray.

With a nod and yet another curtsy, the maid hurried back to her duties in the kitchen.

Everyone had a function, it seemed. Apparently hers was to be served a luxurious breakfast and thereby provide employment to others.

Picking up the cup of steaming chocolate, she listened to the sounds enclosed within the glass walls and ceiling.

She walked over to the glass wall and gazed out at the garden and the apartments across the way.

Grandfather stood on his balcony, sipping a cup of what she guessed to be coffee. From this distance she could not know for sure, but she thought he was smiling. It occurred to her that this was the first time in her life she had not lived under his roof.

At least his roof was not far from hers.

Clementine returned her attention to the conservatory. There must be an aviary tucked among the greenery, because along with the steady pattering of rain, she heard the twitter of small birds.

From where she sat she could see the terrace and the

garden beyond. Out there, past a tall, swaying hedge, was the fountain where she had first met her husband.

Last night he had mentioned being required to attend Parliament this morning, but he was up and gone so early that she hadn't had the chance to speak with him about what she was to do with her time today.

He had suggested shopping. Apparently it was her duty to spread her fortune. While she understood the need of supporting business, she did not intend to pass money about willy-nilly and dump Fencroft back into the ruin she had just rescued it from.

For now she was going to eat her breakfast and enjoy the great variety of greenery in this room. If she was not mistaken, there were citrus trees growing in a brick-edged planter in the center of the room. Lemon and orange, she thought, judging by the shape of the fruit that was not yet ripe. The trees must be quite old given their great size.

Funny how much comfort one could take from a common tree. Well, common for Los Angeles, but probably quite rare here.

Something touched the toe of her shoe. She heard a shuffle, then a giggle.

Lifting the edge of the tablecloth she peered into a pair of violet-blue eyes.

"Why, hello," she said. The young boy's expression was full of mischief, but sweetly engaging even so. "You are Victor Shaw, are you not?"

"Noooo…" He shook his head, setting his blond curls a-jiggle. "I'm a cowboy from America."

"Oh, I see—and why are you under the table?"

"Hiding. You can't tell."

"I will do my best not to."

"It's all one can ever do, says Mother."

"She is right, of course."

"Not all the time. If she was I'd not have that mean old Mrs. Bentley as my governess."

"Is that who you are hiding from?"

"Mmm-hmm." He put his finger to his lips.

Just beyond the conservatory doors, Clementine heard Olivia calling for her son.

She dropped the tablecloth into place at the same time her sister-in-law swept into the room.

"Victor, is that you under the table?"

Clementine felt urgent scratching on the toe of her shoe.

"It's only a small cowboy under there," Clementine answered.

"That's a relief." Olivia rolled her eyes heavenward. "I feared it might be the pirate who was hiding under there last week."

Olivia yanked up the cloth. "Mrs. Bentley has been looking for you for half an hour. Now back to the nursery with you."

"But, Mother—" he scooted out, dragging his knees and pouting. "—she wants to make me read and I want to play."

"Did you know, Victor, that where I come from even cowboys can read?" Clementine said.

"Bet pirates can't." With his arms folded across his narrow chest and his knees locked, he marched from the conservatory.

"I daresay not," Olivia mumbled, a smile teetering at the corners of her mouth. "Such a little scamp."

"Oh, but he looks so sweet."

"Yes, he's that, too."

"I've breakfast enough for a dozen. Won't you join me?"

Olivia smiled and sat down. She lathered butter and jam on a piece of toast and ate it quickly.

"I've only a moment. I need to make sure Victor goes back to Mrs. Bentley. It seems my boy can be a handful."

"I have the impression he is quite bright."

"And imaginative. His habit of running off and hiding has me on edge. I know it's not likely and Fencroft House is safe enough, but that Abductor has me on edge."

"Abductor?"

"You'll not have heard of him, then? He's the devil is who he is. I have nightmares that he's somehow gotten into the house and snatched away Victor. I wake up screaming in my bed. Oh, I know it isn't likely to happen here at Fencroft House, but since when do dreams make sense? Why, not long ago, he snatched a child right out of its mother's arms and then kidnapped them both."

"That's horrible! Did it happen close by?"

"No. It was behind Slademore House. The poor mother was taking her newborn to that blessed place hoping to give it a better life when he came down upon her and snatched the baby from her arms."

"Surely not!"

"It is too wicked to imagine, but there were two guards who saw the whole thing and told the story to the newspaper." Olivia shook her head, frowning. "You can be sure she will never be heard from again."

Clementine set her toast on the saucer beside her tea, stunned that such a thing could have happened.

"They will catch him, I'm sure."

"But how many will he kill in the meantime? Has my brother not told you about Wilhelmina?"

She shook her head.

Was she an old flame?

The very last thing she should do was ask Olivia about her brother's relationship with an earlier love.

Unless she was not an earlier love.

"Oliver believed—well, it's not my story to tell and Oliver might have had it wrong." She stood up. "I'd best be after my child. There is every chance he did not return to the nursery."

"Olivia?" Clementine called after her.

"Yes?" she answered, turning at the door.

"Never mind." If there was something she needed to know about Wilhelmina it would be better to ask Heath about it.

Heath wondered about the necessity of having a footman standing in attendance near the dining room door even though there were only four people gathered at one end of the long, formally set table.

Olivia would think it was. His sister liked things upper crust—proper. Perhaps he would get used to the formality in time but he would be glad when Parliament was dismissed so he could return to Derbyshire and a less decorous way of life.

He would still be required to make frequent trips to London. The Abductor still had his work to do. Unless he and Creed could discover the identity of their informer they were obligated to continue on as they were. But so far the only thing they knew about the person who was having notes delivered to Creed was that she was female.

It was a bit much to hope that she would reveal herself and what she knew about Slademore House, since doing so would put her in peril. It would be a daunting thing for a commoner to stand up against the baron and the powerful people who would vouch for his philanthropy.

Even he, the sixth Earl of Fencroft, would not be believed if he spoke against Slademore with no hard proof of wrongdoing.

"How was your day, Clementine?" he asked, trying to divert his mind from Slademore.

He'd heard that she had taken breakfast in the garden room.

The household had been abuzz over her break with tradition. No doubt this would not be the last time his American bride set tongues wagging.

Now, why was it that it made him smile?

It occurred to him—midbite into a lamb cutlet—that she was like a breath of fresh air, the kind that swept across the open fields of home.

Odd, how he'd been miserable and yet smiling all day long. And doing both for the same reason. That reason being he was a married man and his wife was a better woman than he could have hoped for.

Too many of his acquaintances complained of the bad matches they were forced into.

It might be easier to resist joining his wife in bed if he could contribute to the men's discussion of marital woe. If Clementine was shrewish he could roll about in his misery like a pig in mud.

But no, she was a delight, a fact that had left him teetering between despair and bliss all day long.

"Informative." She gave a one-shouldered shrug and glanced briefly at Olivia. "I explored the house and discovered what was in every nook and closet."

"Sounds a fine way to spend a rainy afternoon," James Macooish said with a nod to his granddaughter.

Did the man really think so? While Heath had not known his wife for long, he did think her mind too inquisitive to be entertained by searching out closets.

"It is a beautiful home," she said.

Heath could guess what she was thinking behind her smile. He tried to look at things as she must be doing.

Parlormaids, footmen, scullery maids and grooms all had a part to play. The role that she would have taken in the natural hierarchy of things was already being performed by Olivia, and Clementine had stated that she would not take it from her.

There was visiting to be done and there were callers to be received, but his bride had made it clear that such pursuits would make her miserable. The very last thing he wanted was for her to be miserable.

She must have noticed him staring at her, because she turned her smile upon him—at least, he thought it was a smile.

In trying to decide if the turn of her lips was genuine or a gesture to hide her thoughts, he missed his mouth and stabbed the fork into his lip.

Whichever it was, it was beautiful. In fact he had been seeing it all day long.

If the lords had somehow managed to pass a bill in Parliament this afternoon, he'd failed to notice the event. He could keep his focus on nothing but Clementine.

How could he avoid it when fellow after fellow clapped him on the shoulder asking what he was doing here when he ought to be home entertaining his bride?

And now, here he was with only moments left before they would finish the meal and retire upstairs.

He'd told her that he wanted to wait to bed her in order to give her time to adjust to the idea, but it wasn't true. If his situation was different, he would do his best to convince her that waiting was foolish. As her husband, he had a right and a duty to teach her the ways of—

Macooish stood up, nodding to the footman. "Please extend my gratitude to everyone in the kitchen, sir. Dinner was most excellent."

"Give them mine, as well," Clementine added.

Macooish patted his trim belly and announced, "I'm off on a short trip to Scotland in the morning. Lord Guthrie and I have business in Inverness."

Clementine arched her brows, one slightly higher than the other. He was coming to understand that this gesture meant that she was questioning—challenging. For some reason it pleased him to know this little thing about her.

He also noticed that in the instant before she schooled her expression, her eyes blinked in dismay.

An understandable reaction, he thought, given that her grandfather was the only person she really knew in London.

She ought to be able to find companionship with her husband, but at this point, they were still so new to each other.

Only a scoundrel—a knave of the worst sort—would erect an emotional wall between them now. Which, until this moment, had been his plan. He detested what he was doing, and yet it was a necessary course of action.

A trip to Scotland! Of all the low-down—

Clementine stood up. In the silence following Grandfather's statement, the screech of the chair legs on the floor was pronounced.

"Inverness is a wonderful place this time of year," Olivia declared in a clear attempt to ease the tension.

"I'll walk you to the door, Grandfather."

"There's no need."

He took a stride away from the table, which she matched.

"Oh, indeed there is." A very great need.

Once outside in the garden, she rushed ahead of him, spun about and blocked his way.

"You cannot go to Scotland! Not now!"

"And why not?"

"Because you cannot leave me alone among people I barely know."

"Ah." He placed a hand on her shoulder, his grip firm. She was certain the squeeze was meant to be reassuring. "But you've a husband now. You aren't alone at all."

"A husband who is all but a stranger."

"My sweet Clemmie, that is exactly why I must go." He bent down to kiss her cheek. "This is a time for the two of you to forge a bond. It will be easier to do if I'm not here for you to turn to. You're his now. It's for him to see to your needs."

"And just how long have you been planning this treachery?"

"No matter what it feels like, this is for your benefit. Besides, it's not treachery, it's business. You know I've been in negotiations for some time."

He hugged her quick and tight and then set her away. With long strides he walked briskly across the garden toward the apartment.

"You, Grandfather," she called across the way, "are—" A rogue? A trickster? A hoodwinker? There was not a word to describe him. Except the one she did not care to accept in the moment because that word was "—correct."

She did need to form a bond with the man she'd married and it would be harder to do with Grandfather living just across the garden.

Given the choice, she would turn to Grandfather for company, go to him with a problem. He had been her anchor the whole of her life, after all.

Passing the fountain, he turned about with a grin and a wave. "I'll be back before you miss me. And perhaps you'll have some happy news to gladden this old heart."

"Canny heart, more like it. And do not hold your breath for that news!"

The echo of his laughter only quit once he closed the apartment door.

Oh, drat him. Without question he'd go to bed dreaming of bouncing baby earls on his knee.

At about midnight a great wind swept across Mayfair, rattling windowpanes and allowing cold air to seep in around the frames.

Sadly, no mere bluster would keep Grandfather from leaving. His mind was set on this new business venture, and when Grandfather's mind was set, there was nothing anyone could do to change it.

Well, here she was under the covers of the Countess of Fencroft's bed, living proof that when he decided he wanted something, he got it more often than he did not.

Ah, but he might not get everything. No matter how he schemed, some things were beyond his control.

For instance, even though her husband shared her bedroom, he did it crunched into a pretzel shape on the chair beside the window.

This situation would be a great disappointment to Grandfather.

Whether it was a disappointment to her or not remained to be seen.

Or, that was what she wanted to think. Clementine would have liked to believe that she was in control of what she was beginning to feel for her groom. That she could determine the course her heart would follow.

She liked him. There had been a draw between them from the very first.

It was her sense that he had a good heart. But she could not help wondering if it already belonged to someone else.

Olivia had hinted that it did—in the past or in the present. How was she to know? Who was this Wilhelmina?

One could hardly fault Heath for having a life before he married her, a life that had been ripped from him by the death of his brother.

She'd had a life, as well, even though it did not involve a man.

Chilled, Clementine drew her knees to her chest under the comforter. The tame fire in the hearth was no match for the encroaching cold. The melancholy voice of the wind whooshing under the eaves made her shiver.

Peeking over the comforter, she watched Heath twitch. The blanket slipped off his shoulder and slid onto the floor.

She thought she heard him curse but perhaps it was only another groan. He'd made several within the last hour.

For pity's sake! This sleeping situation was as ridiculous as it was unnecessary.

Tossing the covers off, she eased off the high bed and padded barefoot to the chair.

Even the floorboards were chilled. She curled her toes against the nip, but it didn't help.

Heath must not have heard her approach, because when she touched his shoulder he lurched and nearly fell off the chair.

"You must be half-frozen," she muttered.

"I'll do." He was looking at her bare feet when he lied.

"This is absurd, you know." He resembled an owl blinking up at her. "You, shivering in the chair, and me in the bed unable to sleep because of it."

"I did say I would not force my attentions on you. Get some sleep, Clementine, you needn't worry."

"We are married. It is perfectly acceptable for you to join me under the covers."

"I don't think that would be—"

"If you do not get up and into the bed, I'll ring for someone to remove the chairs from the room."

She looked down her nose at him. He ought to have cringed, or at least frowned. Drat the man for smiling.

She had a feeling—an unwelcome one—that in times of contest between them his smile would be her undoing.

"What if I can't keep myself from—?" Heat curled curiously through her because while he spoke, his eyes grazed her, from the hair hanging loose over her shoulders to her half-numb toes.

Moments ago she had wondered if it would be a disappointment if he did not come to her bed. She no longer wondered. In fact *disappointed* was rather a mild term for what she would feel if he remained in that chair.

"You needn't worry. I've enough restraint for the both of us." Even though she spoke the words she was not confident they were altogether the truth. "Frankly, I see no reason we cannot keep warm. The mattress is big enough for two."

"All right, then." He stood up and walked ahead of her toward the bed.

As she watched him approach the bed, the breath hitched in her lungs. What had she done?

Oh, dear, his pace was bold, manly, confident and possessive. For all that she bragged about being able to resist his charms, there was a chance she could not.

He lifted the covers for her to climb in and then hopped in after her.

He lay beside her, arrow straight and rigid. His long, hard, muscled body was as frigid as an icicle.

"Thank you, Clementine. I was coming to hate that

chair." Hearing his breathing, feeling the rise and fall of his lungs shifting the blankets, was an intensely intimate thing.

It felt deliciously wrong to be so close to him, even though nothing could be further from the truth. Man and wife were intended to be this close—closer even.

But before they grew closer, there were things they needed to discover about each other. A deep friendship to be forged before anything else.

"Your feet feel like ice cubes," he said.

"The whole length of you is an iceberg."

"I think—" He turned toward her, slipped his arm under her shoulders. With the other he crossed her middle, touched her back and drew her closer.

She thought they had been close before, but now—well—just well.

When she'd thought to share warmth under the covers she'd supposed it would be like when she and Madeline were little and shared the heat of a bed.

How naive she had been to expect a husband's heat would be anything like a cousin's.

There was nothing for it now but to go along, accept that it might have been wiser to leave him to suffer on the chair.

Oh, but all of a sudden he no longer seemed like a block of ice. Heat thrummed from his body, and even his breath brushing across the top of her hair felt delightful and toasty.

Wiser? Possibly, but then again he was her lawfully wedded husband.

"Do you like it?" he asked.

"Very much." The comforting sense of security in lying beside a man was not something she'd given a great deal of thought to in the past. But security was only part of it because at the same time her nerves skittered with an intimate awareness of him.

"It's a grand house, to be sure."

House?

What a lucky thing she did not prattle on about how lovely it was to be so close to him, how good he smelled and how she felt the rumble of his voice all through her.

"Your home is lovely."

"It is your home, as well, now." He nuzzled his chin against her hair.

"It's all so very different from what I'm used to."

"Tell me, Lady Fencroft, what is it you are used to?"

"Warm sunny mornings, for one. Although I do enjoy the rain. Being able to walk about on my own without it causing a stir. Even though Los Angeles is growing, there are not nearly as many people bustling about."

"You don't enjoy the crowds?"

"I might if they were not staring at me. I'm used to going about my business mostly unnoticed. It's Madeline who caught everyone's attention."

"You caught mine." He was twirling a strand of her hair around his thumb. She wondered if he even noticed he did it.

"I would have had to, wouldn't I?"

"Even wet as a duck, I thought you were uncommonly beautiful."

Was that what he had been thinking? As she recalled the event he had a look confused more than anything else.

"What can I do to make all this better for you? What thing can I give you to make you feel at home here?"

"Are there schools in need of instructors?"

"Teaching is that important to you." His sigh sounded resigned.

"Until my cousin ran away it was my purpose for getting up in the morning."

She pushed against his chest, putting a scant distance between them in order to better see his expression. "Everyone has something constructive to do. I have no idea what I will do tomorrow morning. What exactly does a countess do? If you tell me to pay social calls I'll go mad. In any case I doubt anyone would receive me—the foreigner who robbed them of the chance to lie here beside you."

She clapped her hand over her mouth. What was it about Heath Cavill that made her feel so free to speak her mind?

But here she was and those women were not.

"I'll do what I can to keep you entertained."

His fingers swirled slowly down her arm. She felt her skin tingle even through her cotton sleeve.

All of a sudden he clenched his fist. She felt the thump on the mattress when he let it fall.

She was the one to have thought it would not be wise to become intimate without becoming friends first, and yet, it troubled her in some odd way that he would want to keep his distance, as well.

How could she not wonder if he was feeling unfaithful to someone else, even though it was Clementine who was his wife?

Perhaps the woman Olivia had half mentioned—Wilhelmina?

The idea of that should not bother her. She had gone into the marriage knowing it was not a love match. She had recited vows in the full knowledge it was not a love match for him, either.

Which did not make her feel any better about there being someone else he would rather have warming his bed.

"I just want you to know, Heath," she said, thinking he might be wondering the same of her, "until we nearly kissed in the Lady Guthrie's garden, I'd never nearly kissed anyone else. I did not leave anyone brokenhearted when we wed—just in case you were curious. I would not want the doubt to come between our friendship."

"Are the men in Los Angeles fools, then? That's the only way I can account for it."

"Not fools so much as fortune hunters. I knew what they wanted of me and I was not willing to give it."

"And yet you gave it to me?" And there was his hand on her arm again, his fingers gently plucking at the fabric of her sleeve.

She sighed, because the heat of his hand on her arm seemed to be seeping deeper than flesh and bone. She was certain she felt it simmering in her heart.

"I did, yes. In part for Grandfather's sake, although I would not have done it for that alone. And of course, we did get caught in a compromising situation… But no, it was because the reason you wanted my wealth was not out of greed. I had been assured it was for the very good cause of keeping people from being turned out of their homes and losing their employment. If you had your druthers, I suppose you would rather be walking your bucolic fields in Derbyshire."

"And do you regret it yet?"

"How could I? Not without feeling the worst sort of human?"

"What I mean is, do you regret me?"

"Well, you are very warm." She resisted snuggling farther into him even though a gust nearly shook the window from its frame. "And handsome. And to be completely honest I do enjoy looking at you. You have the most compelling eyes—so no, I think I do not regret you."

"I don't regret you, either. And I also enjoy looking at you. You have the most—"

"No more, Heath." He really should not say anything else, nor should she, not if there was another woman to whom those words belonged.

"May I not return the sentiment?"

"I told you that I broke no hearts when we wed. I was free to speak my mind. But perhaps the same is not true for you? For all I know there might be a woman longing to hear the words you are saying to me."

"You have the most exquisite nose and the loveliest hair, and those words belong to no one else."

"But your sister—"

"She told you I have a mistress?"

"Some gentlemen find it acceptable."

He was silent for a very long time. She had a dreadful feeling that he was deciding whether or not to be truthful with her.

"I am not among them. If you trust me even a little bit, know that I do not, nor will I have, a mistress."

"I would hate it if you did." Even a woman in her situation wanted to be her husband's only attachment.

Perhaps the mysterious Wilhelmina was no one important to him after all.

"I like you, Clementine Cavill."

"I like you, too, Heath Cavill." The plain truth was, moment by moment she liked him more.

"Did you know that you have the most fascinating hairline? It's very attractive the way it dips just so right there." She could scarce believe that she had the boldness to reach up and touch the spot.

"Your eyebrows arch in the most becoming way when you challenge someone. Has anyone ever mentioned it to you?"

"Why would they?" She had to laugh. "No one likes being confronted."

"Hmm…well, I think I rather do."

And so the night went. He told her about his life on the country estate; she told him about hers in Los Angeles.

In the deep wee hours of the dark he spoke of Oliver. Of the heartache of missing his brother, of how even in despair he'd felt betrayed by him for leaving everything in financial ruin.

In turn she spoke of Madeline, how afraid she was for her cousin, and yet at the same time how she felt betrayed.

They had that in common, guilt and grief, even though to her knowledge her cousin still lived. But it did remain that she was bitter at Madeline for breaking Grandfather's heart.

Now, looking at her husband's profile while he gazed up at the ceiling talking about something she had lost track of, she knew she did not resent her cousin on her own behalf.

Try as she might, she could not see Heath and Madeline being a good match. On the other hand—

Warm lips brushed her cheek. Yes, on the other hand, she wondered if she and Heath might do very well together.

"We need to get some sleep," he said. "I've a surprise for you in the morning."

He gathered her closer to him, rested his cheek on the top of her hair.

"What is it?"

"Shh…it's a surprise."

She felt her hair stir when he smiled.

Chapter Eight

Dressed and ready for the day, Heath stood beside his bride's bed, watching her sleep.

While he was anxious to reveal the surprise, that he was taking her on a trip home to Derbyshire, he wanted to savor the moment of simply gazing at her.

She had not stirred earlier when he had eased out of their warm bed, touched the cold floor with his bare feet.

Nor had she moved when he stroked her fine red hair and brushed his lips across her forehead. No doubt if she knew what he had been thinking about in the moment she would have leaped from the bed in outrage.

She claimed to have enough restraint for both of them. He, on the other hand, had the restraint of a bee buzzing about a spring blossom.

As eager as he was to take her home, he was just as eager to climb back under the covers with her and finish a conversation they had been having last night about the hot winds that swooped out of the mountains near Los Angeles in the wintertime and turned everything dry and brittle.

Or perhaps he was happy enough to just stand beside the bed and watch one corner of her mouth twitch, to memorize the fine arch of her brows.

Clementine's eyes blinked open. She stretched and smiled, and he found he could not speak a word. All of a sudden Heath forgot there was a reason he was standing here at all. The only thought in his mind was that she was completely and utterly beautiful.

"Good morning," she said, snapping him out of his odd daze.

"Good morning." Better than good, he expected it to be grand. "Are you ready for your surprise?"

She eased up to her elbows, glancing at the rumpled bedclothes and then at her sleeping gown. "It depends upon what the surprise is."

"I'm taking you on a visit home, to Derbyshire."

She leaped from the bed with a laugh, her wild red hair in a riot of curls over her face and shoulders.

The moment, as common as a moment could be, seemed to him like it was a bit profound, and shook him in a delightful way.

For the first time in his life, he had been with a woman when she woke in the morning.

It left him feeling husbandly, protective. It was as if he had been entrusted with something—not helpless, she was not that—but something precious.

She was his to watch over and he found he was grateful for it.

He might easily have been resentful, angry to have been forced into a life he hadn't chosen—but no, he was thankful.

Because of his position, marriage was something he was duty bound to carry through with. Any woman with a fortune might have been his lifelong companion. She might have been an unlovely shrew.

Now, watching Clementine's joy over the prospect of visiting her new home, he felt quite blessed.

* * *

"I can't imagine what it must have been like for you, grieving for your brother and at the same time having to leave this place. Derbyshire is breathtaking."

He gazed out of the carriage window, imagining he was seeing the rolling green hills for the first time, just as it would look to her.

Had he been able to look ahead in time to this moment it might have eased the crushing blow of his brother's death somewhat. Foreseeing that he would continue to breathe, would rise in the morning and do what was required of him and, in the end, be bringing his wife to Fencroft Manor—yes, he would've been very grateful.

He'd heard that adage—"Life goes on"—and now he knew it firsthand. While he would always shed tears for Oliver at unexpected moments, he would also laugh.

"You would know something of that since you did the same thing."

"I'm not grieving for Madeline. Only heartsick with worry. And as for having to take her place?" She swung her gaze away from the window, let it settle upon him. "Things might have been a great deal worse."

"I hope in time—" once the business with Slademore was finished, once and for all "—we can spend most of our time here. It's beautiful every season of the year."

"Everything looks so green and fresh. Are those white buildings the town?"

He nodded. "Village more than town. Sometimes I like to get out of the carriage and take a walk through before going on to the manor house."

"Oh, yes! Let's do that."

Heath tapped on the carriage roof. The carriage slowed down and a moment later Creed opened the door.

Stepping down quickly, Heath turned and took Clementine's hand to help her down. He might have let his coachman do it but he did not want to miss the chance to touch her, even for the briefest moment.

She was his wife and by rights he ought to be able to touch her whenever it was proper. He would have to keep reminding himself that what was proper was not what was right, at least not for him. Not until Slademore was no longer a danger.

Heath stood still, closed his eyes and breathed in deeply. Fresh country air filled him up, cleansed his body of the smog of London. The sounds of birds in the bushes and the gurgling rush of the river nearby cleansed him of the hectic noise of town.

He opened his eyes and saw that Clementine appeared to be doing the same thing.

"We can walk through the village or along the river," he suggested, letting go of her fingers. "Whichever you prefer."

"The village, I think. Your tenants will want to know you are home."

They walked up a low grassy rise to get to the road leading to the village.

"I've no doubt they already know." He touched her under the elbow to lead her up. "But it's you they'll be anxious to see. Fencroft Manor has been without a mistress for a long time now."

"Perhaps the river, then."

Before they could shift course, a child emerged from the blacksmith's and ran across the knoll, carrying a handful of wildflowers. It was too late to take the river walk.

He was only the first of dozens of people to come out of the half-mile-long row of shops and homes, bearing flowers and good wishes.

Clementine tucked the bunches of flowers into the

crook of her arm, smiling graciously as each one was presented.

As soon as they left the village Clementine spotted the manor house, its roof just visible beyond a large grove of fruit trees.

"There are a great many children living here." Clementine glanced back over her shoulder to see them standing at the edge of the village, waving their hands.

He stopped, touched her elbow. "They do not know how close they came to being put out. Because of you they never will know. We really have no way of giving you the thanks you deserve."

"The flowers are thanks—but tell me, do they know how to read?"

"Yes, and write. Most of them anyway. We have a teacher who lives in the village."

"I see." The flowers sagged in the crook of her arm and she watched the ground while she walked.

"Teaching means so much to you?"

"It rather does, yes."

"Working for a wage is not what a countess does." But surely if it was what she wanted? It was not right that everyone benefited from this marriage but her. "But they do volunteer. Charity work is acceptable. Would you want to do that if I can find a good cause? Will that suit?"

She gasped, lunged for him and squeezed him tight. Blossoms and leaves from her bouquet tickled the back of his neck.

"It would suit." She let go of him far too quickly. "Honestly, Heath, I was within a moment of stealing away to the stables to teach the chickens."

The image put a picture in his mind—Clementine standing in front of a row of hens clucking on a fence, while she instructed them in their ABCs. It made him laugh out loud. By the time he had finished chuckling over it, the house had come fully into view.

"What do you think?" he asked.

"It's not so grandly formal as some we've passed by, and I adore it!"

"You do? Truly?"

"I can scarce believe I will get to live here." She hugged the flowers to her chest.

Nor could he. Somehow this marriage of convenience was becoming quite a bit more.

If Los Angeles was the City of Angels then Derbyshire would be the angels' vacation spot.

Clementine stood on the wide front porch, watching the sun go down. In the distance she saw daylight dim on the tops of village buildings. Night shadows crept across emerald green hills. From where she stood, she saw sheep huddling together for the night.

The manor house was large, but for all its size it felt comfortable. It would be a fine place to raise children if she were blessed with them. Of course it was far too soon in her unusual marriage to give the matter more than a passing thought.

So far there had been only two kisses between her and Heath, the splendid one when they'd become engaged and the one to seal their vows. She did not know a great deal about the marriage bed, but she did know that children did not happen because of a kiss.

All that might come in time, but for now her mind was happily occupied wondering about Heath's promise to find a way for her to teach.

She hoped it would be soon, or she really would begin teaching livestock.

A figure on horseback emerged from the grove of fruit

trees between the house and the village. Her heart softened when she recognized that it was Heath.

He drew the horse to a halt at the foot of the porch steps, giving her a wide, happy grin.

Oh, but that smile was finding a place in her heart. And didn't he look happy to be home? It was as if, in leaving London behind, a load was lifted from his shoulders.

"Come. The tenants are having a celebration in honor of your arrival." He straightened, reaching his hand for her.

When was the last time she had ridden double on a horse?

Never was when. She was not sure—

Heath wagged his hand at her. "You will enjoy this."

So far she had enjoyed everything about Fencroft Manor, so she skipped—nearly skipped, anyway—down the steps.

Heath leaned down, placed his arm about her waist and swept her up behind him.

Oh—my, but he was strong. For some reason that made her insides shiver.

Coming out on the far side of the orchard path, she heard music—happy music. If she was required to dance to it she would not know how.

As they entered the village, the laughter of men and women along with the higher voices of children came to her.

The aroma of a dozen different kinds of food filled her senses at one time.

In California they would have called this a fiesta. Many times Madeline had sought Clementine out in the seclusion of the garden and whisked her off for an evening of fun.

This, she thought, glancing at fiddlers, dancers and

children dashing happily about, was nothing at all like a ball.

Instead of sidelong glances making her feel unwelcome, greetings, smiles and wishes for a blessed future met her.

"You are tapping your foot to the music." Heath nudged her in the arm with his elbow. "Would you like to dance?"

"Oh, that would be lovely, but I don't know the steps to these dances."

He winked, smiled and led her by the hand to the spot by the river where the carriage had let them off. The music was fainter here but she could still hear it clearly enough.

"Now we can dance in any way we choose and no one will see us," he said, sweeping his arm about her waist and pulling her close to him.

He took a small step sideways and then another in the other direction.

"I do not recall this dance, Heath."

It was more like swaying to the music.

"It's better for conversation."

"Hmm, I believe you are right."

From the side of her vision she saw their moonlit shadows meld into one. Saw the dark shape of Heath's arm come up and toward her face. She felt the rough texture of his finger when it stroked her cheek.

"You are very soft," he whispered.

"Am I? No one has ever pointed that out."

"I am honored to be the first, then."

He would be the first for many things—she hoped.

"Are you warm enough? It's getting chilly."

"Just warm enough." The truth was, cool air was beginning to seep through her gown, but she would not give up this moment for a mere chill.

She closed her eyes to better hear the violin and the

rush of the river flowing past—to better appreciate the warmth of Heath's hand at her waist, the hint of his heated breath on her nose.

"Are you lonely?" he asked. "You must miss your grandfather."

"It's not the first time he's gone away on a trip, but—"

How did she explain what she was feeling?

"But you have never been without everyone and every-place familiar to you?"

"There was always Madeline, and some of the staff at home were like family, so I always felt secure even when Grandfather went away."

"And now?"

"I'll be glad when he returns." Of course she would. "But I like being here in this moment. In this place—with you."

"This is your home now. You see how welcome you are." He caught her chin, lifted it so that she could look nowhere but into his eyes while they "danced." "And I am your husband—you will always be safe with me."

Chapter Nine

The visit to Derbyshire had not lasted nearly long enough. She hadn't wanted to leave. Neither had Heath, but he had promised they would return soon.

Even given the short time she had spent there, it had begun to feel like home.

Today, walking in the town house garden, Clementine found she did not keep constant watch on the balcony of Grandfather's apartment in hopes of seeing he had returned.

While she did miss him, she did not think of him with endless longing. She wondered how he was faring. But as far as yearning went, her feelings had shifted.

Just now she yearned for the night to come in hopes that Heath would once again share her bed.

It was all very chaste but she was glad he hadn't chosen his own room to sleep in. Given that he was gone all day, nighttime was the only time they had to get to know one another more deeply.

At the same time, she was not so naive as to not realize there was some simmering going on under the covers.

Just how well would they need to know one another before he would act upon it? Last night, she'd felt that with only the slightest encouragement, he would have kissed her. She was certain it would not have been his usual buss to the tip of her nose and a "Sweet dreams, sleep well."

For now she would focus her thoughts on his promise to find her a voluntary teaching position.

He was, she thought, a man she could trust to keep his word.

To keep his word in everything. Olivia was mistaken in her belief that he had a mistress. When he vowed he did not have one, she believed him.

She sighed. The large shrub beside her rustled. Surely she had not exhaled that hard.

While she stared at it a flash of blue fabric moved within the leaves.

"Hello, kitty, kitty," she crooned.

"Meow," purred a familiar four-year-old voice.

She crouched down, parted the branches and looked into a pair of blinking violet-blue eyes. It was Victor. "Poor kitten, are you hiding from your governess again?"

"Kitties don't need them."

"I suppose not." She touched his hair, as if petting it. "If there was a boy hiding in here, why would he be, do you think?"

"His mean old governess would want him to read a book and he doesn't know how to."

He pushed her hand away. The leaves hid him once again.

"I would imagine not, if the boy was only four years old."

"He would be."

"I suppose someone of that age might be curious about the story, though. He might even have stuffed the book in his back pocket."

"Meow."

"Poor little fellow might like to have it read to him."

A small hand shot out between the leaves, gripping the book.

Settling down upon the chilly stones, Clementine arranged her skirt around her.

When she opened the book and began to read, what was out of kilter in her life shifted back into place.

"Master Victor!" a strident voice called, silencing the happy twitter of birds.

"I believe you've been found out," she whispered toward the bush.

"If you tell on me I'll never know if there's really a giant at the top of the beanstalk."

"Where did you get to this time, you miserable brat?" the governess mumbled while rounding the corner of the path. "Oh, Lady Fencroft, I didn't see you."

"I imagine you did not."

She shifted her weight to further disguise Victor's hiding place. But given that she was sitting on the stones with the book open on her lap, Victor was sure to be revealed.

But what was also revealed was the true cause of Victor's habitual hiding. His governess was a tyrant.

"Good day, Mrs. Bentley," she stated, then nodded by way of dismissal. With some difficulty, she resisted the urge to address her as Madame Oppressor, since a countess was supposed to be regal-mannered in all situations and in control of her tongue at all times.

Mrs. Bentley curtsied while her gaze darted from shrub to fountain to tree.

"Are you searching for something?" Clementine asked.

"Master Victor has run off again. Have you seen the boy?"

"I'm sure he will turn up in good time." While this was not an answer, neither was it a lie.

"May I ask what you are holding in your lap, Mrs. Cavill?"

Clementine pictured the notes Grandfather had written about the correct forms of address. She was fairly certain her title had been disrespected.

The crafty old bosom must think her dim-witted because she did not acknowledge the insult, but there was a more important issue at hand.

"As you can see, it's a child's book."

"It belongs to my charge." The governess did have an impressive frown.

Still, it was no match for a Macooish brow arch. "Yes, it does."

"If you know where he is, and I believe you do, you must tell me. He's a stubborn learner and requires a firm, strict hand."

"He's a small boy and must be taught with patience."

"I have many years of experience. I do know what is best in this matter."

"When it comes to her son, it's Lady Shaw who knows best. You may take the afternoon off while I discuss the matter with her."

"Lady Shaw understands the importance of a strict education. But you are an American. I suppose I must make an allowance. You do come from a country of illiterate cowboys, so one could hardly expect more." Mrs. Bentley's expression was the most snobbish she had seen— even among the aristocracy. "But if you like, I will teach you to read *Jack and the Beanstalk* along with the boy."

Victor lunged from the bush and landed in her lap.

"Cowboys can read! My auntie says so!"

"There you are, you little beas— Master Victor."

Clementine wrapped one arm about Victor's small ribs. With her free hand, she motioned for the governess to keep her distance.

A dozen censorious words leaped to the tip of her tongue but another voice spoke before she could settle on one.

"As it turns out, Mrs. Bentley," Olivia declared, stepping out from behind the shrub, "having been standing on the other side of this bush for the better part of your conversation, I now understand a good many things."

She reached a hand down to her son. He leaped from Clementine's lap to hide among the folds of his mother's skirt.

"My sister-in-law is correct in that you will take the day off. Spend the time packing your belongings, for I am terminating your employment as of this moment."

It felt diminishing to be sitting on the ground and having to look up. And her bottom was chilled through. Clementine stood, clutching the book to her chest.

"Lady Shaw! That woman is turning you against your own kind."

Mrs. Bentley made an odd sound in her throat, turned toward Clementine and launched a glob of spittle. It missed her skirt by an inch.

Clementine withdrew a handkerchief from her sleeve and held it out to the woman. "Surely you did not expect someone to clean up after you."

Victor emerged from a swath of brocade and squatted down to give the slime closer inspection. "I'm not allowed to spit since I might be an earl one day—unless I go to America and be a cowboy."

"Whatever made you think you are my own kind or the countess's?"

' Mother is not allowed to spit, either," Victor explained.

* * *

Two weeks after the spitting incident, Fencroft House hosted a ball.

The affair was not his wife's idea but his sister's.

Olivia had been disturbed at the disrespect shown to her sister-in-law by a mere governess and was determined that the Cavills would demonstrate to society, from the highest level to the lowest, that Lady Fencroft was not a despised necessity but a member of the family.

A masterpiece of organization, the gala had come together splendidly. Olivia had a gift for entertaining, and Heath thought the ball would benefit her as much as Clementine.

Olivia liked a display of pomp when it came to hosting a ball. She was something like Oliver in that. In her opinion there needed to be thousands of candles, lace swags and satin pillows on every chair.

Clementine allowed it but only to a financially responsible degree.

In the end the presentation was elegant, with satin cushions for every chair, a smallish twenty-piece orchestra and huge bouquets of flowers everywhere one looked.

The flowers were requested by Clementine and they filled the air with springtime fragrance, even though it was early autumn.

As far as balls went, Heath was enjoying this one. Now that he was a married man and his wife was standing beside him, he was no longer pursued by fresh-faced debutantes.

Standing beside the most beautiful woman in the room and being able to call her his made this more than a pleasant event.

When he'd first seen Clementine descending the grand staircase in her exquisite blue gown, Heath had nearly tripped on the rug.

Tenderness overwhelmed him. Admiration caught his breath and snatched it away.

The Countess of Fencroft was the belle of the ball, her beauty well-bred. From his mother's comb tucked becomingly in her curls to her slippers winking in the gaslight, she was as much a lady as the queen herself.

If Clementine was ill at ease being the center of attention, it did not show. Even though he well knew she did feel uncomfortable with it, she put up a good account of acting a peer. She smiled graciously at everyone, even those who clearly resented her for being "the ruin of polite society."

Not everyone did, though. Both Olivia and Lady Guthrie made a great show of treating her with respect.

Since everyone wanted to be in the duchess's good graces, they would probably follow her lead.

It could not be long before those who were willing to would know his wife for the genuinely compassionate and sensible countess she was.

Hours passed, swallowed up in chatting with this baron and that marchioness. All at once he noticed that Clementine was no longer at his side.

He glanced about but did not see her anywhere.

"If you will excuse me," he blurted to the clear surprise of a woman discussing the Plumage League's campaign to outlaw feathers from hats.

No doubt his bride had sought a moment of peace. He decided to follow her example.

His office was the closest place to escape to.

Walking down the long hallway, he looked at the line of large, potted shrubs spaced a distance of ten feet apart along each wall.

The greenery reminded him of Derbyshire, of the precious moments he had danced with Clementine beside the river.

Coming to the spot where two hallways intersected, he heard whispering. There were always whispers. No interesting gathering would be without them.

He hesitated to cross the hall for fear that he would interrupt a secret liaison.

Which left him hovering at the corner, a voyeur to each quietly spoken word.

As it turned out, they were not lovers but gossips. Three of them, perhaps four.

"Don't be silly, Glenda. I'm certain the earl would have picked you had he not been forced to marry that American woman."

"You do know she planned the encounter in the garden in order to catch him. Why else would he even have looked at her?"

Because she is exceedingly beautiful, he refrained from shouting. He peeked around the corner so he could see who the women were who thought to judge his wife.

Three heads were bent together, the speakers so intent on their ugly talk that they did not notice him.

Even if his marriage had not been arranged with Clementine, he would not have chosen one of them. Not that their plain faces would have mattered, but their mean, shallow attitudes would have.

"And she is as ordinary as a mouse."

"Oh, quite. And not at all interesting. I hoped she would be as lavish in her entertainment as the Duke of Farelone's American heiress was. Don't you remember how she hired a trapeze act? Set them up over the ballroom?"

"It was scandalous how they were dressed! And swinging so low we could nearly touch them."

"Emily Blaine! You loved every second of it. In fact, you did try to touch the man. I clearly saw you reach for his—"

Giggles, giggles and more giggles made him cringe. Made him know how lucky he had been to marry a woman and not a cackling girl.

He had his mouth open to tell them so, when across the hallway he saw someone emerge from hiding behind a potted plant.

A red-haired, blue-gowned someone.

Clementine was hidden from the women since she was in the same spot he was, just on the opposite side of the wide hallway. She motioned for him to stay silent.

"Mark my words, the new countess is going to be as dull as her gown."

Dull? Her gown brought many images—tempting, alluring, bewitching—to mind. They were as far from dull as one could get. Luckily, Clementine did not appear to be offended by the comment. She looked at him and shrugged her shoulders.

Of course, she would not want to cause a scene. To give even more reason for their tongues to wag. He understood and respected that, but at the same time he didn't know how many more insults he could listen to.

"She might look frugal, but mark my words, she will run the earl's fortune into the ground."

To that Clementine arched a brow. He rolled his eyes, which made her smile. How close a bond was growing between them that they might carry on a conversation across a dim hallway with no words spoken?

If he was not falling in love, he did not know what this peculiar turn of his heart might be. Only the fact that Clementine did not seem overburdened with the whispered nonsense kept him from charging to her defense.

"I shouldn't talk about it, and it's to go no further—"

"You know us, Emily. We are as discreet as—well, anyone."

"I heard that the Fencroft estate was bankrupt and that is why the earl married her."

What? He'd been nothing but discreet about that. So had Olivia. Apparently one of the creditors had not been.

"I thought it was because she seduced him in Lady Guthrie's garden."

Across the way, he watched Clementine tap her lips with one finger, clearly reminding him that the seduction had been half on her part.

"It's true, she did. I was there that night."

Heath frowned, thumping his chest with his thumb. He wanted to make it clear that he had been the seducer and she the innocent.

For some reason she must have thought it funny, for she attempted to hide her smile behind a balled-up fist.

"As I see it, now that he's got her money, he can divorce her and marry you, Glenda."

All of a sudden Clementine's fist fell away, and her smile vanished.

Evidently the option of divorce had not occurred to her any more than it had to him.

He shook his head vigorously: she had to know he would never do it.

"It's not as though there will be an heir."

Clementine crossed her arms over her middle, staring down at the floor.

"Quite. Everyone knows American women aren't fertile."

"Maybe they are but their husbands don't want to touch them."

This husband did! The need to do so was a constant itch.

"Well, even if she does manage it, the baby's bound to be a girl."

Enough! He dashed across the hallway behind the gossips, hardly caring if they saw him or not.

He caught Clementine around the waist, briefly hugged her and hurried her away toward the door that led to the garden.

"Ill-bred magpies." Heath's voice rumbled in his chest. Clementine felt the words thrum against her arm. Truly, if he hugged her any tighter she would not be able to breathe.

A door at the end of the hallway led to the patio and the garden beyond. He ushered her outside.

Rain poured down upon her head. Surely the stars had been twinkling only hours ago.

If she could do things over again she would not have tried to escape the ball.

Really, the affair had been lovely, but one could only carry on starched conversation for so long.

Over the years she'd learned that hallways made excellent retreats. So she had made her escape, meaning for it to be a brief one.

At first, overhearing the whispers of those women had not overly disturbed her solitude. Women did like to prattle and they hadn't said anything that she would not have expected them to.

American heiresses were infamous—whether the reputation was deserved or not didn't matter. The flighty image was accepted to be true.

What she could not fight she would not let bother her.

And then Heath had appeared on the far side of the hallway intersection. They had been carrying on a rather nice conversation without words.

Being familiar enough with another person in order to be able to indulge in that skill was an intimate thing. She could only describe those moments as tender, wonderful in an uncommon way.

But then—oh—the things the women said had pierced her heart, squeezed the joy out of it.

Divorce? She hadn't considered it—and in that moment she found she did want a child. Girl or boy, it hardly mattered. But suddenly it mattered to her that there be one. And not for Grandfather's sake, but for her own.

Heath hugged her, caressing her back as though trying to wipe away what those girlish women had said.

Rain pattered loudly on the stones. It sluiced down her nose and made her hair sag.

Heath took off his coat, placed it over her shoulders and tugged it about her throat.

Water soaked his thin lawn shirt. It became translucent, revealing the ruddy hue of his skin, the glistening line of shoulder and bicep.

She had to place—simply could not resist—her palm on his chest, tipping her forehead close and breathing in his wet male scent.

Over the pelt of rain and her heartbeat, she heard his intake of breath when he brushed his cheek across the top of her head. Felt the exhalation before he kissed the crown of drooping curls.

He dipped his mouth close to her ear. "I wouldn't."

She drew back to look at his face. "Wouldn't?"

Water slid off the tips of his hair and washed off his lashes.

"Divorce you—I would never."

"And I would never squander your fortune."

He cupped her cheeks with his thumbs, wiping away the moisture. The calloused tips felt delightfully abrasive.

"Clementine Jane Cavill, I think, I believe I want to—"

His mouth came down upon hers, slick with rain.

She touched his hair, felt wetness and the heat of his scalp under her fingertips.

"I believe," she murmured once she caught her breath, "I want you to do it again."

All of a sudden he tipped his face up at the rain and laughed quietly.

"Last time we were in a garden at a ball…" Funny that a simple smile could make her feel warm when she ought to be shivering. "I thoroughly compromised you without even getting to kiss you."

He touched his lips to hers again, playfully this time, just a quick nip.

"Yes, well, I do recall the event."

"What those women in the hallway said? About you seducing me? That was on me alone. I knew what I was doing. Kissing you was the most important thing on my mind. I'm only grateful it all turned out as it did. I'm not certain I could have gone through with it—getting married I mean—had it not been to you."

"As I recall the way it happened, I'm the one who invited you to fly away. It was overly bold of me and did smack of seduction, you must admit."

"Ah, but in the sweetest way."

In the distance she heard raindrops tapping an umbrella. As much as she wanted to ignore the intrusion she could not. Footsteps marched purposefully toward them.

"There you are!" It was Olivia's voice and it did not sound pleased. "People are noticing their hosts are missing. I suggest you get back inside before you create a scandal."

Clementine's lips twitched because, really, the situation was funny if one looked at it right.

"We appear to be making a habit of creating a scandal,"

she said, watching Olivia balance the umbrella while trying to hold the hem of her skirt out of the water.

"Don't be foolish." For some reason her harsh words did not match her softening expression. "Go back to the house and change into dry clothes."

Spinning about, Olivia hurried back toward the house.

Heath slung his arm over her shoulder, leading them behind his sister.

"What if we don't?" he said.

"As nice as it sounds, we've got to go back. You know we cannot really fly away."

"If only we could, but what I meant was, what if we don't change into dry clothes. Let's go back in dripping wet."

"Now that would cause a great hubbub."

He really did have the most captivating grin when he was up to mischief.

"Oh, the infamy!" He winked at her. "Come on, let's cause a fuss."

Chapter Ten

As it turned out, Clementine could not go through with the daring escapade.

When she and Heath turned right at the hallway leading from the patio to the ballroom, they ran headlong into Trudy.

The poor maid was horrified at what had become of her hard-fought battle to make Clementine shine.

The stricken look on her face was enough to make her realize that what was a spot of fun for her might cause her maid shame.

The girl was nothing if not dedicated to Lady Fencroft's appearance.

She turned to Heath.

"Perhaps we might scandalize everyone another time?"

"Indeed we shall, Lady Fencroft. I've no doubt about it."

He kissed her cheek and then dashed away to find his valet.

While Clementine dutifully followed Trudy up the back staircase, the lingering warmth of Heath's lips on her cheek chased away the chill setting in from her wet clothing.

So now, an hour later, she found herself in a dry gown

with her hair only half-damp, speaking to someone seeking a donation for the betterment of birds.

"How would you like to be plucked?" the lady asked.

That all depended, of course, upon what was being plucked and by whom. If it was Heath and he was plucking off her garments, one by one…

She shook herself, mentally.

"I'll be delighted to donate."

"Why, thank you, Lady Fencroft." The woman's smile turned her cheeks into a pair of pink balls. "I, for one, rather like American heiresses. Naturally, had you been sporting bluebird wings in your hair I might think differently."

She cast a frown back over her shoulder at someone who was.

"Good evening, Countess, Baroness. I quite like American heiresses, too," said a masculine voice. "But for their charm as much as their generosity."

Baron Slademore presented a neat bow.

"Good evening," Clementine greeted her guest with a genuine smile.

There were many people in the ballroom whose names she could not recall. She did remember the baron's, even though the only time she had met him was in the reception line after her wedding.

He was dashingly handsome and had a reputation for good works. She'd even seen him sitting in the front row at church last week smiling all through the service.

"Would you care to give a donation to our avian friends?" her companion asked.

"Yes, certainly." Nodding, he dipped his head slightly to one side while his smile ticked up only one corner of his mouth. "The world would be dreary without them. In fact, we have an aviary at Slademore House for the enjoyment of the children."

With a nod of thanks the woman hurried away, presumably in search of another donation.

From across the room she noticed Heath look up from his conversation. His gaze settled on Slademore.

She wondered if the same thought occurred to Heath as it just had to her. It was so logical it must have.

"Baron Slademore," she said. "I would like to make a donation to your charity."

"You are generous as well as beautiful. I'll admit it's always a relief when I don't have to ask people to support the dear children."

"I'm grateful to be able to help." That was a part of it, naturally. "Each week I will bring a donation, and three times a week I will come and teach the children to read."

"I can't recall ever having a more generous offer, Countess, but you needn't come at all. I'll send a man to collect. I prefer not to have my benefactors inconvenienced. Besides, Slademore House is not in a part of town fit for a lady."

"Naturally, I'll bring an escort."

"Let me be frank, my lady. The children in my charge will not grow up in a world in which a formal education is required. It is the way of things. I'm certain that on their own they will pick up what they need in order to get by."

To get by in poverty, the same as their parents had, which no doubt contributed to the children ending up where they had.

Slademore House might be a respectable shelter, but still, had the parents received an education, they may have been able to keep their children.

"We do live in changing times, Baron. Children will need to read. If you do not accept my offer, and along with it my substantial donation, do you then intend to provide public instruction for them?"

"You have a tender heart, and that is to your credit, but I feel you are misguided."

"I am not misguided." He did have a winning smile. She wondered if he used it as a deceptive trick in order to get his way. If so, his effort was wasted. She had a worthy purpose and she would not let it go. "You have only to look at the changes going on in our world to know the truth."

She nodded, giving the appearance of the conversation being at an end. Deliberately, she turned as if she meant to walk toward Heath but he was already pushing through the crowd toward her.

"Oh." She glanced back over her shoulder, making it appear that what she had to say was an afterthought. In truth it was of utmost importance to her. "My offer will stand until the end of the evening if you wish to accept it."

An hour later the baron sent a note by way of a footman, accepting her offer to teach the little ones to read.

Whether he accepted for fear of losing the funds or because of a change of heart about the necessity of the children learning to read, she did not know.

What she did know was that she had gotten what she wanted and now felt like she was walking on air, or rather dancing on it.

Heath came upon her, snatched her about the waist and led her to the dance floor.

Life was lovely. She was floating on her dreams. She was smiling into Heath's eyes, feeling her heart expand, stretch—was this love?

Perhaps it was too soon to know for sure. But perhaps it was not.

For the moment, it was good to swirl about in his arms.

In only hours she would tell him she had found a place to teach.

No doubt he was going to be as overjoyed as she was. Life was lovely.

Even though Heath was now a city dweller, his body kept country time. Early to bed and early to rise, and all that.

As late as it now was, he excused the footman standing in attendance near the coat room for yawning. He had sympathy for the matron snoring softly in a chair while waiting for someone to take her home.

It was past midnight and yet the guests lingered. Hadn't they homes and beds waiting for them?

Enough, then. He would set the example.

"I bid you good-night, gentlemen," he said to a group of fellows with whom he had been discussing the sad state of politics. Or rather they had been—he'd only nodded his head at what seemed to be crucial points.

For much of the evening he had been Clementine's shadow. When he'd seen her talking and smiling with Slademore his blood had gone cold—or hot. Whichever, it had made him charge across the room with the intention of yanking her away.

Luckily, by the time he reached her, Slademore had turned his slick charm on someone else.

If it was up to him, the man would have been cut from the invitation list. Unfortunately, he was a respected member of society and could not be.

But where was Clementine now?

He glanced about and spotted her near the punch bowl, speaking with Lady Guthrie.

He strode across the room.

Simply looking at his wife made him smile. Clearly,

the late hour had not diminished her energy in the least. She looked as if she still had hours of socializing in her, but he did not intend to go upstairs without her.

Even though he'd been married to her for such a short, chaste time, he'd become accustomed to spending his nights with her.

Coming from behind, he caught her hand and swung her away from her conversation with the duchess without a word of explanation or apology.

However, it was with a great grin.

He could not recall ever acting so impulsively or improperly. But what was one more impropriety when he had been guilty of so many recently.

No matter. Since he'd met Clementine he'd found that a dash of scandal was—well...*fun* was what it was.

When was the last time he had been this happy? Never was when.

Clementine shot him a wink, lifted her skirts in one hand and dashed out of the ballroom, her hand gripped tight in his.

Halfway up the grand staircase, she pulled against his lead.

"Slow down," she gasped. "I can't laugh and breathe at the same time."

With his foot poised on the next stair tread, he looked down at her face—or near it. What caught his attention was the way her chest moved when she panted.

Madness had taken him. He was acting like a man who was free to be a real husband.

Over Clementine's shoulder he spotted one of the gossips from earlier in the evening standing at the foot of the stairs. She stared up at them, her mouth sagging open in an unladylike gawk.

Just went to show who was the lady and who was not. Clearly, it was the woman he had married.

In noticing the direction of his gaze, Clementine looked down. She speared the gawker with a regal nod accompanied by an aloof smile to match the best of them.

Then she dropped his hand and raced up ahead of him, all the while laughing out loud.

Not only was Clementine more a lady, she was vastly more entertaining.

Reaching her bedroom door, she spun about and leaned against it.

Running up three flights of stairs had left her winded, out of breath. She pressed her hand to her side as if she had a stitch.

In a moment her breathing would return to normal.

Even when it did, he feared he would never be normal again. He liked having fun. Liked having it with her.

It might be possible to keep his secret while being the husband he wanted to be, a tempting voice whispered in his mind.

"Wouldn't it have been proper to say good-night to our guests?" she asked. He completely and utterly adored the twinkle in her eyes. "I think we might have created a new scandal. That woman looked ready to drag us through the briar patch."

"We did miss causing one earlier, so I figure we had one coming."

The exertion of climbing the stairs made a vein throb in her throat, just below the delicate curve of her jaw. Unable to resist, he pressed two fingers to the spot and felt the warm, quick thud.

The thrum tapped faster.

He had caused that. Knowing that she reacted to his touch in such a way corrupted his reason.

It had to have, otherwise he would not be putting his mouth where his fingers had been—would not, with his lips still hovering over her skin say—

"You haven't seen my quarters. Would you like to?"

She touched her throat, nodded.

He took her hand again because it felt good to do so, then led her three doorways up the hallway.

This was wrong, but at the same time, right. Anyone would agree that it was not fitting to leave his wife untouched. Did he not have an obligation to her—and really, to God, to "know" his wife?

He was expected to produce an heir. If he did not people would lay the blame at Clementine's feet. The whisper in his mind continued its assault on good reason.

Opening the door, he drew her inside.

"Oh, this is a wonderful room," she said, glancing everywhere at once.

He tried to look at it the way she would be doing, as if for the first time: the huge bed, the warm gold-and-brown tones of the drapes and rugs, the high sheen of the wood furniture, the cozy hearth in which his valet had already set a fire.

"It smells like you," she observed.

Did it? He would not have known that.

"This might be the best night of my life, Heath."

It might be if—

Surely he could be a husband and the Abductor, because he had to be. It was becoming harder each day to be only one or the other.

Clementine would keep his secret if she knew. In fact, she would probably insist on helping!

What was he to do? Risk her freedom for the sake of his pleasure?

Not likely! He'd be a villain of the worst sort to allow that to happen.

He had taken a vow to protect her, not condemn her.

All at once she let go of his hand and twirled away, spinning slowly across the room.

The back of her knees hit the bed. She fell backward, arms open wide. The mattress gave with her weight and bounced in an inviting way.

He sat beside her, gazing down at her face. She reached up and traced a line along his jaw with one slender finger.

A strand of red hair sagged out of the loops on top. He captured it with his thumb, twirled it and drew it over her chest, forming a crimson blaze across her heart.

What he was not going to do was trace the blaze with his fingers and then his lips.

"Tell me, what was the most wonderful thing about the best night of your life," he murmured.

All of a sudden she sat upright. "Well, this, of course, being with you, but you won't believe what else."

"It must be astounding." Whatever it was her joy over it washed through him, made him want to rejoice with her even if he had no idea what it was.

"I—" she pressed her fingers to her cheeks as if she still could not believe the wonderful thing "—have found a place to teach."

"That's wonderful!" If the charity work made her this happy he hoped she could do it every day. "Who are the lucky children?"

Her eyes glittered with her good news.

"The children at Slademore House!"

"No."

A blow to the gut could not have cut him to the quick as badly.

* * *

"No?"

There was not a "no" involved here.

"I forbid it."

She leaped off his bed.

"You…" She pointed a finger at him and saw that it was trembling. She curled it into a fist. "You may not forbid me."

"Of course I may forbid you." He stood as well, breathing hard with his arm braced on the bedpost. "I am your husband."

"You are an arrogant beast."

"See me any way you wish to. The fact remains that you will not spend a moment in that place or in Slademore's company."

Where was the man her heart had softened toward? The one she had been so gleefully ready to give herself to only a moment ago?

This fellow—this vexatious, bullheaded, imperious— clearly she would need *Roget's Thesaurus* to find a word awful enough to describe him.

"You've gone daft." Yes, that was it. Daft. "It's not as though I've decided to become a streetwalker or wear feathers in my hair."

"If you trust me even a little, accept the fact that I have a very good reason for forbidding you."

Did she? How trustworthy was he when he'd promised to find her a charity position and, now that she'd found one on her own, was forbidding it?

Forbid? The word flashed in her mind in big, red, angry letters.

She could not recall being confronted by it before. Grandfather would "strongly advise" but never outright prohibit her from doing a thing she had her heart set upon.

"And if you trust me even a little—" she arched her brows at him, lifting her chin "—accept the fact that I have the good sense to know what I am doing."

"In this case, you do not."

A light tap sounded on the chamber door.

"There's an emergency in the stable, my lord, involving one of the mares."

Heath made a sharp, guttural sound under his breath. She'd had no idea he used profanity. It went to show it would be best to know a man thoroughly before one committed certain parts of her life to him.

"I'll meet you there, Creed," he said, hurrying to the coatrack and snatching off his coat.

She thought he had forgotten her presence in his rush to aid the horse, but he turned at the door to pin her with a glare.

"I expect you to obey me in this."

Forbid? Obey?

Did her headstrong, irrational—oh, did she need to carry the thesaurus on her person?—husband realize he had just tossed down the gauntlet, waved the red flag in front of a bull?

A skirmish was coming between them because tomorrow she had an appointment to teach. She was not going to miss it because there were "things she did not know."

There were things she did know. Those children needed her. Their futures depended upon them being able to read and write.

If Heath's concerns were valid, he should have taken a moment to explain them.

The next morning Clementine picked up a piece of bacon and yawned at it before she put it in her mouth.

She hadn't slept well and it was all Heath's fault. Having become accustomed to his company, she could not now easily fall asleep without it.

And she ought to be able to. She had done it quite well for all her life.

She watched him from across the table, taking note that he did not lift his slice of toast off his plate. He frowned silently down at it.

"Is the mare all right?" she asked because she did want to know, and at the same time she wanted to appear congenial so he would not suspect she was in rebellion against his dictate.

He nodded, glancing up at her. The blue-green glint of his eyes seemed washed out. She noticed a bluish shadow on his cheek. "She'll do, I suppose, but the child is weak and I'm not certain it will survive."

"Do you mean the foal?"

"Is that not what I said? Filly?"

"I think you ought to skip Parliament today and go back to bed."

"I've yet to get to bed."

Good. It would work nicely in her favor to have him sleep the day away.

"About last night." He drummed his fingers on the table, reached for hers. While she did let his hand rest atop her knuckles, she did not return his squeeze. "I regret the way I spoke to you."

Blame it! Why did his fingers have to feel so—so right, stroking her skin?

"Think nothing of it. I'm sure I have quite forgotten the incident." She had not. Not anymore than she would forget how she melted inside when he touched her just so.

Confound the man!

"I only want what is best for you."

That was a very good thing since if he ever found out

what she was about to do she could remind him he had said that.

As a dutiful wife, she ought to obey her husband's whim, but how could she when children's futures were at stake?

If no one stood up for them they had no hope of a prosperous future.

Well! She intended to be that one no matter how the Earl of Fencroft felt about it.

"Good morning," Olivia announced, coming into the morning room. "You look horrid, Heath."

"Where is Victor?" he asked.

"It's his first morning with the new governess." Olivia rolled her eyes. "I'm hoping not to find him hiding under furniture again. She seems a pleasant young woman, but I did have to promise you would read to him each afternoon, Clementine. I hope you do not mind."

"That would be lovely. I'd enjoy it."

"You see?" Heath said, smiling for the first time this morning. "It has all worked out."

Let him think so. "Your sister is right, Heath. You ought to go to bed."

He stood, snatching up the slice of buttered toast to take with him. "I wish I could."

Olivia watched her brother turn to leave the room, then turned her gaze upon Clementine.

She appeared distressed about something.

"I know it is not my business, and I do love my brother. In so many ways he is a very good man, but still he is a man. And truly, Clementine, I care for you, so I must ask." She hesitated, sighing and shaking her head. "What excuse did he give for being out all night?"

"It wasn't an excuse." Even as angry as she was with

Heath, she did feel a need to defend him. "There was a mare in distress. He had to help with the foaling."

"With my late husband it was that his ailing mother needed help at all hours."

"I'm sorry to hear she was in ill health."

"She would be, too, if she knew. Victor's grandmother was, and is, the healthiest person I know."

"Then why would he—?"

"So he could spend time with his mistress. Have a care, sister. I would not want to see you with a broken heart."

"Heath told me he did not have a mistress."

"I would like to think he is a better man than most. His story will be easy enough to prove, though. All you need do is go to the stable and see if there is a horse that gave birth last night."

"I have no reason to distrust him."

She was angry at his high-handedness, certainly—but the Earl of Fencroft was a decent man. She knew this in the bottom of her heart.

"I was you, once." Olivia stirred her cocoa, looking into the brown, swirling liquid. "There was a time when I loved my husband as much as you love yours now."

Perhaps she was beginning to, but to a depth that it was evident?

"And that's why I feel a need to warn you. To trust a man who is supposed to be yours and then find out he is not? I tell you, the only thing that makes the pain worth it is children."

Olivia set down her spoon with a clink on the saucer.

"I must confess, I did not know what to expect before you came. I believed what people said about American heiresses, that they were spendthrifts and gauche. But you are none of those things—you have become dear to me and so I don't want to see you hurt. That is why I have told you what I have. I know you don't believe it, but be careful, Clementine."

They sipped their hot cocoa, each to her own thoughts.

"Do you know," Olivia said, smiling over the rim of her cup, a bit of chocolate smudging her lip, "I never dreamed I would enjoy having a sister. And I do, quite."

"So do I."

And Clementine never thought she would enjoy a life Grandfather had foisted upon her—and yet she did— quite.

Even if her husband was behaving like a beast.

Chapter Eleven

Standing on the front porch of Slademore House, Clementine thought the building looked like a pearl nestled in a trash heap.

There was a decrepit building on the north side and an abandoned one on the south. Being abandoned did not mean uninhabited. Equally decrepit-looking men and women cast sly glances at her while they lounged on the front stairs, smoking and spitting.

It hardly seemed possible that this depressed neighborhood was only a carriage ride from the wealthy streets of Mayfair.

One could only wonder why the baron had founded his orphanage here. It was certainly not convenient for his benefactors to visit.

Indeed, she imagined many of them did not come at all.

The only reason she could think of for him to open a sanctuary in this spot was that this was where women in need tended to live. No doubt he had their needs in mind, rather than the needs of the rich.

It had taken a huge amount of money to convince the hackney cab to wait here an hour for her. She might have come in a Fencroft carriage but Heath would discover where she went.

She nearly sighed her relief aloud when a woman wearing a white apron and a cap over her graying hair opened the door.

"Good day, Countess," she said with a curtsy, when Clementine came inside. "I'm Mrs. Hoper, the children's nurse. It is good of you to come and read to them. We were not expecting you for another half hour, but I'm sure that's all right."

The parlor she was led into was bright and cheerful with white paint on the walls and blue damask curtains drawn back from tall windows.

It was hard to imagine what Heath could have against Slademore House. So far it seemed more than respectable. Any orphan would be lucky to live here.

"I'll let the baron know you are here and then I'll bring a spot of tea."

"Please don't bother. I'd like to meet the children."

The nurse glanced at a closed door, her brows knitted in a slight frown.

"Is there something wrong?"

"Why, no! What could possibly be?" She smiled and, in a blink, looked like Mrs. Santa Claus, with her round figure and her rosy pink cheeks. Clementine half expected a plate of sugary treats to magically appear in her hand. "It's just that you are early and I'm not sure the children are finished—"

The woman cracked open a door and peeked inside.

"Oh, there the lambs are, just come inside from playtime in the garden." She swung the door open wide to reveal several children.

Seven girls wearing blue frocks the same shade as the curtains stood in a line with five little boys in white shirts and short pants.

Standing beside them, a young woman, but barely so,

cradled an infant in her arms. She appeared pale, gaunt to the point of looking unhealthy. Clementine suspected the girl had borne the babe without a husband to protect them.

Bless Slademore House for taking them in.

"Children, this is Lady Fencroft. She has come to teach you to read."

The young woman cast the matron a half-lidded glance. Unless Clementine was mistaken, the lowered lids hid a look of apprehension.

"Books," Clementine said in the face of the children's confusion.

Had the poor dears never heard of a book? This was inexcusable. They might live in a fine home now, but they could not stay here forever. If they did not want to take up residence in a building like the one next door, they would need to be able to read.

"Welcome, Lady Fencroft!" Clementine turned to see the baron stride through the doorway, a great big smile on his face. "The children have been eager for your visit all morning."

Perhaps one or two of them had, but the rest just seemed perplexed.

One small girl looked at the baron and began to whimper. Two girls of about three years stepped closer to each other and clasped hands. A boy, no more than three feet tall, puffed up his skinny chest and glared at his benefactor.

"They're not happy that I called them in early from playtime." He shot the children a smile, which was not returned.

"May I give you a tour of the home before you begin? I find the children's patrons like to see the good their money is doing."

"Yes, if it's no bother." She was eager to see the rest of

the home. Everything she'd seen so far made Slademore House a shining example of what a charity ought to be. "Do you live here with the children, Baron?"

"I have quarters here, of course. Sometimes the children need a father's presence. But I do have a residence in Mayfair that I must keep up for the sake of the barony. But my heart is here, as well as the better part of my time."

"Mrs. Hoper, will you give the children their tarts and milk while I show the countess about?"

"Yes, my lord," she answered. "Come along to the dining room, my pets."

The first room the baron showed her was his office. This had to be his way of asking for her donation. Given what a beautiful haven Slademore House was, next time she might give a larger sum.

Next he showed her four bedrooms that were as fine as the rest of the house, with big, stuffed mattresses on the beds and closets filled with frilly dresses and small suits. In the corner of each room was an open toy chest overflowing with dolls, balls and other treasures. These were not the cast-off playthings of more wealthy children. They appeared to be new, or very lightly used. Clearly, the home had generous donors.

Last of all he took her to the dining room, where the children sat at a long, highly polished table, gobbling up their pastries and gulping down milk.

Baron Slademore clapped his hands. The children set down what they were eating. "It is time for your lesson. I'm sure we do not wish to take up too much of Lady Fencroft's time."

"I have an abundance of time, my lord," she answered, walking beside him while the children went ahead of them to the playroom.

They certainly were a quiet and well-behaved group.

"I'll be on about my business, Lady Fencroft. And thank you for coming." He gave her a brief nod, then turned to go. "Oh, if you would not mind sending word ahead of time when your next visit will be it would be most appreciated. Just to be sure the children are not at play when you come."

"I'll come every Monday and Wednesday at this same time. If I cannot make it then I will send word."

"As you wish."

He smiled in parting but she had the distinct impression the gesture was not sincere. She did have some experience at pasted-on smiles.

A chair had been set for her beside a large window with sunlight streaming through it. The children sat down on a rug in a semicircle in front of her. The young woman with the baby sat in a chair behind them.

Clementine withdrew a copy of *Rip Van Winkle* from the books in her satchel.

After reading a chapter she handed the book down for the children to pass about. Feeling and smelling a book was all a part of the pleasure of reading, and it made it easier for them to look at the pictures.

She watched them for a moment. One by one they were beginning to smile. Seeing the dawning of pleasure as the book went from hand to hand, she was reminded of the flame of one candle being passed and lighting many others. There had to be a poetic way to express that thought. Later it would come to her and she would write it in her journal.

While the children took their time, she gazed out of the window to the children's play yard. It was a lovely green area with flowers and trees. The only trouble she saw with it was that it was adjacent to an alley at the back of the house. But the wall was tall and would keep the children safe while they played.

It was an odd thing, but the house looked longer outside than what it seemed inside.

While she was wondering about it, she heard a child crying. Were not all the children with her?

The sound seemed to be coming from near a great shade tree. A large woman wearing a gray gown emerged from the part of the house that seemed too long. She dashed across the yard and snatched a boy of about four years, with curly red hair, from behind the tree trunk.

The little fellow was dressed in rags. Perhaps he had wandered over from the building next door. The woman yanked his thin arm while she dragged him across the yard.

There was a gate in the tall wall. The woman and the child exited through it. When the woman returned, she was alone.

That answered the question of who he was, then. As she suspected he was from next door.

A little girl tugged her skirt and handed the book back. Clementine caught her tiny hand to give it a gentle squeeze in thanks. She'd expected it to be soft and baby-like the way Victor's were, but they were calloused, red and chafed.

The poor child must have come from hard times. At least here at Slademore House she would be well cared for.

While Clementine continued to read she had a difficult time getting the image of the weeping boy out of her mind.

Without an education he would be lost and would have no hope of a better life. The very sad fact was, there was nothing she could do for him.

But she would do something for these gathered about her. No matter what, she would not let them down.

* * *

No doubt there were worse husbands in London, but in the moment Heath felt the lowest of them all.

Even though he'd announced that everything had worked out well for Clementine given that she had Victor to read to, he knew it was not true.

Had it been so he would have gone to her room last night and spent the night the way they normally did, in laughter and companionable conversation. And severe temptation, at least on his part.

Things were far from what they ought to be between them. Even looking out the conservatory window and seeing Clementine walking in the garden, he felt the aloofness of her attitude toward him.

She didn't even know he was watching and he felt the chill. Not that she was intentionally doing it. She was unfailingly polite, answering with a smile when he spoke to her, but something was missing and he wanted it back.

A carriage ride in Hyde Park might help. The leaves were beginning to turn and today the air was crisp and fresh.

An outing might be the thing to restore her spirits. Autumn air and sunshine would be just the thing.

That was what he tried to believe, walking out of the conservatory toward the fountain, where she had just sat down on a bench. But he knew what would make her happy and it was not in his power to give it to her.

He sat down beside her and would have reached for her hand, but her fingers twined together in a determined knot on her lap.

"It's a lovely afternoon," he said.

"Isn't it?" She smiled, but it was the same, half-stiff one she gave to strangers.

"Let's go for a carriage ride in the park."

A flash of interest flared in her eyes.

She stood up, tweaked her bustle back into place and nodded. "It is a lovely day for it."

He sat where he was for the simple pleasure of watching her walk away with her back straight, her hips subtly swaying. It was a sight all the more tantalizing for its modesty.

She spun about and caught him grinning.

"Bring the carriage about. I'll meet you in half an hour."

This time there was a hint of the smile he missed, although barely.

It was no more than he could expect. He had to seem an unreasonable lout in her eyes.

And yet she had consented to this outing, which gave him hope that they might get back to the easy friendship they had before.

Within thirty minutes they were in the park, slowly traveling under a bower of branches hinting at autumn's rich shades of yellow and red. He'd requested the open-air carriage in order to take in the full beauty of the park.

Beside him Clementine leaned back into the cushions and looked up at the leafy canopy.

"Are you thinking of a verse for your journal?"

"Not one, but several."

The park was not crowded this afternoon, for which he was glad. It would be difficult to focus his attention on Clementine while having to greet every passing peer.

"Tell me one."

She turned her head on the cushion to look at him. "You tell me one."

The very last thing he was, was poetic, but he did want to please her so... "Colorful leaves on a tree. Oh, happy me."

She sat up straight, suppressing a laugh by pinching her lips together. "It does rhyme."

"Now I want to hear yours."

She tapped her lips in thought, a gesture he had to glance away from.

"Red and yellow treasure, drifting down, riches finer than gold."

"That is beautiful, Clementine, truly."

"It's average, Heath. I'm the only one who gains pleasure in it."

"But I wonder…" Hmm, he might have thought of a way for her to teach after all. "There might yet be a way for you to be an instructor."

"Oh." She glanced at a passing carriage, nodded to the passengers. "I thought you forbade it."

"I forbade you going to Slademore House, and I still do."

"I see," she muttered, seeming to give her attention to a squirrel scampering across a branch with a nut in its mouth.

But she didn't see, not yet. "What if you invite a few ladies for an afternoon gathering and teach them to write poetry?"

"What?" Her full attention suddenly settled on him.

"Yes. Engage their minds. I wouldn't know this firsthand, but I expect spending one's afternoons stitching doilies would be tedious."

"It has caused a few minds to go daft. But I hardly see what good it will do society to have a few poetically gifted ladies. And no doubt it would ruin my love of poetry forever. But, if it will ease your conscience, I will consider it."

Never mind, then. Put that way, his idea seemed rather feeble.

"I only hoped to—" To redeem himself in her eyes. It was true and she knew it. "I missed you last night."

He put his arm across the back of the cushions, an act that also placed it across her shoulders without quite touching her. He did this, testing to see if she would shy away from his advance. Perhaps she would not turn from his attempt to restore the natural way things had been between them.

She sighed and leaned against him. She sounded resigned rather than relieved, as if being close to him was against her better judgment but she was giving in to it anyway.

No matter, there she was in the crook of his arm.

Given a few more moments of friendly conversation, she might be happy to be there.

Once he gave her the gift in his pocket, all would be well. He'd be completely forgiven.

Women adored anything bright and glittering. At least that was what was said in private conversation in Parliament. Man after man had been restored to his wife's good graces with a pretty gift.

Clementine, however, had not been pleased with the first gift he'd given her. Not until she discovered it had belonged to his mother. Now the comb was something she cherished every bit as much as his mother had.

He loved her for that.

The thought settled in his mind like a rock tossed in deep water. It went down deep, leaving behind ripples, each one echoing the thought.

Did he love her for that? Or did he simply love her?

He loved things about her. He loved being with her. He loved the sound of her voice and the arch of her brows. He loved the way she smelled sitting so close to him. He loved that she would rather teach school than reign as countess.

Ripples of the thought smoothed out, but the stone that had caused them lay deep in his heart.

He loved her.

"Heath, you are looking at me oddly."

That would happen when a man discovered he loved a woman and could not tell her so.

"I have something for you." He wondered if his voice sounded as thick as it felt. "A peace offering."

He withdrew the small package and placed it in her hand.

She hugged the box with the pretty white bow to her heart but then glanced away.

Was his perceived offence too grievous for a trinket— an expensive trinket—to fix?

When she turned her face to him again, she was smiling, truly and sincerely smiling. The world fell back into place around him.

She untied the ribbon, opened the lid and withdrew the string of pearls.

"Oh, Heath. These are exquisite!"

They were, which made them an exquisite match for her.

"Were they your mother's?"

"No. They are only yours."

She held them up to the sunshine. A subtle glow winked warmly on the strand. Then she handed it to him, nodding for him to fasten it around her neck.

It was a fortunate thing her gown had a high, tight neck. At that moment he could not be responsible for what he might have done had it not had. He was a man in un-requited love holding on by a mere thread of self-control.

"Pearls suit you," he said, putting his mouth to use with compliments instead of kisses. "They are subtle, yet all the more beautiful for it."

"The necklace is wonderful and I adore it, but if you

think to earn my pardon with it, it will not work." She rolled the small miracles of nature between her fingers. "You had it already."

"You're stealing the heart right out of my chest, did you know that?" Maybe he should not have admitted that much, but it had to show anyway. He did owe her some honesty.

Clementine had never been anything but forthcoming. It grieved him deeply that to be forthcoming with her, to make her privy to what he and Creed were doing, was to make her complicit in it.

If he was free to, he would declare his love this moment.

It had always been urgent to expose Slademore's treatment of the children in his care, but it was now more than ever.

In a very real sense, his marriage depended upon it.

"I've missed you," Clementine said and kissed his cheek, right there in an open carriage in Hyde Park. "Will you come back to my bedroom?"

The kick to his heart was such a blow it felt as if he'd fallen from the carriage and onto the path.

The obvious answer was yes. And yet how could he? It was impossible for now.

"The mare—she is not well enough to be left alone." Curse Garret Slademore for forcing the lie.

If she wondered, and who would not, why a veterinarian did not care for the mare, she did not ask.

"Yes, I see." She called to Creed, "Would you mind taking us home now?"

She did not speak to Heath the rest of the ride home.

But neither did she toss the necklace back in his face.

Standing by her bedroom window, Clementine watched the light of a full moon cast the garden in eerie white light.

She rolled the pearls of the necklace between her fingers, absently caressing the smooth, hard surface.

For all her confused feelings when it came to Heath, she hadn't wanted to remove the gift he'd given her.

Chilly air seeped through the glass. She tugged her robe tighter around her even though her room was warm from the fire in the hearth.

Wind and cold had swept across Mayfair from the moment she set foot down from the carriage.

Below in the garden a white cat dashed from one bush to another, appearing to be spooked by the lashing branches.

Had her husband been here with her they might be snuggled up in easy conversation, sharing the affection that came so naturally to them.

From the very beginning, that connection had been there.

Tonight, bedtime was anything but close and snuggly. She had invited him back to her quarters because it seemed that the rift between them was healing.

Then he'd claimed the mare needed him.

Had she so misjudged the way things stood between them that the fact that a horse might or might not need him in the night was enough to keep him away?

Perhaps Olivia was right and he did have a mistress. The pearls might be a gift to appease his guilt.

Ninny. If she truly thought that, she would not have them around her neck; she'd have dumped them in the commode.

At any rate, she might just as well go to bed since he was not coming.

Not only was she a ninny but a fool. The reason she was standing at the window was to see if the stable lamp would go on, because the mare needed him.

Not the stableman, not the veterinarian, but Heath Cavill, sixth Earl of Fencroft.

Olivia had suggested she would discover the truth by going to the stable and seeing for herself if there was an ailing horse and her sickly foal.

Doing so would either put her mind at rest or increase her uncertainty.

Given that she was already brokenhearted, she had nothing to lose by investigating.

She would have to walk through the garden with its spooky, shifting shadows, with leaves blowing madly in every direction, but so be it.

Facing the elements could be no worse than the doubts assaulting her mind.

On the way out the door she clutched the pearls, holding them as a talisman. She had no idea what she would find at the stable but until she had proven reason not to trust Heath, she would wear the necklace.

Moments later she leaned into the wind, wishing she had taken a moment to put on her coat. Clearly, her mind was in too much turmoil. Imagine forgetting to put on a coat in weather like this.

Blowing leaves slapped her head. Droplets from the fountain, being carried on the wind, smattered her face and dusted her hair. But it was the wind that was the worst. It cut though her clothes, making the short walk from the conservatory to the stable feel hours long.

It was a relief to finally step inside and get out of the wind. With no lamps burning, the place was dark. Moonlight streaming through the windows helped her see where to put her feet, but beyond that cold light, everything was dark and quiet.

It smelled like hay, horses and the fading stench of

pipe smoke. Someone must have been here recently but they were not now.

It didn't matter, since she was looking for a sick horse, not a man.

The rustle of shifting hay broke the silence, then a horse's quiet nicker.

Moving out of the moonlight, she walked in darkness, feeling a way with her hand on the wood rails of a stall.

Hooves shuffled on the straw-strewn floor.

"Hello, horsie," she whispered.

The animal whickered and walked toward her. She saw the bold, strong lines of its body through light trickling in from the slats of a wooden window.

The creature hardly looked ailing. It stuck its head over the gate, seeking attention. She petted the thick muscles of its neck, felt the coarse texture of the mane.

"You are not a mare at all, are you, you great beautiful animal?"

Her answer was a snort of warm, moist breath on her face. Even though the stall was dark, she had seen enough through a stab of moonlight to know this was true.

There was a horse in the next stall also. As far as she could tell it was in good health.

Before she could make her way farther along the rails, the scent of pipe smoke came again. This time it was fresh, drifting toward her on a draft filtering through the barn.

"Hope you are rested, fellas," a voice said in the same instant a lamp flared to life. A beam of soft light leaked from under the door. "We'll be going out tonight."

Oh, dear. She really had no wish to be caught out in the stalls wearing only her nightclothes.

She rushed to the far end of the barn, exiting through the same door she had entered.

Cold hit and hit hard. Wind buffeted her this way and that, slapping her with icy breath.

Coming into the conservatory, she was shivering to the point her teeth chattered.

"Blasted cold stones," she muttered on a half run across the room.

All of a sudden a large, faceless shadow blocked her path. A pair of gloved hands gripped her arms.

"What are you doing here?"

"Having the daylights frightened out of me is what!" She tried to wrench away but Heath held her fast.

"You shouldn't be alone in the garden at night. Anyone could wander in."

"The only person I've encountered is you."

He had to have heard the accusation in her voice but he did not loosen his grip.

"Why were you outside?" It sounded as though he had to strive to remain patient. Well, let him stew, then.

"I was worried about the sick horse."

Dead silence lasted for a full five heartbeats. She knew because she counted them.

"You went to the stable?"

"What would I find if I had? A sick mare and a foal that might not live?" She was warming up quickly, heating from the inside out. "Or a pair of perfectly healthy carriage horses?"

He let go of her. She stared at his face in the darkness, waiting for him to explain—to give her something that was the truth.

He did not.

She dashed out of the conservatory.

Heath and Creed had saved a child tonight but not without a fight. Heath had taken a hard blow to the gut and another on the shoulder from the guards, but managed to escape on foot while Creed raced with the infant to the safety of the seaside cottage near Folkestone.

Even with the help of their informer, this rescue had been more difficult than the rest.

The baby had been where she noted it would be and at the right time. Heath thought he might have seen a slightly built woman peeking around the corner of the building, but then again, it might have been a shadow.

If only he or Creed knew who she was, they might speak with her, convince her to tell what she knew. And clearly she did know.

This time the message had come while Creed was sitting in a tavern. The serving girl handed him a crumpled note. The waitress did not know the person who gave it to her. "A gutter waif" was all she'd told him.

So still, all they knew of her was—nothing.

Walking from the stable to the house, he rolled his injured shoulder, trying to ease the ache. He glanced up at Clementine's window and saw a dim orange glow.

He guessed the fire was dying and she was asleep. There was no help for it but to wake her.

Having been caught out in his lie he would have to tell her something—not the truth—but something.

He entered the house through the conservatory, the same way as he'd gone out. On every night but this one it was the safest way to leave without being seen.

Once inside he took off his shoes. He should not have to sneak about in his own house, but not many peers of the realm were wanted men. The more secretive he was the safer he would be. There was Creed to be considered, as well.

Both of them were the Abductor.

At the top of the stairs he did not bother to go to his

own room and change clothes. First he needed to make things as right as he could with his wife—his friend.

He wasn't sure it was possible, or what he was going to say.

Relief made his hand clench on the doorknob. She hadn't locked him out.

If she had not locked him out of her room, perhaps she had not locked him out of her life.

He glanced at the bed. It was empty; so was her chair.

Clementine stood beside the window, looking down at the garden, a shawl drawn over her nightclothes.

"Hello, Heath," she said, turning her face toward him.

It seemed to Clementine that it had been a dozen hours between the time Heath had crossed the garden to the stable and the time he returned. In truth it had only been two. Two hours in which she stood by the glass looking out, watching for him.

The voice she'd heard in the stable had spoken to the horses about going out—in the dead of night.

To her way of thinking, it also meant they were taking Heath to do something secretive.

Exactly what, she could not imagine. But whatever it was, he'd done it before, using an ailing animal as his excuse.

"Clementine," he said, his voice low and seemingly anguished, in response to her cool greeting.

He closed the door and stood beside it as if he did not quite know what to do.

"I'm glad you are back," she told him, giving in to the softer emotion that suddenly came over her at the sight of him, finally home and safe.

Yes, he had a secret. But so did she.

He rushed across the room barefoot and wrapped her

up in a great hug. He winced as if in pain when he pulled her tight against him.

"I can't imagine what you must think of me."

"I can't, either," she answered, lightly touching the shoulder he was favoring. "Perhaps you should tell me."

"I should—yes. But that does not mean I am free to."

"You make it sound so mysterious." She eased out of his embrace…reluctantly.

Until an understanding was reached between them it was better to remain clearheaded.

It wasn't easy keeping a distance, since all she wanted was to stand in the bay of the window, feel his arms wrap her up, relax in his solid presence and rejoice in the fact that he was here and unharmed—mostly unharmed.

All manner of horror had romped freely through her mind while she'd watched for him to come back.

She patted him lightly, playfully, on the cheek in order to lighten the moment.

"Surely you are not going to admit to being the Abductor." She smiled, winking.

"I am not." He curled his fingers into the edges of her shawl and drew her back to him.

"I wonder if you have a mistress after all. Everything does point to it."

"Not everything, Clementine."

Slowly he drew her until she was flush against him. His mouth settled on hers, gently probing. She melted to him, either forgetting about her determination to remain aloof, or ignoring it—yes, ignoring because she did recall it, dimly.

Like a match to dry grass, his kiss ignited within her a blaze burning away common sense and leaving only an urgent need to be even closer to him.

"I do not, nor will I ever have a mistress," he whispered. She only needed to look into his eyes to be sure of it. "But there is something."

"I'll not be tricked by an ailing horse again, so you might as well trust me with whatever it is."

"One day I will." He lifted her hand, kissed her knuckles. "But not tonight."

For an instant earlier she had thought to become his wife in the way God intended, but he'd said it with his own lips—not tonight.

Until there were no secrets between them, she could not.

Neither would she send him away as if his silence on the matter meant betrayal. How could she? Not when she concealed something of her own.

"Stay with me, Heath. It's cold outside and I can't seem to get warm without you."

He glanced at the chairs. She nodded at the bed.

"Do you trust me? Even though you do not know what I'm doing?"

She nodded. "Would you trust me if I had a secret that I could not share with you?"

"I would, of course. Unless it was a terribly wicked one."

He might think her blatantly disobeying him was terribly wicked. To her it was terribly necessary.

Dishonesty was a nasty burden to carry.

"Come to bed, then. Tell me what you can of your day."

She eased out of her shawl and set it on the back of the chair. She walked toward the bed but he caught her hand, turned her to face him.

"I've another secret, Lady Fencroft. It's one I can tell you."

"Oh, good, then please do." He had the most peculiar look on his face.

"I love you."

Her breath caught. It took a moment for the words to settle in her brain, wrap around her heart.

She could not imagine his other secret, the one he refused to tell her, would be bigger than the one he'd just revealed.

Stepping close to him, she touched his chin where the bruise from the other morning had begun to fade. She guessed the injury, along with his sore shoulder, had to do with whatever he kept from her. For now she would not question it.

"Love, my husband, is not a secret. If one looks closely enough it's plain to see."

"You are still wearing the pearls." His smile grew wider.

"What might that reveal, do you think?"

"I'd like you to tell me."

He tugged her closer. She felt the thump of his heart. Inch by slow inch his lips came nearer.

"It reveals that I love you, Heath. I would not have expected to, not given how things started—"

His kiss said he did not care to hear the rest of what she had to say. And why would he? He knew how things had started between them.

The way they ended up? It would depend upon the secrets kept from one another.

But love was a start.

Chapter Twelve

Hours later, Heath stood beside the window in Clementine's bedroom. He watched water from the fountain blow sideways in the wind.

He ought to be sleeping. He was due in Parliament within four hours.

Ah, but he'd like to see the man who could resist the woman slumbering so contentedly only feet away. His mind pictured her even when he wasn't looking at her.

She lay on her back, red curls splayed across the pillow. Her left hand brushed the curve of her cheek, palm up and fingers curled. Her wedding ring glowed warmly in the light of the fire he'd just rekindled.

It was wickedly cold and he wanted nothing more than to get back in bed with her, soak up her warmth and give his heat back to her.

The problem was, it was getting more and more difficult not to touch her the way a man ought to touch his wife. There was a flame within the woman. Passion simmered just under the surface of her reserved demeanor.

Knowing this, and finding that his touch brought a temptress to life, it was becoming nearly impossible to restrain himself. He was a man—a newlywed man. Just because he had set down restrictive rules did not mean he did not have strong desires.

It was why he was standing at the window shirtless, without feeling the cold draft seeping through the glass. Burning up with want of a woman would do that to a man. Make him edgy and frustrated, as well.

Leaving the window, he crossed to the bed and stared down at her. He clamped his hands behind his back because his control would not hold if she moved and inadvertently made a seductive gesture—there was only so much he could take.

Slowly her eyes opened. Even in the dim light they glowed nearly emerald.

"You aren't wearing a shirt," she murmured dreamily. "You are quite well made—so handsome and manly. I want to touch you."

Clearly she was still dreaming. That was not how she acted while awake.

She reached her hand toward him. Heaven help him. He allowed her fingers to trail a path from his chest to his navel before he ended the intense pleasure by catching her hand.

He sat down beside her on the bed. "Wake up, love."

Long-lashed eyes blinked, came into focus on his bare chest.

"Heath Cavill, you'll catch your death. Put on a shirt." She sat up and shoved a hank of hair back over her shoulder. "Why are you smiling?"

Was he smiling? That was surprising, given that he was about to tell her something he would regret. Then again, how could he not smile knowing how she really felt about his bare chest?

"You make me smile, Clementine."

"Call me 'love' again. I like it."

"Love," he said, leaning forward and causing the mattress to dip. He kissed her nose—he truly did love that nose. "There's something I need to say."

"Might you be able to say it under the covers? It's frigid even with the fire going."

"That's the thing. I think it best I sleep in my own room from now on." That was not quite right; it wasn't best, only necessary.

"Oh, I see."

He didn't think she did. But then she sighed, yanking the covers to her chin.

"That thing you are keeping from me is also keeping us apart. And now that we have declared how we feel about each other, intimacy on a friendly level has become more difficult. Isn't that right?"

"Yes. That's it."

"Well, please do find a solution to the issue you are embroiled in. If not for us then for your own safety."

With that, she lay back down, flipped onto her side and drew the blanket over her head.

"Good night, Heath."

He stood up. "It's morning."

Apparently she had nothing else to say, so he went back to his own cold bedroom, where no one had bothered to light a fire. Why would they? Married men slept with their wives on cold nights—as well as hot, sweaty, fervid ones.

Using a word that a gentleman ought not to utter, he grazed his hand over the stubble that had begun on his chin.

How early did Creed rise? he wondered.

They really did need to make contact with their informer. Taking children from Slademore House was about as effective as putting a bandage on a gushing wound.

For every child they delivered to Rock Rose Cottage, the baron took two more in.

Heath put on his boots and heavy coat and went out into the predawn.

Creed was more of a man than he was, Heath thought, wondering how he was able to sleep after the ordeal they had been through in taking the baby.

He heard the coachman's rhythmic snoring through the closed door of his quarters in the stable. He pounded upon it, heard a curse and the thump of feet across the floor.

The hinges groaned when the door opened. So did the man looking at him with bleary eyes.

"With all respect, my lord." He scrubbed his large hand across his chin. "I'm in no shape to go out again. The horses aren't, either."

"No, I wouldn't ask. But would you mind speaking with me for a few moments?"

"I'll set a fire in the stove." He waved at a stool, indicating that Heath should sit on it.

Creed sat across from him on a saddle placed over a sawhorse.

"We need to make an end to this, Creed. It's past time we exposed Slademore."

"Aye, the rescues are getting more risky. I'm thinking that even the girl can't keep on with what she's doing without getting caught."

The thought was one that had occurred to Heath, as well.

"We've become predictable. Each time the risk of getting caught gets greater," Heath said.

"Do you suppose the girl would be bold enough to speak against Slademore?"

"I wonder. It depends in part what her relationship

is with him." Heath shivered. "Has it always been this drafty in here?"

"A fellow gets accustomed to it."

"I'll hire someone to make repairs." He rubbed his hands together briskly, trying to ease the ache setting in from the chill. "But about the woman, is there anything else the tavern girl said?"

"Oh, aye—she said she'd not give me a kiss no matter how I begged. But about the other? Only what we already know. A female, slightly built and waifish looking."

"I can only think she has some sort of connection with the place or she would not have seen us that first time when we took Wilhelmina's baby. She would not have known to send messages to you."

"If she's seen us, someone else might, too. I wonder if we ought to stop this. We won't do anyone any good in prison."

"We ought to do what is safe."

"But—" the stableman stomped on the floor with his bare foot, stirring up straw and dust "—we will not."

"No, we will not. I'll pay a call on Slademore House. See if anyone reacts to my presence."

"All due respect, sir, if there's danger, it should be me facing ruin. The whole of Fencroft depends on you."

"I'm proud to call you a friend, Creed." The man had put himself in enough peril as it was. To be caught snooping around Slademore's place would mean certain prison for a man of his station. "But I'm going."

"You are a married man, my lord. I am not." Creed shook his head. "It ought to be me."

"How would you get into the house? You can hardly pay a social call on Slademore. No, this is for me to do."

To do for Willa.

To do for Clementine.

* * *

Clementine read a book to the children gathered about her on the floor with only half her attention on the story.

Worry for Heath took up a good bit of her focus. He had not revealed what he did during the nights he was away, but whatever it was, it was not safe. His mysterious scrapes and bruises attested to that.

Did he lead a secret life as a cat burglar? Operate a clandestine gambling hall in a seedy part of London?

While not impossible, she thought it highly unlikely. He was a better man than that.

But what was it? How was she ever to sleep another night while wondering if he would return home safe and hale?

Simply said, she would not. No, she would be forced to spend her days yawning, trying to concentrate while her thoughts skittered every which way.

Refocusing her attention on *Jack and the Beanstalk*, she made a great show of describing Jack's bravery in climbing the stalk.

The dining room door creaked open. The frail-looking young woman she'd seen on her first visit to Slademore House came into the room carrying a tea tray instead of an infant.

She set the tray on a table beside her chair. She looked even paler than she had the first time Clementine had seen her. Clementine hoped the baby was not ill.

At about the time Jack reached the top of the beanstalk a child began to weep. A small girl had her hands balled into fists while she pressed them against her eyes.

Clementine motioned for the child to come to her.

Leaping up, she ran forward and hid her face in Clementine's sleeve, whispering through her tears.

Mrs. Hoper, who had been lightly dozing through the tale, came suddenly awake and lurched out of her chair.

"What did she say?"

Clementine took her time answering, wiping the tearstained cheeks with her fingers.

Once the child was calmed she gave her attention to the nurse.

"She wants a beanstalk so she can climb to Heaven and see her mother."

"Magic beans won't do it," the woman mumbled.

"A word, if you please," Clementine stated.

The woman blushed and followed Clementine to a more private corner.

"That was a rather harsh thing to say to the child."

"I imagine it sounded so. It's just that I am rather tense this morning. That Abductor kidnapped a baby from us last night."

"Oh, I see." Clementine's heart rolled, quivered.

"We are all distraught, but the girl, she's been carrying on over it all morning."

"It's understandable. I'm surprised she was able to serve tea with a steady hand."

"One does what one must. A lady of your breeding would not be expected to understand." She anchored her fat fingers at her waist, nodding her head sharply. "To survive we must toughen our hearts. Even these children must, as young as they are. Crying is strictly forbidden."

"Living here at Slademore House, I would think they would be protected from the harshness of life to some degree."

"Yes, well, filling their minds with a belief there is magical treasure to be had at the end of a beanstalk will only make dreamers of them."

"That is an odd thing to say in regards to young children. Dreaming is a part of childhood, is it not?"

"Oh." Mrs. Hoper's face blanched. "I did not mean that so much as—that didn't come out right. I'm not in the habit of conversing with an American countess and I quite chose the wrong words."

"Regardless, I will continue to read about magic beanstalks and the like because it might lift the sorrow over what they have lost, even if it is only for the moment."

"As you say, Lady Fencroft." The woman bobbed a half-hearted curtsy and then went back to her chair to sit down.

She would have words with Baron Slademore today about this employee. He could hardly refuse to hear her given the amount of money she was donating, and also because of her higher social standing.

Perhaps there was an advantage to bearing the title of Countess of Fencroft. People had to listen to her whether they cared to or not.

Returning to her chair, she sat down and resumed the tale.

Finding her place was not easy because once again her attention was on something else.

The sixth Earl of Fencroft.

Was her husband going out in the night trying to apprehend the Abductor?

While that was a noble thing to do and she loved him all the more for trying, it was also extremely dangerous.

The Abuductor was the vilest of the wicked. Depraved in the worst way. Harming a child was the worst thing she could think of.

Still and all, it was for the constables, not Heath Cavill, to apprehend him—if in fact that was what he was up to.

* * *

Heath sat in a bathtub placed in front of the grand fireplace of the master suite. Warm water laved his muscles and washed away the aches of the day. Spending hours sitting on a bench, discussing every aspect of a political point of view, could be grueling on joints that were already sore. For all that men argued their opinions, nothing was settled.

No more than anything was settled in his own life.

Today they had discussed forming a committee to address—what was it? The day blurred in his mind, but whatever it was, the discussion over forming it had been going on for ten years with no resolution, or so he had been told.

To Heath's way of thinking it was a ridiculous situation. Nothing of importance should be dragged on for so long. If it was not worthy it should be dropped once and for all.

Anything of consequence ought to be dealt with straightaway.

Not only in Parliament but in his own life.

Especially in his own life! His marriage was of great consequence.

He clenched his fingers on the lip of the tub.

He'd hoped to see Clementine before retiring—needed to see her.

Things could not go on as they were. Now that they had admitted to their deepest feelings, declared their hearts, everything had changed.

He looked about the room, gazing at the large window, the huge hearth and the great four-poster bed.

The space was elegantly appointed. A perfect blend of refinement and comfort.

Flames in the hearth reflected warm golden light off

the drapery and papered walls. It cast flickering shadows on the bed, a reminder that the room was lacking the most important thing.

Lady Fencroft—Mrs. Heath Cavill.

Without her, there was no point to any of these fine appointments. He might as well live in the stable for all the joy he took from the surroundings.

It was enough!

If she was willing to have him, to accept that sometimes he would be called away in the night, and if she was willing to not question it—if she could trust him that much, then—

He stood up from the bath, felt the chill as warm water slid off his body and cool air nipped it. He plucked up the towel and rubbed briskly if not efficiently.

Still half-damp, he snatched the robe from the chair and shoved his arms in the sleeves. He yanked the sash into a knot. Water droplets fell from the tips of his hair to dampen the silky cloth but he had no time to deal with it.

He was going to claim his bride.

Clementine sat on a stool in front of her small mirror, absently watching the movement of her fingers while she plaited her hair for bed.

Bedtime had become a lonely affair of late.

Funny how she had slept alone her whole life and not been lonesome or cold. Evidently once one became accustomed to the presence of a large, warm man in one's bed there was no going back from it. Especially when one had come to love that man quite desperately.

Tonight even the bright fire snapping her hearth was inadequate to warm her completely.

But where was he? Having a late night at Parliament? Out doing whatever secret, dangerous thing he did?

She had not heard him come home but he might have. He might be sleeping soundly while she worried and fretted.

If that were true she would have a thing or two to say about it. He ought to have let her know he'd returned.

He ought to be here—with her. It was where he belonged.

The more thought she gave to the matter, the more wrongheaded he seemed. A man did not declare his love and then keep his wife at a chaste distance. That was hardly the way to fill the manor with happy little heirs.

Upbraiding him for his neglect of her would be a relief, since if she was able to do it, that meant he was safely in his bed. Clementine let go of her braid, watched it unravel.

Enough was enough! There was only one way to let go of this worry and that was to go to his quarters and see for herself.

Without bothering to put on a dressing gown, she rushed across the room, the words she was going to use to scold him dancing on the tip of her tongue.

He claimed to love her? From now on he was going to act like it!

Flinging open the door, she rushed into the hallway.

And there he was. Large, damp and so close she felt heat pulsing off him.

He gripped her forearms. A strand of wet hair dangled across his forehead, skimmed his dark brows. It dripped on the bosom of her nightgown and then her nose, when he drew her closer to his chest.

"I'm done." His voice sounded deep, raspy. His warm, moist breath puffed on her face.

"Done with what?" She knew what, of course, but the words did bear saying.

"Done with waiting for everything to be right."

"It's right enough."

A decided draft whooshed along the hallway. It stirred the hem of her gown, ruffled the bottom of his robe. As always, her long toes felt icy.

All of a sudden he scooped her up. She'd never thought of herself as the swept-away type but found she rather liked it.

Oh, yes. When he carried her toward his suite, she liked it more than a little. Maybe because his arms were so strong, the muscles around her back and under her thighs so firm. Or maybe because she had the odd sensation of floating.

No doubt the sensation had to do with the fact that he was kissing her while he carried her, robbing her of breath and sensible thought.

Whatever, it was delightful and she did not want it to stop.

"You will not be sleeping in your room tonight."

"Good, then." Her room was lovely, but this was where she belonged.

Right here on the vast, canopied bed he was setting her down upon.

"Do you trust me? Even not knowing everything, do you trust me enough to give yourself to me?" he whispered against her hair.

The mattress gave when his greater weight settled next to her. She tipped toward him, felt his warmth seep into her.

"The secret I'm keeping from you—it's nothing immoral."

"Only dangerous?" She touched the bruise on his face, which was only beginning to heal.

He nodded. Turning onto his back, he stared at the ceiling with his hands cradled under his head.

She eased up on her elbow and traced the shape of his eyebrows with her fingertip.

When her finger drew close to his mouth, he caught her hand, kissed it.

For some reason, she could not catch her breath.

"I want you," he murmured. "But sometimes I'll get called away in the night. Do you trust me enough not to ask me about it?"

He trailed one finger from her jaw to her throat to the curve of her shoulder. As if by magic he summoned a line of gooseflesh on her skin.

"This is the second time you've asked that question. I'm still here in your bed, so yes, I do, Heath."

He really did have the most compelling smile.

"Do you want to know one of the things I love about you?" He kissed the tip of her nose.

"Don't you dare say my nose." She snuggled closer to him because it felt utterly natural to do so. "And, actually, I want to know all the things you love about me."

"Your forthrightness."

"Honestly, Heath." She poked him in the belly, felt the smooth satin of his robe slide against his abdomen. "Those are not the romantic words every girl dreams of."

"No?" He rose above her, lowered his mouth and gave her a long, sultry kiss. He hadn't fully lifted his mouth from hers when he uttered, "What if I said you were the most open-hearted, guileless woman I have ever met?"

She would say he was mistaken in thinking so. He was not the only one with a secret he was unwilling to reveal.

Perhaps that was what made overlooking his secrecy something she could do.

And at least she knew she was overlooking something while he did not.

"I love you for your honesty," he murmured.

Oh…well. She nuzzled him with her icy toes because she did not want to dwell on dishonesty in the moment, not his and certainly not hers.

What was honest, what was true, was what mattered.

She honestly loved him. He honestly loved her. No other truth was necessary.

"You're freezing!" He gasped when her toes poked his knee.

Sitting up, he caught her leg and made slow, circling motions with his fingers as he stroked a trail down her calf. He cupped her foot.

"Oh, that's heavenly." She sighed, closing her eyes. "Your hands are like heaters."

"Are you cold anywhere else?"

"Everywhere." Actually, she was fevered everywhere, a condition she suspected he was well aware of.

"Well, then, sweet wife, it would be my pleasure to ease your suffering."

She could not say it was suffering she felt so much as a craving, a yearning that pulsed in her veins with the intensity of an ache.

His hand, tangled in the hem of her nightgown, created urgency in her nerve endings of a sort she had never experienced.

"There's no going back for us," he murmured, shifting his weight over her and sliding her gown up at the same time.

How had she never noticed how the cotton slid over her skin in such a tantalizing way before?

But then she was being washed in a thousand sensations she had never experienced.

"I don't want to go back."

* * *

Heath woke in the deepest part of the night hearing wind-driven rain batter the window.

He didn't mind being woken by the storm, not when he could draw his wife's warm body into the curve of his and wrap his arms about her.

The rhythm of her steady breathing, the slow beat of her heart, was the most wonderful thing he had ever felt.

Perhaps he ought to have shown more restraint during the past hours, but Clementine did not appear to want restraint. She had been wildfire in his arms. A blaze that burned away everything he had ever been and left behind a husband, a true one in the way God intended.

Also a contented one. Wouldn't it be fine to spend the rest of their lives just so, curled together, with nothing, not even a breath of air, between them?

He traced his thumb along the delicate line of Clementine's collarbone. She smiled in her sleep.

He could not imagine how life had delivered such fortune to him—a wife who was virtuous and earthy, all in one beautiful body. A body he intended to enjoy one more time before sunrise and the demands of being Earl of Fencroft called him away.

Chapter Thirteen

Clementine stepped down from the cab, lifted her skirt and stepped carefully over mucky puddles. She climbed the steps of Slademore House a little slower than she normally did.

To the casual eye she might appear normal. Ah, but there was the most delightful glow within her that felt like a smile radiating out of every part of her body.

In some sense she felt like a new person.

One who woke this morning to kisses, sweet nuzzles and declarations of love.

She was a married woman, bonded to Heath by the most intimate and personal of acts.

How was she to keep her mind on reading *The Prince and the Pauper* when all she wanted to do was race home and meet Heath beneath the covers of their great bed?

"Good day, Lady Fencroft." It was the thin young woman opening the door to her today. "The children are waiting for you."

"I do look forward to reading to them today. I'm sorry," Clementine said. "But I did not get your name on my previous visits."

"It's Lettie, my lady."

"Lettie, I can't say how sorry I am for what happened to your baby. If there is anything I can do?"

"Oh, he wasn't mine. Just one here that I cared for."

"I must have misunderstood Mrs. Hoper."

"Well, they do all feel like mine."

"What a horrible thing to have happened! But how are the others?"

"They don't know about it, poor lambs. T'would only frighten them if they did."

"I hope the police will catch that villain soon." This could not go on much longer without it happening. Everyone was on edge.

"I fear he will—" Lettie clasped her hand over her mouth and coughed. "Will not be, that is. Not soon."

"I imagine the children were not able to play in the garden this morning because of the mud," Clementine said, in part to direct the conversation another way.

"No, they did not play in the yard." The girl glanced down and then away.

"They will be restive, then. I hope the story holds their attention."

"These children need you, Lady Fencroft," she murmured. "Are you—"

Mrs. Hoper stalked into the room. A guarded expression crossed Lettie's face.

"They need you to read to them," she said in a louder voice.

"Will you be here to listen, if you haven't had the opportunity to read Mark Twain? He's quite good."

Lettie glanced at the nurse, clearly seeking permission.

"Oh, I'm sure that would be acceptable." Those were the words Mrs. Hoper spoke but Clementine sensed the woman did not truly find it acceptable. "Just as long as your chores get done."

Mrs. Hoper was a woman with secrets. It seemed that lately, everyone had them.

Clementine entered the parlor and sat down in her customary chair. She greeted the children with smiles, opened the book and showed them a page with artwork on it.

While they looked at the drawing she spotted a boy she hadn't seen before.

No. That was not right. She thought she might have seen him. With his shock of red hair he resembled the urchin she'd noticed from the window the other day.

She could not be sure, of course. That boy had been dirty and this one appeared freshly scrubbed.

At the same time, she noticed another child absent. The little girl who had been crying and wishing for a beanstalk.

"Where is Lucille today?" she asked Lettie, who had taken a chair near a window that had a view of the street.

It was Mrs. Hoper who answered. "Sick. The doctor says she must have bed rest."

"I'll be sure to visit her on the way out," Clementine said.

"That would be lovely. Lettie will make sure she's not sleeping. If she is, perhaps you can see her another time."

Lettie turned her gaunt, sallow-cheeked face away and stared out the window. The crown of a top hat bobbed past the window. Lettie seemed to be watching its progress going by.

What an odd day this was. There was a sense of something being amiss here that she had never noticed before.

No doubt it was because of the missing baby and because Lucille was ill.

Mark Twain, she hoped, would be able to brighten things up.

"'In the ancient city of London,'" she read, "'on a certain autumn day in the second quarter of the sixteenth century, a boy was born to a poor family…'"

This ought to capture their attention since the same could be said of each child sitting at her feet. Wealthy orphans had relatives to take them in. These sweet ones had only Baron Slademore to depend upon.

She regretted the doubts she had just entertained about Slademore House. This home was a great blessing. Everyone praised it.

And yet the one person whose opinion mattered very much to her had forbidden her to come here. Knowing him as she did, she thought he must have a good reason for it.

Still, whatever the reason might be, it was not good enough to make her desert these children.

Lettie was correct. They did need her.

She read on about the birth of another child, this one to a wealthy family.

Clementine's children would be born to wealth and privilege. Love was all they would ever know.

For a moment she sat silently with the book open on her lap. She tapped the page with one finger, feeling that she wanted to run outside and gather up orphans, bring them home and keep them safe.

"Did the poor one die?" the red-haired boy asked, his young brow wrinkled in worry.

"No, no, he didn't. And you are all quite safe here with the baron to watch over you."

All of a sudden Lettie gasped.

"There's a visitor, Mrs. Hoper," she said more calmly than her first reaction accounted for.

That was odd.

A knock rapped on the door.

"How delightful," the nurse stated. Funny how her expression did not reflect delight when she rose from her chair and walked into the foyer to open the door.

"Lord Fencroft. Welcome to Slademore House."

"I've come to call on Baron Slademore."

"I'll see if he is in, my lord. But won't you join the countess in the parlor while I find him."

Clementine dropped the book on the floor.

"Which countess?" he asked through gritted teeth, even though he was certain he knew which one.

"Why, your countess, sir, Lady Fencroft."

The very Lady Fencroft he had forbidden to come here?

The same one whose honesty he had praised—loved her for, only last night?

Had his soul suddenly been cast in lead it could not have felt any heavier. Who was this woman he had taken to his heart?

Coming into the parlor he saw her sitting on a chair, her face pale as a bleached sheet. A dozen or so small children sat on the floor gathered about her skirt, looking up at him in wide-eyed fascination.

Perhaps they had never seen an earl. They had, however, seen a countess. He could only guess how many times.

"Lady Fencroft," he said once he gained control of his voice. "What a surprise to see you here."

"Did I not say I wanted to read to the children?" Color was beginning to rise in her cheeks. "I'm certain I did mention it."

"We mentioned many things, as I recall." He forced his voice to sound pleasant. The last thing he wanted was to scare the little ones. They had enough be frightened of as it was.

He glanced about. For all that Slademore House looked like paradise, he was not fooled. Not like his wife clearly was.

He'd come here for a reason—which was not to catch his wife disobeying him, but to try to discover a waifish-looking woman who might be working here. One who knew the secrets kept within these walls.

The nurse hurried back into the parlor, looking flustered.

"I'm afraid the baron has stepped out."

No doubt. He probably escaped out the back door as soon as he saw Heath coming to the front.

For as much as Heath tried to hide his animosity when around Slademore, the fellow had to feel it.

The baron would feel more than a scorch as soon as he found the informer and convinced her to reveal all she knew.

For a man to take copious donations for orphans, then keep the funds for himself, and to let the children go hungry and tattered while his dog wore diamonds made him the worst kind of human.

Clementine would think these children pampered because that was what she saw. What she did not know was that as soon as she went home, the fine clothes would be stripped from them and they would be taken to that dark room in the basement and fed gruel for dinner while the dog ate sumptuously.

Picturing it made him half sick.

What would his wife think if she knew those children would be sewing shirts by the light of grease lamps when they ought to be sleeping? Engaging in labor meant for adults, making a wage.

And all to earn Slademore a few more pounds?

Heath could only wonder why Slademore valued

money more than a child's welfare. The baron was fond of adoration. That was part of it, no doubt. Perhaps the more prosperous he appeared, the more respected he felt—the more envied.

Too fond a love of gaming might have to do with it. Heath had seen Slademore in gaming rooms a few times. He always appeared to be anxious, great circles of sweat dampening his fine clothing.

One time Heath had seen him forget the presence of his bejeweled dog while deep in a game of whist. The pet had wandered out into the garden and become lost. It had taken a dozen servants the better part of an hour to find it.

A fondness for games of chance combined with an expensive image? No doubt the man was in debt.

He was certain that not all Slademore's orphans were in this room. In another part of the house there would be others hidden from the public eye.

But he was going to end this. As long as he could find the woman and convince her that he would protect her if she told what she knew.

He would need to deal with his wife's disobedience, but that was for another time. He was here to find what he could of the informer.

"This is a sweet group of children," he said to the nurse. "I wonder how you care for them all. It must be a challenge."

"Well, it's like you say, Your Lordship, they are a sweet group."

Looking at their faces, he thought they were distrustful of the nurse. Did Clementine notice?

A shadow moved across the doorway, there and gone so swiftly he could not tell much. But the figure was small and very likely female.

"Who was that?"

"Just Lettie," the woman said.

Clementine stood up, her arms crossed over her middle while she glowered at him. A little girl peeked out from behind her skirt, her eyes wide and blinking.

Mrs. Hoper, he was certain, knew everything. He'd see her in prison as well as Slademore.

"May I meet her?" Was she the waif?

"She'll be in the kitchen preparing biscuits and honey for the children." The nurse snapped her fingers. "Come along to the dining room, children."

"Shall we join them?" he asked Clementine.

With a curt nod, she walked beside him.

"Stop scowling," she said. "You'll scare the children."

"I'm not scowling. Surely you know a smile when you see one."

She turned on him. He had no idea brows could lift that high.

Taking his coat sleeve, she pivoted him so that he faced a large vase. The mirrored surface was shiny enough that it reflected his face.

"You see?" she said.

It did look like he was scowling. "The vase is curved. It's a distortion."

"Heath Cavill, I will not let you go in there and upset those babies. They've been through enough with the Abductor snatching away a baby."

As much as he wanted to crow about that rescue, he kept quiet.

"I want to meet Lettie."

"What? Why would you?"

Why? He could hardly admit why!

"I do not need to explain myself."

"I rather think you do."

It would make life easier to be able to. But no, it was

impossible. It was bad enough that she was even here. If he were caught it would be difficult for her to claim she had no knowledge of his activities.

The need for her to stay away from here was even more urgent than it had been before.

It looked very much like she was going to spit fire at him!

"I'm taking you home." He captured her elbow to lead her toward the front door.

"You are not!"

She swiped a handful of flowers from the vase and faced off with him, gripping the roses in one fist as if wielding a lethal weapon.

He glanced about. Luckily no one was nearby to witness the rebellion of Lady Fencroft.

He reached for her.

She shook the petals at him. "Keep back, you—you—"

While she clearly considered what wicked word best suited him, he bent, scooped his shoulder into her soft belly and lifted her off the floor.

"Brute! Pillager!"

Maybe he was all those things but he was also Earl of Fencroft.

She was his wife, obliged to be obedient.

"You will do my bidding," he announced against her jostling bustle.

All of a sudden she went utterly still.

What had he done?

It was possible he had just declared war between them.

A war in which she had the more powerful weapons.

Silence.

It was quite possible that she might never speak to Heath William Cavill, sixth Earl of Fencroft, again.

* * *

Clementine watched out of the carriage window, her hands clenched in her lap, taking note of how the scenery gradually changed from impoverished to affluent.

The man sitting across from her, all stares and frowns, was despicable—a heinous wretch. A contemptible rogue.

While the description did fit him she could not say so aloud. Not having taken a vow of silence against him.

As a mere woman who must do his bidding in all circumstances, no matter how foolish those circumstances were, she must use the weapons available to her.

The first of those was to remain silent; the second was acting aloof.

She hoped he wouldn't try to carry her off to his bedroom tonight, because—well, because she would drag her heels on the carpet. She would batter his chest and turn her face away from his ardent kiss. Because she was absolutely not going to his room tonight!

It was growing awfully warm in the carriage. Somehow it must be Heath's fault.

Of course, he might creep into her bedroom and sneakily convince her to succumb to his desires. Blame it! She was too overheated to give that possibility further thought.

She huffed out loud, but that was not speaking, in truth.

"I forbade you to go to Slademore House because this part of town is far too dangerous."

She dearly wanted to point out that there was a woman on the corner selling bread and no one was assaulting her.

By inclining her head in that direction and giving Heath an accusatory look, she made her point without exactly speaking.

"She is not Countess of Fencroft."

For the few minutes remaining of the ride she gazed

straight ahead, watching the fringe decorating the ceiling as it swayed with each gouge in the road.

She wanted desperately to ask her husband what he had been doing at Slademore House. It was not likely that he'd come to retrieve her. He'd seemed genuinely shocked to find her there.

He would be, of course, given that he considered her the soul of honesty—a saint in the cause of truthfulness.

She huffed again, shot him a scowl and then snapped her attention back to the fringe.

The carriage came to a stop in front of the townhome stairs.

She stood up, reached for the door. The last thing she was going to do was let him assist her down. The door handle turned from the outside. Heath caught her hand to prevent her exit.

"When are you going to speak to me?"

She yanked her hand out of his grip. Cool air from the open door rushed inside but did not do much to salve her temper.

"When you learn to behave like a civilized human being!"

She placed her hand in the waiting coachman's and turned to step down.

"My sweet Clemmie."

"Grandfather!" Reaching the bottom step, she flung herself into his arms, hugged his neck. "I've missed you! Oh, welcome home!"

The coach creaked with Heath's weight when he stepped down behind her.

"Son!" Grandfather loosened her stranglehold about his neck and set her aside in order to greet her husband. "I'm delighted to know you and my girl have made a good match, after all."

"I believe you left your wits in Scotland, Grandfather."

He grinned, arched his impressive brows.

"Yes, an excellent match!" He winked.

As it turned out she needn't have worried about Heath carrying her off or invading her bedroom. She had spent the night undisturbed.

Except that she had been disturbed.

Watching from her window she'd seen Heath pacing the garden for hours on end.

Clementine stooped to slip her shoes on her feet. Straightening, she leaned closer to the mirror and touched the bluish shadow. "Oh, never mind," she grumbled.

She went out of her room and took the two flights of stairs down to the conservatory. On the way she met two servants going about their duties and thanked them for their efforts.

Their smiles back at her were not as guarded as they had been in the beginning. No, indeed, they appeared comfortable in encountering her.

Continuing down the steps, she thought about what she had said to Grandfather.

Welcome home—not welcome back.

It was true that this was where she now lived, but was it home? She found that she did think of Los Angeles less and less, but if she were gone to a faraway place, which spot would call to her?

She stopped for a moment, letting her heart feel the way.

Fencroft House. She would want to return here, to Fencroft House.

The realization came as a surprise since in the beginning she had been resentful of being forced into coming here.

This morning, walking into the conservatory to the sound of small birds twittering in the aviary, the scent of lush green foliage and the sight of Grandfather waiting for her at the small white breakfast table—she'd known this was home.

She would always love where she had come from, but when she went away on trips or whatever, this was where she would long to come back to. And not only here. For as short as the visit to Derbyshire had been, she felt strongly drawn there, as well.

Or, perhaps it hadn't so much to do with a place as a person.

To her Heath.

"Good morning, my Clemmie!"

She kissed Grandfather's cheek and sat down across the table from him.

"I said it last night and will again, I'm so happy to have you home."

"As I am to be here. Are you still not speaking to your husband, though? You have tears in your eyes."

"Do I?"

"Ah, sweet Clemmie, sometimes, the ones we love the most are the ones who cause us the most grief." She wondered if he might be referring to Madeline but thought it had more to do with her. "But love forgives all things."

"This," she said, blinking and finding it was only a slight misting in her eyes, "is not over Heath Cavill."

"Is it not?"

"All right, it is, but not in the way you think. It is more that I only just now realized how deeply I am attached to this place, and again to the man who owns it."

"And yet you continue to be at odds with him? I don't understand." Grandfather's quizzical expression confirmed that he did not.

Given that he was a man, she could not hold it against him. Like her husband, her grandfather was under the mistaken belief that being a male meant that he was in charge of her decisions.

Apparently, one could love a person and want to throttle them all in the same breath.

Since this was a conversation she did not wish to continue, she turned its course. "Tell me more about your trip."

"Scotland is a wonderful country and the business was a great success. Having the duke a part of it helped a great deal with the negotiations, and he was there because of your title."

"I'm glad my sacrifice helped in your endeavor."

"Sacrifice, Clemmie? I think you are not unhappy about it." He smiled, winking. "You met your match in Heath Cavill. Had you been given the choice of a thousand men you could not have picked better. I am not mistaken in this."

Indeed, Heath had some flawed beliefs, but he was not flawed. He was wonderful.

"It is true, you are not mistaken." She rested her chin in her hands. "I'm quite happy being married to him on most days."

"Perhaps you have some blessed news for me?"

"You weren't gone all that long. And no, I do not have blessed news."

"Ah, well, no matter. It will happen. But in the meantime—here."

He withdrew a large box from under the table and handed it to her.

"I visited a doll maker in my travels." A wide, satisfied smile spread across his face.

She lifted the box lid and stared into the blue marble eyes of a life-size baby doll.

"It's very well made." She lifted it from the box and held it up to the light streaming through the window, in order to get a proper look at the finely painted porcelain face. "Thank you, Grandfather."

"I thought it might give you a smile until a living one comes along."

It made her sad, was what it did. Not the doll itself. It was the fact that a toy was dressed better than some living babies were and it broke her heart.

This was not right.

There had to be something she could do. She had thought her calling to be teaching but very clearly the door to that had been unreasonably slammed in her face.

She might take the dress off the doll and donate it, but that would only help one child and only until she outgrew it.

What if she—?

"How many bedrooms are in this house? I wonder?"

"You could ask your husband."

"Yes…" She supposed she would have to. "I imagine he knows how many there are in Derbyshire, too."

"You must be planning on having a large family, Clemmie."

The thought had occurred to her too suddenly to be considered a plan, really.

"Something like that."

Once again, Heath felt like a very poor husband. Marriage was not the easy thing it appeared to be.

Especially when secrets were involved. And his skeleton in the closet was rather large.

What must she think of him, dragging her away from a place known for good works?

That he must be daft—or worse—unhinged.

No matter that she reviled him, he could not relent on his decision to stop her from going there. She had no idea what the cost would be to her if it all fell apart.

He would not change his mind on this.

Any lady of society he might have married would respect his decision and dutifully obey it.

Ah, but his Clementine was a blazing flame in comparison to their polite candle glow.

Heath walked across the entry hall toward the front door. Ramsfield, the butler, stood at attention with Heath's coat hanging in precise folds over his arm.

Ramsfield returned Heath's smile even though in truth Heath hadn't directed it at the fellow, but rather at the about-face of his mental wanderings.

Strange that he should be smiling when his life was in upheaval. But how could he not grin? His wife was fun, she was lively and spirited. He could not recall ever meeting a more fascinating woman. It was all he could do to keep from blatantly staring at her, even when his attention ought to be directed somewhere else.

Truth be told, he did not want a meek lady who would never dare to question a man of title.

He wanted the one he had. The issue was, did she still want him?

His behavior yesterday hadn't been exemplary. While it had been within his rights to bring her home, in reflection, he might have done it more circumspectly.

It was a very good thing Clementine had vowed for better or for worse. Also a very good thing that he had lain with her as a true husband.

She was good and stuck with him now.

Going down the front steps, he rolled his shoulders, appreciating the shaft of sunshine warming them. It was another mostly clear day and very welcome after the rain.

Creed stood beside the carriage, holding the door open.

"Good day, my lord." The coachman slanted him a grin. "I trust you spent a restful night."

"You trust no such thing. You saw what I did yesterday."

"When you behaved like a barbarian, do you mean?"

"There was no help for that. The countess refused to come along."

"I suppose there wasn't. It wouldn't do for her to be part and parcel with us."

Heath shook his head firmly. "Lady Fencroft is to have no part in this."

"We'd best expose Slademore soon, then. The countess is a sharp one. When she figures it out, she'll be right angry at you."

"My situation with her could hardly be worse than it is now."

"Aye, well, you did carry her off like a sack of wheat." Creed chuckled while closing the door. "Don't know how you can expect anything else."

Even though Heath was within his rights to protect his wife and would do the same again if need be, he was deeply sorry he had done it quite that way.

Perhaps in America men did not guide their wives in what was best for them. It was known to be a wild and lawless place in some parts.

He leaned back against the seat cushion and closed his eyes.

What he ought to do was go back inside the town house and find her, work this out before the hurt festered beyond healing.

If she was hiding away in her room weeping over his imperious behavior, he was twice over a cad.

He thumped the roof of the cab, signaling for Creed to stop, then realized the carriage had yet to move.

The door flew open even as he reached for it.

Clementine stepped inside and closed it after her. The carriage started to roll.

Her breath came in short, quick gasps as if she had been running.

Sitting across from him she leaned against the seat-back, her arms folded at sharp angles across her middle.

Mutely, she stared at him with round green eyes. He adored her eyes.

Was she going to speak to him?

She had sought him out on his way to Parliament. Judging by the high flush in her cheeks, the slight lift of her chin, she had something to say.

However, the steadiness of her gaze suggested she had questions more than anything else.

"I miss you, Clementine. Won't you talk to me?"

"I miss you, too."

"I'm sorry I treated you so disrespectfully." He reached his hand toward her across the jolting carriage. "I love you. Come back to me."

She placed her fingers in his hand. He swallowed them up in his fist and yanked, propelling her toward his side of the cab.

At the same time the carriage wheel hit a divot in the road, tossing the cab left. Clementine's balance listed toward the door.

He clasped her about the waist and hauled her onto his lap.

"Do you forgive me?"

"Do you mean for making a decision that was mine to make, or for acting like a beast?"

"There is a very good reason for keeping you away from that place. I promise it won't remain a secret forever. I've asked you to believe I'm acting for the best—

more than once. Now I'm doing it again." He stroked her bottom lip with his thumb, wanting desperately to put his mouth on the spot. "I do ask your pardon for carrying you away and behaving like a heathen."

"I can accept that you believe you are acting for the best. But as for behaving like a heathen?" She sighed, placing her hand on his heart. "I think I'll need to give it more review."

"What kind of review?"

"Oh, I should call it a demonstration, more than that."

"Does this demonstration involve pillaging a kiss?"

"Not at first, but if the heathen proves to be strong and diligent in his perseverance, it could result in a bit of pillaging."

"How would said heathen go about this without offending the lady?"

"He could steal into her chamber and forcefully remove whatever clothing was not strictly needed for warmth. At that point she would not likely find it amiss to be tossed over the heathen's shoulder and carried off to his lair."

"To be pillaged?"

"A lady would hope."

"Barbarian that I am, I'll not wait for the cover of dark to begin my ravishment of you."

He plucked the pins from her hair and tossed them someplace where they hit with little pinging sounds. Winding his hands in her hair he tugged her face down to his, looting the booty of her lips, plundering where he wished.

"Heath the Heathen," she whispered into the sweat-dampened hair at his temple.

It was so very private with the drapes drawn in the carriage, as if they jostled along in a world of their own where nothing could intrude.

Nothing but—

"Drat Parliament," he said, his breath coming hot and fast. He set her off his lap. "I'll have Creed take you home after he drops me at the blamed place."

Clementine laughed low in her throat. She shifted her weight and climbed back on his lap, this time straddling him.

"I've instructed him otherwise."

"You intended to waylay me from the beginning."

"I did not." She rose up, cupped his face in her hands and came down upon him in a long kiss. "I meant to talk to you, but then I was distracted by an uncivilized rogue and quite lost my wits."

"Is what you have to say something we can talk of later?"

"I fear we'll have to since in the moment I can't recall what it was."

In the end he had no idea how many times they circled the streets of Mayfair, but by the time Creed stopped the carriage in front of the town house stairs, the sun was slipping behind the horizon.

They'd have barely enough time to straighten their appearances before dinner was served.

Chapter Fourteen

At dinner Clementine stared past flower arrangements and candelabras at Heath sitting at the far end of the table.

Having been so close to him all afternoon and being able to touch him as she wished and as often, this distance seemed vast although it was only feet.

Grandfather sat on her right and Olivia on her left.

Her heart warmed as she watched their faces while they ate and chatted. In only a short time the four of them and small Victor had become family.

She did not know how it happened but a bond of belonging joined them one to another—and it was wonderful.

If only her cousin was here. Madeline's presence would make the circle complete.

"And the fear is he will begin kidnapping children from other areas," Olivia said.

Evidently the conversation had taken a dark turn while she counted her blessings.

"One source believes he will begin abducting whole groups of children."

That comment must have startled Heath because he dropped his spoon into his soup.

"What source is that, sister?"

"I wouldn't know, but it was written in the newspaper and so it must be true."

"Just because you read something does not make it so. Think of it…" Heath cast a glance at each person sitting at the table. "Trying to snatch several children away from their guardians with everyone screaming and carrying on? It's hard—would be hard, it seems to me, to get one of them away. In my opinion taking several children makes no sense."

"It makes no sense to take even one child. What can he possibly want with a baby?" Clementine asked.

"Perhaps he sells them," Grandfather said. "Some men will do anything for a profit."

"What if the Abductor is not even a man?" Heath pointed out. "No one has actually seen him."

"Slademore's guards have seen him. They reported to the newspaper that the Abductor is a man—an exceptionally stealthy man. Some are beginning to say he's not actually a man and that his black coach has no driver."

One corner of Heath's mouth ticked up. That was an odd reaction. No doubt the turtle soup had given him gas.

"He must be a demon to take orphans!" Clementine looked at Heath when she spoke. "Especially the ones who have been fortunate enough to be taken in by the baron. The kidnapper has no scruples."

As she expected he did not look pleased at the mention of Slademore. One could only imagine there was a long-standing problem between the men.

However, in the few conversations she'd had with the baron, he had never said anything amiss about Heath.

"This whole thing makes me want to strap a holster around my hip and carry a weapon on my person. Isn't that what they do in America?" Olivia asked.

"It's not something you see every day," Grandfather explained. "Especially in the cities. But I haven't lived all my life in polite society so I have seen it."

"Victor will not be pleased to hear that it is uncommon."

"Oh, but cowboys almost always do," Clementine added. "He needn't despair."

"Perhaps I should wed a cowboy, then, so he can protect us from that evil…" Olivia pursed her lips. "I find I cannot come up with a word bad enough to describe the Abductor."

"Fiend," Clementine suggested because she could think of many words. She was not sure she would ever get over the sweet baby being kidnapped from Slademore House. "Wretch, viper, monster, hellhound!"

"Yes!" Olivia exclaimed. "Hellhound is the very word."

"I say we turn the conversation to more pleasant talk." Heath addressed his comment to Clementine more than anyone else. "Did not Lady Guthrie host a flower show today?"

"I would not know." She had to look at her lap, pretend interest in a fold of her napkin. If she did not she feared everyone would see her thoughts, know where she had been and what she had been doing. "I was occupied with other business today."

"Olivia and I attended," Grandfather said. "We spent a few lovely hours admiring the posies, did we not, my dear?"

"We did, actually. I cannot recall when I've enjoyed flowers as much as I did today."

There was a lull in the conversation while everyone sipped soup, each one to their own thoughts.

"Clemmie, my love," Grandfather said, breaking a silence that was not at all uncomfortable the way some tended to be. "I've had news from the Pinkerton man."

"What?" She coughed on her soup. Grandfather reached around to pat her on the back. "Please let it be good news!"

"I can't say whether it is or is not. But Madeline was traced to the docks in New York, where she boarded a ship."

"Bound where? Was she alone?"

"It's a bit of a mystery. The investigator didn't see her, but he did speak with a ticket agent who remembered her. It's no surprise he would." Grandfather nodded at Heath and Olivia. "Madeline is quite unforgettable. He also recalls that a man was involved in some way—but all that was somewhat foggy. She did, however, purchase only one ticket."

"To where?" Clementine gripped her spoon tight. Joy, dread and hope crashed inside her like croquet balls being slammed by mallets.

"Why, to here!" Grandfather grinned. "Where else would she come but to the bosom of her family?"

"I wonder." Heath rolled onto his back, catching his breath. "Which one of us is the heathen?"

Clementine turned on the mattress and trailed one finger down his chest.

"It's you. Did you not carry me from my room to yours slung over your shoulder?"

He caught a strand of crimson hair, trailed the end of it across his nose in order to better take in the scent, which was not so much perfumed as fresh. It had to be a natural fragrance that was her own.

"You must admit you did nearly leap up there."

"That was your imagination. I could not possibly jump so high."

She settled into the crook of his shoulder.

"Do you recall that earlier in the day I wanted to discuss something with you?"

"My mind has been preoccupied with…" He lifted her hand and kissed her fingers. "With other things, but I vaguely remember."

"I need for you to pay attention now because this is important to me."

"I hope you are not trying to convince me to allow—"

"It has to do with the estate in Derbyshire."

That was not what he had expected her to say, although he did not know what he had expected other than an attempt to convince him to let her return to Slademore House.

"What to do with it?"

"Our visit there was so short I didn't have time to see it all. But how many bedrooms does it have?"

"Sixteen, not counting the servants' quarters."

"Oh, good. It should suit nicely."

"For what?" He stared hard at the carved bedpost. He was supposed to be paying attention to what she said, not the curve of her neck or how sweetly round her earlobes were with tumbled red hair tucked behind them.

She smiled. He knew he would give her anything she asked—almost. "I want to open a shelter for street urchins there. Give them food and an education, show them what it means to be loved."

Stunned to silence, he simply stared at her.

"I will not be told it is impossible, that a countess would not do such a thing. I am going to do it. If the baron can, so can I."

She sat up again and folded her arms across her middle.

"You ought to say something or else I will think you disapprove. And if you do we will have a great row—a greater one than fine society has ever seen."

Indeed, her skin was beginning to flush pink all over.

The sight was enough to make him want to hold back his answer a bit longer. Then again, it was not an answer she wanted so much as affirmation.

"Let's do it."

"Good, then." She snuggled back down under the blanket and lay one arm across his chest, hugged him tight. "Will we need to prepare the rooms or can we bring some of the children with us when Parliament is dismissed?"

"We'll bring them."

If it was possible to love another person more than he loved Clementine Cavill, he could not imagine how. He didn't know a way to even express what he was feeling in the moment.

No doubt she would have the words he needed, but he was at a loss.

"I believe that the Good Lord sent me a perfect woman. I love you, Clementine."

The sun was peeking through the window before he finished demonstrating just how much.

The next night, Clementine was exhausted. She ought to be sleeping but her mind would not allow it. Heath suffered no such problem. He lay beside her, his breathing slow and regular.

She'd had an exhausting day purchasing a few of the things needed in order to make a home for her rescued children.

While it sounded a simple thing to say she would pluck them from the streets—not like the Abductor did, but in the open with the full consent of lawyers and magistrates—it was not quite so easy.

They would need bedding, clothing, books and toys.

And education! It seemed she would fulfill her calling

after all. She would no longer teach in a formal classroom, but when she thought about it, this was better.

She had far more to teach her charges than letters and numbers. She would show them how to respect themselves and others. She would teach them how to love, because it might have been lacking in their lives.

Oh, she would teach love but she would also give it.

They would learn what it was like to have a mother. Not that she could remember what it was like, but she'd had one once and knew in her heart that she had been cherished by her.

Who would they be? Sweet little girls? Mischievous little boys? Scholars and tricksters?

With sleep elusive, she got out of bed and put on her robe.

Tonight, she and Heath shared her chamber, so she curled up in her chair beside the window and gazed out.

Fog crept slowly across the garden, its white, wispy fingers searching out corners and obscuring the fountain and shrubbery. The top of a tree was still visible across the way. So was Grandfather's window, where a lamp softly glowed.

He must be up late worried about Madeline crossing the Atlantic Ocean alone. It was not as though she was traveling first class like Clementine and Grandfather had done. Coming over with no money and no chaperone would be a different experience altogether.

A frightening one.

For all the upheaval she had undergone, Clementine had never been alone through any of it. She had gone from the security of Grandfather's watchful eye to the shelter of her husband's home.

Sitting here listening to Heath's even breathing,

wrapped in warmth from the fire's glow, she felt utterly surrounded and protected.

Beyond the walls of Fencroft House, fog would be hiding criminals going about their business. Only streets away, children, possibly ones she already counted as hers, would be huddled in doorways, shivering and frightened of rats and of evildoers who scavenged in the darkness.

They would be keeping one ear open for the worst of them all.

The Abductor.

The doll Grandfather had given her sat in her frilly clothes on the chair across from her. She snatched it up and hugged it to her. She gazed into the blue marbled eyes, wondering what had become of the baby taken from Slademore House.

How was it that law enforcement had not been able to apprehend the criminal?

Surely someone ought to be able to do it! She had entertained the thought that Heath might be trying to, given his sudden disappearances in the night, his bumps and bruises.

It was but one explanation for his odd absences. There could easily be other reasons. Not that she was ever likely to know, since he steadfastly refused to confide in her.

She trailed her fingers over the porcelain head of the doll and wrapped the edge of her robe over it, imagining she was protecting one of the helpless children in the fog.

"There you are. No bad man can see you now."

All of a sudden her hand clenched in the fabric of the robe.

Under the cloth no one would know whether the doll was a real child or not.

Perhaps she was the "someone" who ought to do something to bring the Abductor to justice.

It was a risky thing to do but how could she possibly sit here in her cozy room with the nice fire and her warm husband when young lives were at stake?

A little voice reminded her that she ought to tell Heath what she was going to do. Perhaps he could help.

But no. He would only refuse to let her get involved. If he thought that going to Slademore House in a carriage during broad daylight was too risky, he would never approve of this.

Nor would Grandfather. The truth was, no sensible person would encourage her to take the risk.

Which did not mean that the next time Heath went out in the night she was not going out, as well.

Clementine was far too busy to attend a tea party. Too preoccupied, as well.

Three nights had passed since she decided to pose as a wretched mother giving her child to Slademore House, and still Heath had not gone out in the night.

Olivia was not keen on attending Lady Guthrie's tea, either, but she'd explained that one did not refuse an invitation issued by the duchess.

So this afternoon found the pair of them being ushered into the duchess's presence along with six other young ladies all honored with the same summons.

One of them, Clementine was nearly certain, was one of the women who had been gossiping in the hallway on the night of her ball.

Lady Guthrie greeted Clementine and Olivia last but with genuine warmth.

"We'll take refreshment in the sunroom since the fog is relentless today. I do wish we would finally have a spot of sunshine."

The sunroom was lovely, lush with small trees and

shrubs. It reminded Clementine of the conservatory at home.

Beside a window two tables were set, each with tea and a tower of pastries.

Lady Guthrie indicated that Clementine and Olivia, along with one other lady, should sit with her while the others sat down at the other table.

"My dear Lady Fencroft," the duchess said with a smile. "You look lovely. Marriage greatly agrees with you."

"Not so much as it does my brother," Olivia added, making Lady Guthrie grin and the women at both tables laugh. Except for the one. She was openly frowning.

"I thought it would. I had no qualms about the union whatsoever. Glenda, is there not enough sugar in your tea? You look rather sour."

Glenda blinked and returned her attention to the duchess. "I do beg your pardon, Lady Guthrie. The tea is perfect as it is."

The duchess turned to Clementine.

"Yes, it is apparent that marriage suits you, my dear, but what about us? Do we suit? We must seem so very different from what you are used to, with all our titles and rules. I imagine you miss home very much."

"May I speak openly, Lady Guthrie?"

"Oh, yes, please do."

"I did come to London with a great deal of misgiving. But I'm happy here now. And even though it might look like I was forced to marry the earl, I have no regrets. We were drawn to one another before you came upon us."

She was speaking quietly. Only the people at her table would hear what she was saying. Unless they were intently eavesdropping, which Glenda appeared to be doing.

"I'm telling you this so that you won't feel you made a mistake in forcing the match."

"Oh, I never do." Lady Guthrie patted her hand. "And just so you know, there have been couples in my garden whom I have passed by without a word. But I felt you and Lord Fencroft would suit. And now, my dears, tea is getting cold."

A moment of quiet ensued while they lifted half-cooled cups and sipped.

Whispered conversation continued at the other table.

"She might be happy here but you know, she will always be an American..." someone muttered.

"An outsider." Glenda's whisper sounded like an announcement from a Sunday pulpit. "And you know the chit will not produce an heir. What a shame it will be the nephew to inherit."

Good heavens, ladies of society they might be, but they were not actually ladies. She did her best to ignore the prattle.

"If he does not have a mistress, mark my words, he soon will."

Olivia clenched her spoon while she stirred her tea, her slim fingers turning white, her lips pressed tight.

If only there was something Clementine could do to ease her pain over her husband's infidelity. It would be hard for her to let the hurt go since he had died in the other woman's bed. Olivia had never had the chance to express her anger at him to his face. It festered, trapped within her.

"No." Olivia turned on her seat, pinning Glenda with a glare. Her chair made a long, slow screech on the stone floor when she stood.

Lady Guthrie set down her teacup, clearly waiting to hear what Olivia was going to say.

So did everyone else, including Clementine.

"Glenda, if you think so little of my brother, why were you so het up to have him for yourself?"

Standing, Olivia walked toward the other table. "Lord Fencroft is an honorable man. He has never, and nor will he ever, have a mistress."

"Well, I'm sure I only meant—well, some do." Glenda's glance at Olivia was sly, ugly.

"If you are referring to my late husband, I am well aware of his infidelity."

Olivia circled the back of Glenda's chair. She might have been wounded by the snarky reminder, but it did not show.

"Why would it be a shame for my son to inherit?" She bent forward and whispered as "quietly" as Glenda had been whispering. "In the event my Victor decides not to be a cowboy he would be well suited to inherit the title."

She patted the girl's shoulder. "Being unmarried, perhaps you do not understand how children are created—so to some extent your ignorance is understandable. But I do know, and I assure you there is every chance that my good sister will produce an heir by this time next year."

Olivia straightened and came back to her chair. She sat down and sipped her tea.

"My, my, Glenda." Lady Guthrie picked up her teacup and tipped the rim at her blushing guest. "I believe your tongue has caught up to you at last. If you feel the slightest bit uncomfortable over it my footman will be happy to escort you out."

"I don't know what society is coming to when an outsider—an American—is sided with over a daughter of the realm."

"It is a changing society, Glenda." Lady Guthrie smiled and nodded at her departing guest. "Unless you change with it, it is you who will be the outsider."

Glenda followed the footman but cast a resentful glance back at Clementine.

"Pay her no mind," Olivia said. "Glenda was always judgmental and free with her opinions, even as a girl."

"You were wonderful, Olivia. Thank you for speaking up for us."

She could not recall seeing her sister-in-law's smile so self-assured.

"It did feel rather nice. And I meant it when I said Heath would never have a mistress. I've misjudged him over it and I'm sorry."

Clementine squeezed her hand and Olivia squeezed hers back.

Chapter Fifteen

Clementine stood beside her bedroom door, listening for footsteps in the hallway.

Earlier in the evening, Heath had claimed to have a headache.

Being fairly certain he did not but meant to go out and do whatever it was he did in the wee hours, she had dressed. This was her opportunity to sneak out of the house, too.

All she needed was to put on her coat and then pick up the doll that she'd wrapped in a baby's blanket.

The only thing to do now was to wait, to stand here by the door shifting from foot to foot and wonder if she was doing the right thing.

But she was, of course. She was not going to let a bit of risk stand in her way of protecting children in danger.

She hoped Heath did not come to her room and find her fully dressed. An unexpected visit would ruin everything.

Although she figured he would not, since he wouldn't want to draw attention to the fact that he also was sneaking out.

She'd done what she could to make certain her plan would be accomplished without mishap. Given her title and her wealth she had an advantage that she had not appreciated in the past.

When Lady Fencroft hired a coach to remain a few streets away from the town house and be available to her from the hours of eleven until dawn every night, it was sure to be waiting for her.

She also felt strongly that when she offered the constables who patrolled the area the opportunity to come with her and apprehend the Abductor, they would not refuse.

All she needed was for Heath to leave the house.

It was nearly midnight when she heard the thud of his boots pass by her room. Moments later she watched from the window and saw his dark silhouette cross the garden path going from the conservatory to the stable.

Snatching up the doll, she tucked it under her arm and tiptoed downstairs. Following Heath's path, she left through the conservatory and crossed the garden.

Cold seeped through her shoes, bit her ankles and calves all the way to her knees. Fog curled along the stones and obscured the shrubbery.

She stood still for a moment, listening. Once she heard carriage wheels roll out of the stable and then the clop of the horse's hooves on cobblestones, she exited the garden gate.

The Fencroft carriage, with Creed driving, passed by the one waiting for her. How interesting that anything identifying the carriage as belonging to Fencroft had been removed. It might be any carriage on the way to an assignation in the night.

Walking quickly with the doll clutched to her chest, she came to the hired hack and rapped on the door.

The coachman opened the door, rubbing his eyes.

He climbed down from the cab, nodded and held the door open for her.

"Take me to Slademore House, please," she instructed, going up the steps. He gave the blanket a concerned glance. "And stop when you come to the first policeman you pass."

"Is the child well, my lady?"

Oh, splendid! He thought it was real.

"Yes." She sat down on the bench. "Only sleeping like a lamb."

Within a moment the carriage jolted into motion. She had a very good feeling that her outing would be a success. The Abductor had taken his last victim. His reign of terror would end tonight.

The carriage slowed, then stopped. She drew back the curtain. A pair of constables stood on a corner only feet away.

She felt the weight of the cab shift when the driver stepped down.

"Lady Fencroft wishes a word," she heard him say before he opened the door.

She hadn't meant for her identity to be known but perhaps it was for the best. They would hardly refuse to help a countess.

She explained where she was going and what she hoped to accomplish. They refused to help.

This was no work for a lady, and on and on they went, both of them firm in their objection.

In the end she was able to convince them she was going even without their help, so they climbed inside the carriage.

"Truthfully, I don't know if the Abductor will be there tonight or not, but this is the only time I have to get out of the house without the earl objecting."

"Meaning no disrespect, my lady, but were you my wife I'd lock you in the house, you and the child."

"As would the earl if he knew, but he's stepped out and will be none the wiser."

"Are you sure you want to expose your babe to this? I'd not think it's safe."

She peeled back the cover to expose the porcelain face. "My plan is to save children, not endanger them. Once we have concluded this business, I trust you will protect my identity? As soon as you have caught the villain I will return home in this coach. You may make up any story you like to explain how you have made London a safer place."

"You can count on my discretion," agreed the shorter of the pair.

"I don't approve of any of this—but, aye, I'll not reveal you."

"Of course, we can't be sure the Abductor will appear, but it has been some time now since he has." She folded the blanket over the doll's head, patted the cloth behind. "Perhaps I can call upon you again in the event we are not successful tonight?"

"With a bit of luck the fiend will be in prison by morning."

"I don't like it, but I'd hardly let you face him alone. Yes, Lady Fencroft, you can call on me again."

Leaning back against the bench cushion, Heath crumpled the note delivered to Creed. This had been delivered to the barbershop by a beggar boy who'd dropped it in his lap while he sat in the chair with suds all over his chin.

It had been written in the same feminine hand as the other notes. By the girl Lettie? he wondered.

He and Creed came before the time she had appointed, hoping to intercept her when she left the child.

Whoever the woman was, she was brave. It was a

tricky thing to be able to place the child on the steps while the guards patrolled the other side of the building.

He might be wrong about her living on the premises but it made sense that she did. What else would explain her familiarity with the timing of the guards' routines?

Rescuing the child was their goal for the night, but they also wanted to speak with the woman. Needed to. This business was becoming too predictable, too risky to continue with much longer.

Creed slowed the pace of the carriage, the signal that they were a block from the alley that ran behind Slademore House.

Heath put on his black hat and cape, tied the mask over his eyes and his nose. He drew on a pair of leather gloves.

He disliked the disguise that was loathed by all of London. Every time he put it on he had to remind himself of the good it was doing.

With each rescue he thought of Willa and pictured his friend's child in his mind, how she was growing strong at the seaside.

Creed tapped the roof of the cab twice, the signal that something was not as they expected it to be.

Like he normally did, he drove the carriage slowly around the corner.

One rap hit the roof. Creed had spotted something.

Heath drew the curtain aside and noticed a woman standing in deep shadow, holding an infant. Poor thing, her heart had to be breaking.

Clearly this was not the woman who had been sending the notes, nor was this the child they were supposed to rescue. They had been told to expect to take a three-year-old girl.

The doll Creed had purchased to comfort the girl lay beside Heath's knee.

There was nothing for it but to help this woman first.

He opened the door and stepped down from the carriage in a swirl of fog. His boots clicked on the stones.

The hood of the woman's cloak hid some of her face. White mist obscured the rest.

Funny, but she did not run away from him. She simply stood and stared, first at Creed, only partly visible atop the carriage, then back at him.

She cast a glance over her shoulder. This smelled of a trap, but she was holding a baby. A woman would never let her child be used as bait.

In any case, if she did need help, he could hardly run away and leave her to her fate.

He motioned for her to come. This was where he expected to have to give chase. He'd yet to meet a woman who willingly went with the Abductor.

Why did she not run? She simply stood her ground, hugging the baby to her chest.

It wasn't smart to come this close to the building. For the moment the guards were nowhere in sight but they might come around the corner at any moment.

But he needed to get them into the coach before the informer came out with the little girl.

It would be impossible to rescue them all at one time.

His heart began to thud. His breath came in short, hard pants while sweat dampened his collar and hat brim.

If it came to choosing one child's life over another? No, he could not possibly. He might be doing God's work but he was not the Almighty, and to pick who would survive and who might not?

It was not a choice he could make and so he continued with the deliverance set before him.

He ran hard toward the woman.

She ought to be turning now, to flee from the masked

monster bearing down upon her, his cape flapping like great wings of evil.

Why was she standing her ground? Why had she looked over her shoulder earlier?

From the corner of his eye he saw Creed leap down from the carriage. There could be no reason for that except that he sensed or saw something wrong.

If there was risk, there was nothing he could do about it now. He focused on one goal—getting the woman and the baby to safety.

Once he had them inside he'd need to convince the frightened mother he meant her no harm, and he'd need to do it before the informer brought out the child.

He was not leaving one of them behind.

Clementine needed to scream. To drop the doll and run away, to vanish into the fog.

Out of the mist Evil ran toward her. His dark coat lashed at the mist like wings of death. His boots slapped the stones and brought him closer at a fearful speed.

Run! Run! Run! Everything within her needed to, but...

He is only a man, she recited over and over, *no matter how wicked, still only skin and bones.* And the police were just behind her, unseen around the corner.

Close now—so close she heard his ragged breathing.

He was upon her, reaching for the doll.

Cradling it to his chest as he was, he would know it was not real and that a trap had been sprung upon him.

He shouted at the man racing toward him on a run, warned him to get back. He reached for her hood, yanked it back in the same instant she grasped his mask.

His curse shook the quiet of deep night.

That voice! She recognized it even before the mask fell away from his eyes.

Time slowed. Seconds moved as if wading through mud.

The doll fell from his fingers, shattered on the cobblestones.

She stared at Heath's face, which was frozen in horror, the mask slowly drifting to the pavement, his features dumbfounded.

Helpless to prevent it, she watched while the constables pounced upon him, beat him with their fists and kicked him in the belly and ribs.

She screamed his name.

Creed grabbed her about the waist, lifted her off her feet and carried her away. He shoved her inside the carriage and then climbed on top.

The carriage jolted forward. She grabbed the doorknob, found it locked from the outside.

She heard gunfire, a crack when the shot hit cobblestone.

The driver took a corner so fast the left wheels lifted off the ground.

Eventually the shots grew distant. She collapsed on the floor, weeping.

Heath—not Heath. It could not be! The man she loved was—

No! Not him! But she'd ripped the mask from his face with her own fingers.

All the things she'd said! Called the Abductor a fiend, a monster. All this time she'd been loving the most despicable of the wicked. Had wanted to bear his children!

Her heart fell out of her, shattered on the carriage floor. At that moment she did not even care to pick it up.

Her sanctuary—her children's home! Heath had agreed to it without a single argument. Had it been because he intended to harm the little ones she was protecting, right under her watch?

But no. The husband she knew would never do it. He was a good man, a loving man.

Who had disappeared in the night without explanation.

But his nephew adored him. Would not his innocent instincts have warned him away from a demon?

And Creed! His accomplice was carrying her away from—not to—Fencroft House. They had passed by the house moments ago and were now out on the public highway.

What did he mean to do with her, a witness to the evil he was a part of?

He must intend something dire.

And a part of her didn't care.

It was an hour before the coach slowed down. An hour in which her joints ached from the constant jouncing and her stomach grew nauseous.

One horrid, unholy hour in which she wanted to die rather than remember what had just happened.

In her mind she relived her moments with Heath. Not for one small second had she suspected him of being the Abductor. No, she'd wondered if he was trying to capture the—

The fiend—it was what she had believed about the man—but Heath?

If there was one person in the world she had trusted as much as she did Grandfather it had been her husband.

Yes, she'd known he was keeping a secret. He had admitted he was—but this?

She could make no sense of it—or of anything. She was Alice fallen through the looking glass, not knowing up from down, large from small.

But mostly she could not tell virtue from wickedness,

because when she thought of her husband, all she felt was love.

Clearly she was the worst sort of person. She ought to be cursing him, hating him, but instead she was worried about him. The way the guards had been pummeling him, he must be injured.

It made sense now, why he wanted to keep her away from Slademore House. It had nothing to do with the danger the area presented. It had to do with the danger he presented to it. He did not want her to be near the scene of his crimes. To somehow suspect what he was up to.

Nothing made a bit of sense.

Oh, but her eyes hurt. She touched the skin around them. It was going to take a week for the swelling to go down, but only if she quit weeping.

And that was not something she thought she would ever manage.

This whole thing was very wrong, and yet it hadn't been an unknown monster behind the mask. It had been the husband she was bound to by the deepest of connections.

No matter how she tried—and over the past hour she had tried—she could not hate him. That emotion and Heath were like mismatched puzzle pieces that would not come together.

The latch on the outside of the door twisted. Creed stepped inside and sat down across from her, his expression grim.

"I suppose you mean to toss me in the river."

"Aye, well, I can understand why you might think so." He shook his head. "But no. I mean you no harm, Lady Fencroft."

"Why then have you kidnapped me?"

"I want to show you where we take the children, so you'll understand."

"I fear that is something I would rather not know."

He opened the door and stepped out. She might have taken that moment to try to dash past him, but the area beyond looked darkly wooded and seemed more perilous than remaining with Creed did.

"I suggest you get some sleep. We've still a long ride to the coast. I promise, once we get there you will know the truth about Lord Fencroft."

The cell was not completely dark, but dim enough that Heath could not see the source of the scurrying noises in the straw bed on the far side of the space.

While he could not see the condition of the mound, the ripe smell coming from it indicated it had not been changed in some time.

The stones he huddled upon were cold, but he wouldn't have to share them with rats—or with the many men bedding on the pile before him.

He crossed his arms around his drawn-up knees in an attempt to gather a degree of warmth in his core.

Leaning his head back against the wall, he wanted to pound it on the stones, but the pain would be too great. There was not a part of his body not bruised or battered.

His heart hurt worst of all. He'd thought he might be caught one day, but by his own wife?

She must think him the devil. He did not believe she expected him to be the one behind the mask. She'd have never lain with him, shared her body and risked bearing his child had she suspected him of this villainy.

Remembering her expression when the mask fell away from his face, he wanted to do more than bang his injured skull against the wall. The hurt, the utter shock he'd seen in her eyes made him want to quit breathing altogether.

What happened tonight was completely his fault.

Had he quit being the Abductor, this would not have happened.

Had he told Clementine the truth, this would not have happened.

But what would have happened?

For one, the last baby he took to the cottage would have died. The poor wee thing was barely breathing when Creed got her to the doctor. What kind of foul person was Slademore for not seeing to her health? The kind who counted it a waste of money to get medical help for a fragile infant, was what kind.

Another thing that might have happened was that his wife would have managed to get herself involved. No, not might. She would have. Clearly, forbidding the woman to do something was useless.

Had he told her the truth, at some point, she would be condemned along with him.

He allowed himself the luxury of cursing under his breath. The sixth Earl of Fencroft had handily brought the estate to ruin, so it hardly mattered whether or not a few shocking words passed his lips.

Having it happen the way it had, being turned in by his own wife, was for the best. Clementine was not going to suffer for his crime.

Not in a legal sense at any rate. He'd quite ruined her besides that. What if she was with child? Would he have destroyed his own child's future for the sake of other children's?

James Macooish was going to be unhappy. The man had given him his granddaughter in the firm belief that a title would protect her and her children. How wrong he had been.

In the end it was his wealth that would do it. It was a lucky thing he'd made the financial deal in Scotland;

the family would need it now that Heath had ruined the Fencroft name.

Now he did thump his head against the wall. The intense pain shattering his brain was easier to take than the agonizing grief ripping through him. He wasn't sure he could live through the despair of knowing the next time he saw his bride it would be at his trial.

Try as he might not to imagine the way her gaze would settle upon him in cold loathing, he could not help seeing it.

In case his misery was not past the breaking point, he worried about the small girl he had failed to rescue. Because of his failure she would grow up under the hand of Garrett Slademore. Would she even survive his neglect?

Now that the Abductor was in jail and Slademore the free man, how many children would suffer, perhaps even die because of it?

At least Creed was free. There was some hope to be found there. With the coachman's knowledge of the informer he might be able to find her. If he could convince her to tell what she knew, her testimony might be enough to put Slademore right here beside him.

Heath could do what he felt like—shout, curse and rail—but all it would accomplish would be to make his head hurt. Weeping for his loss would gain him nothing, either.

There was only one thing left to do. He bent his head and prayed.

The jailer's keys rattled in the lock. He didn't bother to look up. The fellow was no doubt here to deliver another blow or dash a bucket of cold water on him.

The Abductor was so hated that rules of decent behavior were ignored when it came to him.

The door screeched when it opened, groaned when it closed.

"It appears you will have need of these, son."

Heath jerked his head up. Pain shot through it.

"Mr. Macooish," he gasped, feeling dizzy, nauseous.

"Grandfather, you mean."

He tried to stand but the old man shook his head, sat down on the filthy floor beside him and gently placed blankets over his back.

"You don't look good, my boy." For a man his age, his fingers were strong. They gripped Heath's chin, turning his face, examining it. "I'll have a doctor here at first light."

"They'll never allow it. I cannot believe they let you in the cell, let alone with blankets."

"Everyone appreciates money, especially when they don't have to go to the trouble to earn it. You can expect to be treated decently now."

"If you knew to find me here, you'll know why."

"I know what they say, but I'm a good judge of character. I'd never have given you my Clemmie if I thought ill of you."

"Did she make it home?"

He shook his head. "But I think she's safe enough."

"How can you be sure?"

"A pair of constables banged on the door of Fencroft House looking for Clementine and told your poor sister why. Olivia rushed to my apartment ready to swoon, which I think is unlike her."

He cursed. It was a good thing Macooish didn't seem to mind; he did it again with even more vehemence.

"I don't believe it, but the police fear she's been kidnapped by your man, Creed. That he means to do her harm because of what she knows."

"If she's with Creed she is safe. I wonder why he did not bring her straight home, though?"

"A good and sensible fellow like him? He'd want to shield her from police banging away on the door in the dead of the night."

Grandfather removed a cloth from his coat pocket and unwrapped a small loaf of bread. "Can you eat?"

He shook his head but took the offered loaf.

"You don't believe I'm the scourge of London's helpless?"

"Tear me off half of that loaf and tell me about this Abductor. Who is he really?"

The sun was coming up. Clementine watched the light around the curtains grow steadily brighter.

Fresh sea air filled the cab. When the carriage stopped she heard the sound of waves crashing on the shore a short distance away.

"And who have ye brought me this time, Mr. Creed?" The door opened. A round, pleasant-looking face peered at her, smiling kindly. "Oh, you poor wee dearie. It appears you've been through an ordeal."

"More than you can guess, Mrs. Pierce," Creed said. It was a good thing he had a firm hand under Clementine's arm. Her legs were nearly too weak to bear her down the carriage steps. "This is Lady Fencroft. She has just seen Lord Fencroft beaten and arrested."

"Arrested!" The woman clutched her apron and backed up several steps as if she had been struck. "No—that can't be true!"

Her wail of despair brought another woman scurrying from the house, a baby at her breast in an interrupted feeding.

"Something has happened to Lord Fencroft?" she gasped.

A boy dashed around the corner of the charming cottage with a great smile on his face. Seeing the women crying, he nearly tripped over his feet. "Where is m'lord?"

"Arrested." Mrs. Pierce dabbed her eyes with the corner of her apron. "In London."

"At Slademore House?" the child gasped, his face turning pale.

"I'm afraid so, Georgie."

"Take me back, sir." The boy dashed past her and climbed into the carriage. "I'll set him free."

"Who are all of you?" Clementine asked, looking from face to face. Whoever they were, they appeared to be as devastated as she was over what had happened. "What have you to do with my husband?"

"I'm Ginny Sawyer. We all, each and every one of us, owe him everything," the young woman sniffled.

"I don't understand." Perhaps she had fallen through the rabbit hole after all.

"Walk to the cliffs with me and I'll explain it," she said, taking a deep breath, steadying her voice.

Moments later Clementine stood on a bluff overlooking the ocean. There was not much of a beach below. Waves crashed on rocks instead of sand. A spray of cold salt water dampened her face.

Thousands of miles west of this spot, waves would be breaking on a wide swathe of warm sand, gently rolling ashore and probably tickling someone's toes.

She was going home. Grandfather might stay and wait for Madeline, but she was going home.

No doubt she would have to remain long enough to testify at the trial, but once she survived doing it, she would book a passage to America.

"You believe your man did this thing? Hurt children?" the young woman asked, holding her infant close to her heart.

"I hardly know what I think. But I'm the one who ripped the mask off his face. I'm the one who made sure the police were there to witness it. I did not expect to find Lord Fencroft—" Her throat closed up, too dry to utter another word.

"It was a brave thing for you to do, my lady. I do recall how I feared for my life when he grabbed my Clara out of my arms. Oh, he was a wicked sight to be sure."

She did not look frightened talking about it now.

"You escaped him, you and your child?" Clearly she had.

"Something like that, my lady. Lord Fencroft lured me to the carriage with my baby in his arms. I wasn't going to let him take her, now, was I?"

"But he didn't harm you?"

"No, he saved my life and Clara's." She hugged the baby tighter. "I didn't know the place I was going to leave her at was so awful."

"Slademore House?" Clementine asked, but where else could she be speaking of?

The young woman shivered, hugged the baby tighter. "It's run by the devil, I've come to learn. Some of the wee ones don't survive the place and the ones that do are treated horribly. Did you know that the baron gives more care to his little dog than to the children he is supposed to be sheltering?"

Oh, she did recall that dog. How his collar had glittered with jewels. How at her ball Slademore had fed his pet quail and caviar.

"But I spent time with the children there. They were well cared for." She had seen it with her own eyes. "They were well dressed and had lovely rooms to sleep in. There were toys and a beautiful yard for them to play in."

And there were calluses on the children's fingers.

"Georgie will tell you that was but a masquerade. Lord Fencroft rescued him from the place. He says they were forced to act at being happy when benefactors came to visit. He didn't mind it so much since it gave him a few hours away from work. They got biscuits, honey and cream during those times."

Clementine felt suddenly dizzy because she did remember those treats being served. She also remembered that the toys had looked new and unused.

An image came to mind. The red-haired child hiding in the garden, the nurse she'd never seen before escorting him to the gate.

This was all true!

Heath was an innocent man, a hero. It shamed her to have doubted him for even a second.

"Would you be willing to come back to London with me? Tell the police that you were not kidnapped?"

"Unless I'm wrong, Mrs. Pierce will be loading up the carriage with all who will fit. My guess is that Mr. Creed is changing out the team with rested horses as we speak."

"Thank you. I'm more grateful than I can say."

"It's all of us who are the grateful ones. If your good husband had not forced me into the carriage, I'd have thrown myself into the Thames. It's what I planned on doing after giving over my daughter. But—" She turned, indicated the cottage above with a wave of her hand. "This is the safest place I have ever lived. All of us love Lord Fencroft deeply."

Chapter Sixteen

Clementine sat up on top with Creed, the cab of the carriage being packed with witnesses to Heath's innocence.

The chill of the autumn afternoon made her shiver, and she shrank into Creed's heavy coat. She had tried to refuse it but discovered him to be a strong-willed man. Just now she was grateful he'd insisted because the temperature was falling quickly.

"I imagine they cannot accuse my husband of a crime if no crime has been committed," she stated hopefully.

"I'm afraid it won't be so easy as all that. The perceived crime is a heinous one. These are witnesses, yes, but they are children and poor women."

"There's you, Creed."

"And I'll say what I can, but if they don't believe these—" he patted the roof of the carriage "—they won't believe me. I'm involved in all this, aye? As guilty of the crimes as Lord Fencroft is."

"So you will be arrested if you speak for him?"

"I'll be arrested before I speak for him, my lady. As soon as they see the coach coming."

"I'll vow you did not kidnap me. As Countess of Fencroft my position should be of help. But still, I think perhaps it would be best if you remain at Fencroft House until the truth is revealed."

"Your position is a high one, my lady, but you are the wife of the prisoner. They'll take my word before yours." He shook his head. "We'd need half of London town, I'm afraid, to make the constables give ear to what we have to say."

"All right, then, so we shall."

"Lady Guthrie," the butler stated, "is not at home."

"Inform her that Lady Fencroft requests a moment of her time."

Either the butler did not recognize her or he did but chose not to acknowledge her. One or both could be the case. She did look like life had stomped on her. Her appearance was a mess. By now she was certainly an object of contempt among peers and commoners.

They would be thinking she was unwise, pitiful even to have married such a man. Some would think she was in league with his crimes. Others would consider her an utter turncoat for betraying her husband.

There would even be those who would have expected nothing else from an American bride.

Judging by the scowl on the butler's face he believed all four things to be true.

She glanced at the carriage waiting beside the curb and nodded to Creed.

He smiled, got down from his perch and then opened the door. For a man facing extreme peril he seemed awfully confident.

Everyone, from Mrs. Pierce to the youngest child, emerged from the coach and joined her on the porch.

"Inform the duchess she has visitors."

"As I said, Lady Guthrie is not at home."

With an arrogantly blank expression, the butler began to close the door.

Why, the churl!

She slapped her hand on the door, preventing it from closing, and stepped inside.

"Come along," she smiled encouragingly at the group because they did look ill at ease to be walking boldly into the elegant foyer.

The butler attempted to prevent her progress by stepping in front of her. She neatly went around him, her wide-eyed flock following in her righteous wake.

"You need not accompany us," she said with a backward glance at the red-faced servant. "I know my way to the tearoom."

It was a breach of the worst sort to rush in unannounced but with Heath's life at stake she did not care.

"Lady Fencroft?" The duchess set down her tea cup. One of her guests dropped hers. The expensive porcelain shattered on the stone floor.

The butler sailed into the room, red-faced and arms waving madly. "I beg your pardon, my lady, but the woman and her ruffians stole past me. Shall I summon a constable?"

"Smythe, inform the kitchen that there will be a dozen more for tea." Lady Guthrie stood, opened her arms.

Clementine rushed into them and all at once her tears began all over again.

"I'm so sorry I forced you into this, my dear, had I any idea—"

"Might I speak?" Mrs. Pierce interrupted. "Me and little Georgie?"

It was highly improper for a commoner to interrupt a duchess, but it only spoke of the desperation of the matter at hand.

"I've something to say, as well," Creed declared.

"As do I," Ginny Sawyer added.

"Come along." Lady Guthrie led the way out of the tearoom, leaving her guests with their mouths open in astonishment.

She led them to the parlor, indicating that those there was room for should sit. The butler followed, his puckered mouth showing his disapproval of their presence.

"You may all speak," Lady Guthrie said. Clementine noted that she stood and allowed three children to take her chair.

Clearly, a true lady did not gain that status by title alone.

One by one, each of them told how they had never been kidnapped, but rather rescued.

"Won't you help us free m'lord?" Little Georgie wiped his nose on his sleeve. "They, the constables, I mean, won't listen to us all on our own."

Lady Guthrie patted Georgie's head. "I dare say they will not. Smythe order my carriage at once."

"But Lady Guthrie!" he gasped.

"Snobbery does not become you, Smythe. Order the carriage, then go to the kitchen and have Cook pack up a meal for the children."

Heath's cell was not so far from the front of the police station that he could not hear his sister's voice.

"I demand to be allowed to see my brother."

"It is against the rules."

What was she doing here? No one detested the Abductor more than she did.

"Then I insist on speaking to someone above you. Someone who has the power to set aside a small rule."

"Lady Shaw, you must understand that Lord Fencroft is awaiting charges for a heinous crime."

"Which he did not commit."

"He was caught in the very act. Exposed by Lady Fencroft, who is now missing."

He could only hope that she stayed missing. That wherever Creed had taken her was where she would remain. The last thing he wanted was for her to become involved in all this.

Now that she knew him to be the most wicked of the depraved, she probably would stay as far from London as she could. He hoped Creed had taken her to Derbyshire.

And yet, a part of him wished that somehow she would feel his innocence. That she would trust him enough to see beyond what appeared to be true. That she would come to him in spite of everything.

That she would love him in the face of what appeared to be the unshakable truth, that it would be her love for him that would be unshakable.

Which, of course, was unreasonable to expect.

At least Grandfather believed him. The old fellow had remained in his cell until dawn. For a man having two granddaughters missing, he seemed unflinching in his belief that all would be well.

"If you do not let me speak to someone who can do something, it will be at the cost of your position." Olivia's voice sounded mild given what she was saying.

"There is no one who will let you back there. The man is dangerous. We have men searching the Thames for Lady Fencroft's body as we speak."

"As much as I appreciate the effort, you may quit looking, for here I am."

Clementine!

"I insist upon seeing Lord Fencroft."

Heath shot to his feet, gripped the iron bars. For all

that he yearned to see her, he did not want her here. She could not be seen to be supporting him.

"I do not know how many times I must repeat that no one may see him."

Not without a bribe, clearly, since Grandfather had spent the night with him on the cold stone floor.

"May not his wife see him, Officer Jones? In consideration of my Christmas donation to the Police League, you might feel more kindly toward the favor."

Lady Guthrie? What was happening out there?

"I demand to see my husband."

What was she doing? Throwing herself into the pit with him? There was no reason for it.

Except for love. There was that reason.

"No!" he shouted but voices were rising in the outer room and he doubted anyone heard him.

Seconds later, Officer Jones unlocked the cell door, secured handcuffs about his wrists and led him toward the growing commotion.

The light out here was bright compared to what it had been in his cell. He blinked, trying to bring the figures filling the room into focus.

Before his eyes adjusted to the change, he felt arms wrap around him, hug him tight.

"I know you are innocent of it all," Clementine whispered.

"You believe it, or know it?"

"Here! You cannot touch the prisoner!"

"Both," she said while the policeman tried to peel her fingers from his shirt.

"Take your hands off my wife." He shoved the fellow with his shoulder, breaking the contact.

"It's against the rules for anyone to touch a prisoner," Officer Jones complained while rubbing his arm.

"I find that I am quite weary of rules!" Lady Guthrie bustled forward. "This man has not committed a crime. You must set him free this moment."

"Meaning no disrespect, but his crime was one of the most wicked we've ever seen. Not even your position can free him."

"Nonsense." Lady Guthrie extended her hand, palm up. "Where are the keys to the cuffs?"

"If he's found innocent, he will be released then."

He wouldn't be, Heath knew. This separation from everyone he loved would be permanent.

As he gazed at the group of children and adults from Rock Rose Cottage who were gathered in the small room, his heart rolled over. He could scarce believe they had come all the way from the seaside to support him.

Looking at them, seeing the children alive and healthy, he knew the price he was about to pay was worth it.

"There was no crime committed, sir."

"And who are you?"

"Ginny Sawyer. It was reported that I was kidnapped, me and my babe. As you can see, we were not."

"Sawyer? But—he was seen taking you."

"That was an assumption. In truth I went willingly. Lord Fencroft has given me and these others a home at his cottage near Folkestone, and all out of the goodness of his kind heart."

"What does he hold over you that you would defend him?" the constable gripping the keys asked in a rough voice. "Everyone knows the Abductor has a black soul."

"Officer, tell me, how many have been kidnapped?" Clementine suddenly sounded as regal, as in command, as Lady Guthrie did. In the midst of everything, he was proud of her.

"Eleven, my lady."

"And how many in this room will avow they were not kidnapped?" She tapped the toe of her boot on the floor, crossed her arms over her chest and speared Officer Jones with "the look."

"Thirteen," Mrs. Pierce said. "Two of them were rescued while Baron Slademore's guards were busy at dice, so they never noticed."

"The charges must be dropped." Clementine slipped under the cuffs. She pressed her back to his chest, clearly daring Jones to extricate her. "All those assumed to be victims were not."

"Which means there is no Abductor," Olivia declared, clutching the hand of four-year-old Julie Anne, who seemed on the verge of weeping out loud. "I told you he was innocent! Unlock these cuffs at once."

Maybe he wouldn't get out of here, but having his wife and his sister support him meant the world.

"A formal charge is about to be filed. It's not for me to dismiss it. This is a matter for Judge Harlow to determine and I imagine he's at home having dinner with his family."

"He was," came a disgruntled-sounding voice from someone pushing through the crowd.

"It was kind of you to leave your meal in the name of justice." Lady Guthrie acknowledged the judge with a nod.

The short, round judge didn't miss many meals, Heath decided. He also hadn't come out of any sense of justice, but because James Macooish had escorted him here.

It was Grandfather's opinion that money could influence anyone to do what was honorable. But it was more than that. He had a manner about him that made people do what he wanted, and oftentimes with a smile.

That was why the doctor had tended his wounds this

morning and why the judge was standing here listening to half a dozen people claim they had not been kidnapped.

Some were too young to speak the words, so Mrs. Pierce did it for them, recounting in detail the circumstances of each rescue.

"I would have died if the earl hadn't taken me. And Baby Millie, too, but Mrs. Pierce wouldn't have it and so she lived." It warmed Heath to hear the shy cook from Rock Rose Cottage speak up for him.

"My ma died, sir. I was cast out from where we lived and then Baron Slademore—" Georgie sniffled loudly. "I don't know what would have become of me if it weren't for Lord Fencroft taking me away."

"Humph—hand me the keys, Mr. Jones."

"But, Your Honor! We've finally got him."

"Got who?" The judge unlocked the cuffs with his own pudgy hands. "There's not a soul who was reported to have been kidnapped who claims they were. In every case the supposed victim is right here in this room and clearly of their own free will."

"But the public wants his blood."

"The public be hanged. I will not charge a man for kidnapping when no one was abducted."

"And you will inform the press of this development?" Lady Guthrie said.

"Ah, well, they are gathering on the pavement as we speak. Macooish and I had to push past them."

"Take the children out the back door," Heath said to Olivia and Lady Guthrie. "I would not have them put through an ordeal."

"We will take my carriage," Lady Guthrie said.

Olivia, still holding Julie Anne's hand, scooped up a small boy. "We will meet you at home, Heath."

In a moment the room was empty of everyone but

Clementine. Tears shimmered in her eyes and he was undone.

He had been given a great gift. A miraculous reprieve.

The only thing he wanted of life was to live it. But this business was not yet finished.

As soon as they came outside Creed was waiting with the carriage.

"I'll take you home," Heath said and kissed her quickly. "But Creed and I need to go out."

"I think not." Her eyebrows lifted and she speared him with the look. "I only now got you back and I will not be left behind."

"Slademore House, aye?" said Creed.

The unmarked Fencroft carriage rolled along the streets of the West End.

Clementine snuggled under Heath's solid arm while they made slow progress toward Slademore House.

She drew back the curtain to peer at the buildings they passed by. Cold, white moonlight shone down to illuminate things better left unseen.

"I suppose there might be frost by morning," she commented. "And there's a woman in that doorway shivering under a blanket."

Heath caught her hand, drew it away from the window and held it close to his heart. "Best to keep the curtain down. That woman who looks like she's in distress might be bait for a crime. I've seen it before."

She sighed and leaned back against the cushion. There had been no time to talk about what had happened—how he felt about her exposing him. If he was resentful over her betrayal it didn't show.

Of course, she'd had no idea it was him she was unmasking.

Later, they would talk. Once this business of shutting down Slademore House was accomplished, they would need to make things right between them. They were solid, yes, but still a bit raw.

"Do you have a plan for getting the children out?"

Tonight's undertaking, the rescue of so many little ones at once, was going to be beyond difficult. She couldn't imagine how it was to be safely carried out.

It would be one thing if Slademore had already been exposed. But he had not and in the eyes of the law, he was an innocent man. They were breaking into his orphanage.

She prayed the next hour wouldn't see them in the custody of the law again.

He shook his head. "I will, once we get there. Something will present itself."

"I hope we have enough blankets." There were a dozen stacked on the floor, which they had collected from Fencroft House before setting out.

"There's one thing, Clementine. I need you to remain in the coach." He took her chin between his fingers, turned her face toward him and gave her a quick kiss. "Please promise you will."

"But the children know me. If they see you they might think the Abductor has come to carry them off. I can calm them and keep them quiet."

"You can calm them once they are in the carriage."

The coach slowed down and stopped. Clementine felt the rocking when Creed stepped down.

"The guards are in their usual positions," he said, coming inside and closing the door after him.

"The news about my release won't be widely known yet, so that's good. Slademore won't suspect anything more than our usual work."

"We'll need to do something about the guards or we'll

never get inside." Creed drew the curtain aside an inch. "I wish we could have made contact with our informer."

"Informer?" Clementine asked.

"Yes, a woman, but we never saw her. She'd have someone deliver notes to Creed when she wanted to sneak a child to safety, tell us when to be here. We suspect she lives at Slademore House."

"We'll need her, aye? To tell what she knows. There's Georgie but he's only a child and his word won't hold up against the baron's."

"No. And the nurse, Mrs. Hoper, she'll side with the baron."

"But no one knows what she looks like? I must have seen her."

"Small," Creed said. "Waifish is all I was told."

"Lettie!" It had to be. "Did she give you an infant?"

Heath nodded. "The babe was sick but Mrs. Pierce and the doctor brought her through."

"I'm so relieved to hear it. It was Lettie, then. One day she had a baby and the next she did not. And of the ones caring for the children, she seemed the kindest to them."

"Now that we know," Creed said, "what are we to do about it?"

"I'll go in. I can convince her to help me sneak the children away."

"You will remain here."

"Have you a better plan, my lord?" Creed asked.

Apparently not, since he stared mutely at the two of them.

"You—" he gave her a stern look "—will stay beside me at all times."

She would do her best, of course. But events might unfold in a way to make it impossible.

Luckily his attention turned to Creed's role before she was forced to give her word on that.

"You'll get the children into the coach as we bring them out? Keep them as quiet as you can?"

"First I'll have a *game* or two of chance with the guards—offer them a drink." Creed withdrew a silver flask from his coat. Waggled it back and forth. "Afterward, it should be safe for you to sneak inside."

"Will that work?" Clementine did not know a great deal about spirits, but she was fairly certain there was not enough in there to put a bird to sleep, let alone a pair of full-grown men.

"Oh, it will, aye. It's a recipe of me mum's. The canny woman's deflected the attentions of a few untoward men in her time."

The coachman got out of the carriage and walked around the corner, making it appear that he had come from the front of the building.

Peeking out the window, she saw him show the men a deck of cards. When they were seated he offered them a few gulps from the flask.

It only took a moment for the guards to slump sideways.

"Let's go." Heath grabbed her hand.

"Ouch!" Clementine whispered as they crept along the back wall bordering the garden. "You are crushing my fingers."

It was true, he was. While she had not said outright that she would not stay beside him every second, there had been a telling look on her face. A quick sideward glance that indicated she had her own opinion on the matter.

"Sorry." He bent down and gave her a quick kiss but only loosened his grip a little.

"I'm sorry, too." She stood still, halting his progress toward the gate. "For getting you beaten up by the constables—I had no idea it was you."

"I should have told you. It was my fault."

He urged her farther along the wall. The guards would not sleep forever and he had no idea how many children would need to be taken to the coach.

"I would have kept your secret, you know."

He glanced over his shoulder at her. "It wasn't that—I knew you would. I didn't want you implicated."

"Just being married to you, I'm already implicated in everything you do."

"You know, that's the only reason it took me so long to—" He stood suddenly still. "What was that noise?"

It was barely discernible even though the night was unusually quiet. No breeze, no crickets this time of year and, oddly, no drunken revelry to block the faint sound of—

"Singing," Clementine said. "A lullaby."

He tried the latch on the gate.

"You'll have to hoist me over so I can open it."

"No." The last thing he was going to do was allow her to be on the other side without him.

"One of us needs to open the gate and I can't lift you."

Heath made a sound.

"You are good at that."

"What?"

"Uttering curses under your breath."

With no help for it, he cupped his hands for her to step into.

"Don't get hung up on your skirt and don't take a step away from the gate until I come over."

"All right." She stepped onto his hand. He pushed her up and over she went.

"Open up," he whispered as soon as her boots hit grass.

"I can't. There's a padlock and I don't see a key."

"Are there any rocks it could be hidden under?"

"Only ones too small—but that's Lettie singing. I can see her under a tree toward the front of the yard. I'm going to see if she'll help."

"Do not—" It was too late. Even if she had been willing to obey his order, she was already too far away to hear the rest of it.

Because she was singing to the fretful baby, Lettie would not hear Clementine's footsteps. The last thing she wanted was to startle the girl and cause her to scream.

Clementine did not have a lovely singing voice, so she began to hum the tune Lettie sang in the hope that joining in would seem friendly.

She came forward slowly.

Lettie continued to sing when she looked up. When her gaze settled on Clementine, her eyes popped open wide in surprise.

"What are you doing here in the middle of the night, my lady?"

"Looking for you, actually...if you are the one who has been sending notes to Creed."

"If I was, why would you be looking for me?"

"Because you know what is happening here. I believe you want to help."

"Please go home. You ought not to be here."

"We are taking the children away tonight. Will you help us?"

"All of them?" Lettie stood up, cradling the fretful bundle to her chest. "How? And who is with you?"

"Lord Fencroft and Creed are outside the gate, ready with the carriage."

"Yes, then. I'll help." She nodded toward the back of

the house and began to walk toward it. "This will be risky. Are you certain?"

"Quite."

"Is it Lord Fencroft who is the Abductor, then?"

"I thought perhaps you knew, since you sent the notes."

"I knew Mr. Creed, recognized him right off. I'd seen him before—he's a hard man to forget, if you take my meaning. But your husband was always wearing that fearful mask and cape."

"Oh, he's not a bit fearful without it." Not even when he was acting beastly. "Is the baby ill?"

Lettie nodded. "It's why we were outside. The baron is here tonight. I didn't want him to know the child is sick."

"Shouldn't he summon the doctor?"

"He will, sometimes, if the child is older and likely to survive. But he believes infants are frail, and spending money on them is futile. I do what I can but sometimes it isn't enough."

Oh, but she wanted to stomp up the stairs and give the baron a piece of her mind, or her fist. What kind of black-hearted soul would refuse aid to a sick infant?

Slademore was no better than a killer.

Lettie withdrew a set of keys from her pocket, taking care that they did not jingle. "The baron is restless tonight."

"It's no wonder with the guilt he must carry."

"I don't believe he does." She took off her shoes, indicated for Clementine to do the same and then unlocked the door.

"It's only a bit of luck I have the keys. Mrs. Hoper keeps them locked up tight," she whispered. "But I know where and I took them because of the baby."

The hallway Lettie led her down smelled dank. No wonder the baby was sick if this was the air it was breathing.

They went down a short flight of stairs. The only light coming in was what moonlight shone through the door Lettie left standing open.

She unlocked another door and handed her the infant. The sound of a match striking seemed louder than it ought to, the lantern blazing to life brighter.

Lettie knelt beside a bed with four children packed into it.

"Lawrence, Mary…wake up. We are going on an adventure, but we must be very silent and brave."

It took only a minute to get the children gathered by the door.

"Will the key work for the gate?"

She shook her head. "The baron keeps that one at night. We don't dare go out the front, though, so we'll have to hand them over the wall."

Lettie began to hurry the children out the door.

"Wait! There's two babies left behind."

"We'll have to come back for them. Our arms are full as it is."

It was true. Lettie carried three toddlers in her arms. Clementine could barely manage the sick baby and a one-year-old in hers.

With Lettie at the head of the line and her at the back they led the children out.

Heath must have brought the carriage close to the fence. He and Creed were crouched on something tall, looking ready to leap into the yard.

She'd done it! Somehow Clementine and the other woman had managed to bring the children without being discovered.

Heath watched them rush silently across the yard, their

bare feet padding across the damp grass and the hems of their sleeping gowns getting wet.

The woman—Lettie, he thought Clementine had called her—got to the fence first. Leaning over the edge, Creed plucked up the three children she carried, one by one. He took them down into the carriage and then within seconds was back helping Heath pull more of them up.

Clementine placed the children she carried into Lettie's arms. She spun about and then, rather than handing up another child, she ran back toward the dark house.

Except that it wasn't dark. Someone was up. Heath saw a shadowed figure carrying a lantern from window to window.

Tall and lean, hunched slightly at the shoulders, the figure resembled the Grim Reaper. Judging by the advancing glow, Slademore was taking a hallway close to the entrance that Clementine had just disappeared into.

Lettie, seeing the same thing he did, gasped. "She's gone for the last two babies. She'll never get them out in time."

Clementine saw lantern light coming from the hallway one floor up. Her only hope was that whoever it was would trip on something and be slowed down.

But she was not turning back and leaving the infants behind.

The children's cell—and that was what it was more than a bedroom—was now in complete darkness. She had to feel her way to the back where the cribs were.

There! Her fingers brushed a warm cheek. She gathered the child into the crook of her arm.

Feeling her way along the wall, she knocked something over. It clattered on the floor.

The light was now in the hallway outside the door, illuminating the other crib. When she picked up the second baby, it began to cry.

If there had been any hope of hiding, or escaping the room undetected, it was gone.

Please! Please! Please let it be Mrs. Hoper carrying the lantern.

Clementine got as far as the doorway before the baron's shadow, looking long and distorted, spread over the stone floor in the hallway.

"Lady Fencroft?" He set the lantern down. The lamp's glow shadowed his face in streaks of orange and red, casting him as the devil he was and not the angel of mercy most people believed him to be. "What are you doing here?"

He glanced past her into the cell. She tried to step around him but he blocked her way. It looked like his face was on fire as his expression flashed from surprise to accusation and then to menace, all in the space of a second.

"Where are the rest of my children?" He reached for her, as if he intended to take the crying baby. She swung away.

"Stand aside." She lifted her chin and looked down her nose at him.

He chuckled under his breath. "I will say, I never expected the Abductor to be Fencroft and his wife. But wait! The kidnappings began before you came to London. Can I assume you are his spy?"

"You can assume to spend the rest of your life in prison for what you have done to the children you were supposed to be caring for."

"But I was caring for them. If I made a bit of money from the arrangement? It's my due." His grin might be the single most wicked thing she had seen in her life. "Now, you will give me the babies."

He took a step forward. She took two steps back.

"I'll use force if need be. I promise you, my fist will not discriminate between their flesh and yours."

He balled up his hand and began a downward swing. She fell on her knees, hunching over the infants, shielding them from the promised blows with her head and shoulders.

She heard a furious roar. Felt air rush past the back of her head but not an explosive strike.

Looking up, she saw Heath crushing Slademore's fist in his hand and watched his foot swing forward.

Scrambling to her feet, she ran outside with the babies, shouting for Creed.

Before his name left her mouth, he raced past her toward the house.

Lettie was already on top of the coach, lying flat and reaching down for a baby. Clementine lifted the squalling baby up for her to take and did the same with the other child.

Stooping, she snatched a stone off the ground. It was slick with dew. She ran back toward the house, gripping it tight.

Halfway back, she met Heath and Creed emerging from the building, Slademore half-limp between them.

She stepped close to the baron and was within an arm's length, before Heath warned her back.

"She wants to smash you in the head with it," Heath told his captive. "I'd let her, too, except that jail cells remind me of the room you kept the children in. You'll have one just like it and you can spend your years thinking of that."

"I'll charge you with assault."

"And I'll say you did murder," Lettie declared.

"Murder? I gave them a place to live. They'd have died on the streets quicker."

"I'll tell how you wouldn't call the doctor when they were sick and how it was you who made them sick by forcing even the smallest ones to scrub your floors into the wee hours, how you made them get up before daylight and clean the kitchen until you could see your face reflected in the pots. I'll tell how you starved them and put them in closets if you thought they would tell something to a visitor."

"Who will believe you? You are nothing. I'm a near saint, ask anyone."

"There's the room where you kept them, aye?" Creed shrugged. "That ought to say something. I suppose your benefactors will be interested to see where their money went."

"Tie him to the top of the carriage, Creed," Heath said.

So he did, securing Slademore's arms and legs every which way.

When the coach pulled up in front of the police station, the sun was nearly ready to rise. Folks beginning their day stopped to watch Baron Slademore screeching in his nightshirt.

Chapter Seventeen

The sun was coming up, bringing dark garden shadows back into the light.

Clementine moved away from the window and knelt beside the fireplace, poking the coals to keep the flames burning bright.

This early it was still cold outside.

She glanced at Heath sitting in his chair beside the window. Lines creased the corners of his eyes while he looked back at her.

He smiled, beckoning her to come to him with a crook of his finger.

Rising, she crossed the room. Sat down on his lap and snuggled into his arms. She breathed in the masculine scent of him deeply, slowly savoring it.

"They look so peaceful," he said of the children asleep on the floor in front of the fire.

Seeing them lined up in a row, lying on quilts and covered with down blankets, she sent up a silent prayer of thanks.

"I wonder what it feels like for them," he said.

She cupped her hand over his where he hugged her close to his chest.

"They are feeling warm and safe for the first time, maybe in their lives, I imagine."

"Because of you," he murmured.

"You and Creed had more to do with it—and Lettie."

"It's you who went in after the last two. I died a thousand unspeakable deaths thinking I would not get to you in time. And then to see you, covering the babies with your own body. All I did was stop a fist. You were willing to sacrifice yourself for them."

"All that matters is that they are here, safe and warm."

So was she. And that was because of Heath. She would never forget what he had done.

"I suppose when they wake up they will be hungry," he said. "From what Lettie told the police, all they got to eat was scraps unless a benefactor was visiting."

"I'll instruct Cook to make plenty."

"I doubt if you'll need to. It created a stir in the household when we carried them in." He laughed low in his chest. "It's fitting, don't you think? You and I causing a stir?"

"It's rather enjoyable—a diversion from the humdrum of everyday life."

"I'm pretty sure I haven't had a humdrum moment since you rescued me from the fountain."

"I love you, husband."

"I love you, too, wife."

"I believe I'd do anything for you."

He sat up straighter, looking at her with a tiny frown right between his brows. She smoothed it away with her fingertips.

"I believe I'd do anything for you, too."

"I want them." She nodded at the children.

"All of them? How many are there?"

"There's the seven here, then the other seven Olivia is watching in your quarters."

"You want to adopt fourteen children?"

"Yes—especially that one with the blond curls just peeping out of the cover. Her name is Lucille. Do you know she wanted a magic beanstalk so she could climb to Heaven to be with her mother?"

"And you want to be her mother."

"More than anything."

He smiled, caught her cheeks between his hands and kissed her for a very long time.

"You're sure? It will be a huge undertaking. Adoption? It's much more than the shelter we spoke of."

"It is what I want."

"Good. It's what I want, too." He nuzzled her neck and sent a tickle up her scalp. "And they say Americans are barren."

"Fourteen Fencrofts ought to prove the myth a lie."

"Grandfather will be beside himself."

"He's worked hard toward this end."

Then he kissed her and didn't stop until the first of the children woke up wanting to eat.

Epilogue

Derbyshire, one month later

Heath should not be surprised to find himself standing on a hilltop at the estate, seeing it blanketed with snow on Christmas Eve.

If the fact that he was watching his wife and six—he squinted at the hill opposite—no, make that seven, of his children sledding down the slope, a foot of snow on the ground was quite believable.

The bundle he cradled in his arms squirmed. He glanced down, watched his baby son smile up at him.

"If I can believe you," he crooned, "I can believe anything, isn't that right?"

"Makes one believe in miracles, does it not?" Grandfather stood beside him, holding another of Heath's babies. "Let's see who has the biggest smile, Leroy or Willie?"

"Goes to show what you know." Lettie laughed, walking past and pulling a small wagon outfitted with skis. "It's Abigail."

Lettie, now their governess, could be correct in that. At ten months old, his daughter never ceased smiling or chattering.

It hit him again, what Abigail's life might have been like if not for Clementine. Then add the fates of his other thirteen to that.

He shook himself because the thought was too horrid to contemplate.

"Will you listen to that?" Grandfather cocked his head, apparently doing just that.

"The children are having a good time."

"Ah, but it's their mother I'm hearing. My Clemmie. I brought her here wanting a secure future for her and the family. But you, my boy, have given her so much more."

"As much as I would like to think I have, it's Clementine who is responsible for all this. I'm only the lucky chap who gets to call her wife."

"I'll not argue that." Grandfather made a face at Leroy and was rewarded with a baby laugh.

"I only hope…" His voice trailed as his gaze wandered. "I worry about Madeline."

"Have you heard something?"

He nodded. "I'll wait a bit to tell Clementine, but I have had word from the Pinkertons."

"Not good news?"

"On the surface of it, no. But Madeline, for all that she seems like a sweet rose, is a scrapper. You will recall that the investigator reported that she boarded a ship bound here. I've had a man waiting at the docks for the ship. It made port with all passengers accounted for, but my girl was not among them. I hardly know what to think."

"She's a Macooish." As far as Heath could tell they had a way of coming out on top of things. "She'll show up here one day soon, telling us all of the great adventure she's had."

"That she will!" He clapped Heath on the back. "And

for now I intend to live this adventure. Can you imagine I've got so many grandchildren?"

"I'm still stunned by it sometimes, but grateful beyond explanation."

"You've a lot of love around you, my boy." Grandfather pointed toward the manor house. "Look over there. Seems your man Creed and our Lettie are knee-deep in it. And I wouldn't be surprised to find some young fellow sweep your sister away before long."

"He'd have to be a determined fellow. She finally trusts me, so I guess that's a start. But the rest of our kind?" He shrugged.

"There's someone for all of us."

"Even you?"

"I've got more someones than I can count at the moment." Grandfather grinned and nodded, sweeping his gaze over the snowy, happy scene. "Look, Clementine is waving for you to come sledding."

He nodded at the baby, reminding Grandfather that he held one in his arms.

"Lucky thing God gave me two arms." He reached for Willie. "Go on now and have a bit of fun with your wife."

Yes, she was nearly hopping up and down, waving her hand madly for him to meet her on the opposite hill.

Heath dashed down the slope. It was slower going up the other side: he had to lift his knees high to climb over the snowdrifts.

It was worth the effort because he was greeted with a great, happy kiss right there in the open.

That was one of the things he loved about his wife. No matter where they were or what they were doing, she always had a kiss for him. Of course, the kind of kiss depended upon the activity they were engaged in. But she always expressed her love.

"I love you, Clementine," he told her—and how many times had he declared it this morning already?

"You'd hardly have adopted fourteen children if you didn't."

She sat down on the sled and motioned for him to get on behind her. He sat down and curled his arms around her middle, ready for the thrill of racing downhill.

She wore her hair loose most of the time here at the manor. Just now it tickled his nose.

"So…" she said, leaning back against him. "I was thinking I would like to purchase Slademore House."

She did have a fine sense of humor. "To burn it down?"

"To turn it into an orphanage. I'll call it Willa's House."

She laughed, leaning forward, and suddenly they were speeding down the slope.

All he could do was hang on and enjoy the wild ride.

* * * * *

If you enjoyed this story, be sure to check out these other great reads by Carol Arens.

The Cowboy's Cinderella
The Rancher's Inconvenient Bride
A Ranch to Call Home
A Texas Christmas Reunion